Standing directly bene... center of the black-and-white-marble-floored foyer, Sutton Vane began taking the final steps in his well-planned, unemotional seduction of Laurette Howard Tigart.

Overwhelmed by his smooth, slow, sensual assault, Laurette felt herself losing control, knew what was going to happen if she was not careful. Suddenly she was uneasy again. She felt as if she were in imminent danger. All at once his very image was both evil *and* erotic. Powerfully provocative. This man whose kisses she craved was, she feared, quite capable of making her lose her head, of behaving irresponsibly. Of causing her to surrender to his dark, irresistible sexuality. Should that happen, she would surely suffer for her unwise indiscretion.

"The pages burn as Nan Ryan works her magic.... This is vintage Nan Ryan: sensual, steamy, titillating."
—*Romantic Times* on *The Seduction of Ellen*

NAN RYAN

The Scandalous Miss Howard

MIRA

MIRA

ISBN 1-55166-893-9

THE SCANDALOUS MISS HOWARD

Copyright © 2002 by Nan Ryan.

All rights reserved. Except for use in any review, the reproduction or
utilization of this work in whole or in part in any form by any electronic,
mechanical or other means, now known or hereafter invented, including
xerography, photocopying and recording, or in any information storage or
retrieval system, is forbidden without the written permission of the publisher,
MIRA Books, 225 Duncan Mill Road, Don Mills, Ontario, Canada M3B 3K9.

All characters in this book have no existence outside the imagination of the
author and have no relation whatsoever to anyone bearing the same name
or names. They are not even distantly inspired by any individual known or
unknown to the author, and all incidents are pure invention.

MIRA and the Star Colophon are trademarks used under license and registered
in Australia, New Zealand, Philippines, United States Patent and Trademark
Office and in other countries.

Visit us at www.mirabooks.com

Printed in U.S.A.

This book is for that bubbly, brash, bouncy, brainy, beguiling blond bombshell Katherine Orr.

K.O., you're O.K.

The door closed quietly behind her.

The only sound she heard was that of a crackling fire. Frowning now, she anxiously stepped into the drawing room where a fire blazed in the grate and a dark, totally naked man sat on the floor before the dancing flames. He sipped brandy from a crystal snifter.

The man looked up, smiled disarmingly, and raising his brandy said, "Welcome home."

The sudden, unexpected sight of him caused her heart to miss a beat or two. Foolishly longing to throw herself into his arms and press kisses all over his handsome face, she glared angrily at him. "How did you get into this house? I always keep the doors locked and—"

"I have a key," he said with no apology.

Her eyes widened. "You have a...? You've no right to have a key to—"

"Ah, but I do," he corrected her. "I own this house."

She shot him a wilting look and shook her head. "For your information, a large company owns this house now. The Bay Minette Corporation." He nodded knowingly. Flabbergasted, she swallowed hard, then snapped, "Just what do you think you're doing without any clothes?"

"My clothes were wet," he replied, "as are yours."

Her chin elevated pugnaciously, she quickly shrugged out of her long, sleet-dampened cape and tossed it over his lap as she ordered, "Get dressed and get out!"

To which he calmly replied, "Get undressed and get down here."

Insulted, she said, "You are an arrogant bastard and if you do not vacate the premises at once, I shall summon the authorities!"

He tossed aside the cape she had thrown over him and rose agilely to his feet. He waited a couple of heartbeats before making another move and she realized that he was giving her the opportunity to turn and flee if she so desired. She strongly considered it.

But how could she leave when he stood gloriously naked before her, his tall lean body, burnished by the firelight, a study in male perfection.

When she didn't move, he reached out and took her in his arms, drawing her against his frame. At first she tried to free herself, but his will was stronger than hers. He kissed her then, and continued kissing her until she was short of breath and her heart was beating rapidly in her own ears.

In minutes they sank weakly to their knees before the fire and continued to kiss each other ardently, hungrily. When finally, after at least a dozen heated, probing kisses, he took his lips from hers, he gently cupped her flushed face in his tanned hands and said, "I cannot wait another minute to make love to you."

"No." Her inborn spirit rose and she declared hotly, "No. You can't just wander in and out of my life and expect me to—"

"There was a very good reason for my absence," he said.

"Fine! I'd like to hear it."

"As soon as we've made love," he replied as he bent and pressed his lips to her exposed throat. She felt the flick of his tongue against her flesh and it made her gasp.

Trying very hard to keep her wits about her, she said, "Don't. Stop it. Either you tell me why you—"

But his masterful lips silenced her and she soon surrendered to the searing passion he had aroused in her. Within seconds she was as naked as he and glad that she was.

While sleet tapped against the windowpanes and the winter darkness engulfed the river city, he stretched out on his back and drew her to lie atop him.

The next few minutes were spent in arousing sexual play as he slid her slender body sensuously against his own, pressing her soft, full breasts into the crisp, black hair that covered his chest. He kissed her, caressed her and murmured promises of forbidden sexual pleasure, promises that she knew he was quite capable of keeping.

Soon he switched their positions, easing her over

onto her back in front of the snapping fire. His dark, chiseled face and wide gleaming shoulders looming just above, he moved so that his slim hips were between her pale, parted thighs. He slid slowly down and, with a hand between their bodies, carefully positioned himself so that only the smooth, hot tip of his throbbing erection was inside her.

It was enough to instantly arouse her to the boiling point.

She looked anxiously up at him and watched as his lips languidly lowered to meet hers. It was a slow, sensual kiss of such potency that she felt as if she were already a part of him. At last his lips left hers. He lifted his dark head and, looking directly into her eyes, eased his hard male flesh up inside her. She sighed with pleasure and gave herself completely to him.

For the next half hour he made love to her the way he knew she liked it. His weight supported on stiffened forearms, he watched her beautiful face change expressions as he slid almost all the way in, then pulled out, stopping when, once again, only the tip of his blood-filled erection was inside her.

He loved to hear the kittenish whimper she sometimes made when she wanted him to thrust forcefully into her; her sweet, pliant body begged for all he could give her, her dark, sparkling eyes glazed with lust. And then after the whimper, she usually made a deep sigh of gratitude as he penetrated fully.

Generally, she flung both her arms and her legs

outward as she enjoyed the incredible pleasure of his sexual torment.

Not this time.

Not now.

She gripped his biceps so tightly her nails cut into his flesh and frantically she wrapped her legs around his back to draw him to her.

Her message was clear.

She desperately wanted to keep him as close as possible, wanted him to stay buried deep inside her, wanted him to never leave her. Which was exactly how he wanted her to feel.

Her eyes slid closed with bliss and she missed his faint smile of triumph. She had no idea she had once again played right into his hands.

He was well pleased. Everything was going according to plan. Soon, within weeks or perhaps a couple of months, she would be hopelessly in love with him, would belong to him, body and soul. And then...

He ground his even white teeth and snapped himself back to the moment at hand. He flexed his firm buttocks and drove deeply into her. She sighed with building ecstasy. He changed the tempo of his lovemaking, thrust more seekingly until he totally possessed her. She responded with a wild sweetness that gave him the same kind of pleasure he was giving to her.

The lovemaking was incredible. Their shared orgasm wrenching. But when at last both were satiated and drowsy, she said, "I'm still angry with you. You should just leave now. Go home."

Never raising his dark head from where it rested comfortably on her breasts, he said, "You don't mean that."

"I do," she said as she made a halfhearted attempt to rise.

He tightened an arm across her waist and accused, "You're behaving like a child."

"What would you know about being a child?" was her retort.

"Even I was a child once," he said with a yawn. "And I remember my childhood well."

PART ONE

One

Mobile, Alabama
Tuesday, July 23, 1844

It was a still, muggy day in the southern port city of Mobile. The streets were near deserted as the hour of 3:00 p.m. approached, bringing with it the hottest part of the afternoon. Gentlemen in offices along Water Street had long since shed their frock coats and loosened their cravats. More than one businessman, face shiny with perspiration, dozed in his studded, high-back leather chair, his well-shod feet resting atop his mahogany desk.

The ladies of the city, having anticipated the oppressive midafternoon heat, had done their errands and shopping early and were now secluded in the relative comfort of their homes. Many had retired to their bed chambers. There they had pulled the heavy drapes against the scalding sun, disrobed down to their underclothing and would attempt to take a nap.

In the bedroom of an eight-columned mansion on peaceful, oak-shaded Dauphin Street, a young woman, drenched with perspiration and writhing in agony, had chosen the blistering hot July day to give birth to her first child.

When the blond and very pregnant Marion Howard had awakened that morning with a nagging backache and the beginning hints of contractions, she had known that her child was not going to wait much longer to enter the world. The baby was not due for another two weeks, but Marion felt certain labor was beginning. Despite her discomfort, she smiled dreamily and gazed at her sleeping husband. It was early morning—not yet 7:00 a.m. She would let him rest. She would, she decided, wait at least an hour before she awakened him.

Marion waited less than five minutes.

Frightened when a stab of pain shot through her lower belly, she laid a hand on her husband's bare shoulder. He came instantly awake. He saw the fear in her large, dark eyes and the discomfort etched on her beautiful face.

Quickly sitting up, he said, "My God, it's time. You're going to have the baby!"

"I believe so, my love," she said, determined that she would remain brave and silent throughout the coming ordeal.

"I'll send Daniel after Dr. Ledette," said the excited T. Hershel Howard, bounding out of bed and anxiously stepping into his trousers. "Ring for Delia, darling! Hurry, sweetheart, the baby may be here any minute."

The statement made Marion laugh. "T.H.," she said, opening her arms wide, "come here, please."

His brow furrowed with concern, the slim, sandy-haired man hurried to his wife. Taking a seat on the bed facing her, he asked anxiously, "What is it? Is the baby already coming?"

"No. Not yet," she assured her worried husband as she took one of his hands in both of hers and placed it gently atop her swollen belly. "But soon. Now, T.H., I want you to promise me something."

"Anything, darling. Name it and it's done," he said, lightly caressing the smooth skin of her belly.

"Promise me you won't behave foolishly today," she said in her most honeyed voice, while she reached up and stroked his unshaven jaw.

T. Hershel Howard frowned, taken aback. Defensively, he asked, "Have you ever seen me behave foolishly, Marion?"

Smiling at the dear, handsome man whom she knew absolutely adored her, Marion reminded him, "Only on those rare occasions when I was sick and you were worried." Remembering, he nodded sheepishly. She continued, "Today there is nothing to worry about, T.H. I am young, healthy, rested and oh so eager to deliver our firstborn." She tilted her head to one side on the feather pillow and confided, "I believe a lot of women carry on over the horrible pain of childbirth to get attention and sympathy. I'll make you proud, darling. I fully intend to breeze through this delivery without a complaint or a whimper. Now kiss me."

"Oh, dear God, nooo," groaned Marion as the tall clock in the corridor downstairs struck the hour of

3:00 p.m. Another deep, painful contraction racked her tired, delicate body. "I can't stand it, I can't stand it," she sobbed loudly, tears spilling down her hot cheeks.

Naked now, her body shiny with perspiration from head to toe, her blond hair lying in damp, matted curls around her stricken face, she lay in the middle of her sweat-dampened bed. Her legs spread, she attempted to follow the stern orders of her attending physician, the portly, white-haired Dr. Gerald Ledette, and the gentle coaxing of her loyal personal maid, Delia.

"You push just as hard as you can now, sweet-ums," the big black woman urged. "Won't be much longer, then all the pain will be gone."

As she spoke, Delia pressed a damp cloth to Marion's forehead and throat and held her frightened mistress's hand. Two younger servants scurried about, doing the doctor's bidding, bringing basins of hot water and clean white towels.

Outside the room, T.H. paced nervously, stopping every few minutes to pound on the door and ask about his wife. He had intended to stay by Marion's side throughout—to watch his son being born—but Dr. Ledette had soon ordered him out, saying he was in the way and doing Marion no good. T.H. was secretly glad that the doctor had made him leave. To see his beloved lying there, frightened, helpless and in such obvious agony, was more than he could bear.

His fists and teeth clenched as he paced, T.H. cursed himself for making Marion pregnant. He was responsible for the terrible pain she was enduring. It was all his fault. He had wanted a son. How ungodly selfish of him! How thoughtless and uncaring. He didn't need a son. Or a daughter. He didn't need anyone but his precious Marion and now he might well lose her.

Something must surely have gone terribly wrong for her to be suffering for so long. Her wrenching labor had lasted for seven long hours now and still she could not expel the child. How much more could such an exhausted, fragile woman endure?

T.H. stopped abruptly as another loud, keening wail came from beyond the closed bedroom door. He clamped his hands over his ears and closed his eyes tightly, knowing that his wife was enduring yet another painful, tearing contraction. At the same time the sound of faint laughter caught his attention. He took his hands from his ears and made a face. He had completely forgotten that guests filled the downstairs rooms.

Earlier in the day, he had sent a quartet of servants to the homes of his good friends, inviting them to the Dauphin Street mansion where a miracle was about to take place.

Colonel George P. Ivy and his wife, Martha, had arrived first, coming from their home in the Oakleigh Garden district. The childless, middle-aged couple said they wouldn't have missed this event for the world. Shortly after the Ivys' carriage had pulled into the drive, the Adairs—prominent attorney Paul Adair, his wife Melba and their twelve-year-old daughter,

Lydia—had shown up. Melba had brought a gigantic bouquet of delicate pink roses that had come from her own gardens, which were considered the most beautiful gardens in Mobile.

Eminent Springhill resident, Judge Noble Parlange and his wife, Lena, also attended. The Parlanges had just returned from South Carolina where their only son's wife had given birth to twin girls in early June. They were joined by the Faradays, the Pirrilliats, the Caldwells and, of course, the Douglas Dasheroons.

A buffet had been laid out in the high-ceilinged dining room where the gleaming cherrywood sideboard and long matching table now held a wide variety of delicacies for the visitors.

In one of the mansion's drawing rooms, the gentlemen, most of whom were standing, spoke of the cotton market, sugar production and Thoroughbred horse racing. In the other drawing room, directly across the wide, marble-floored vestibule, their wives were seated on brocade sofas and velvet chairs, reliving the births of their own dear children.

For some it had been a long time. For others, like dark-haired Carrie Dasheroon, who lived with her husband Douglas directly across Dauphin Street from the Howards, it had been only one short year to the day.

The child, their dark-curled little boy with his olive skin and deep blue eyes, had just now climbed down off his mother's lap to go in search of his father. As Carrie watched her adorable son in his short white trousers and starched white shirt make his unsteady way past the smiling ladies who reached out to touch him, to tousle his hair, her heart swelled with maternal pride.

Carrie thought Ladd was the prettiest, sweetest little boy in the whole wide world. She marveled every time she looked at him, almost unable to believe that such a perfect child actually belonged to her. From the minute Ladd had opened his eyes, he had been a constant joy. So beautiful and bright and affectionate and curious.

Her gaze following him, she saw him stumble and fall in the foyer. She started to rise, but settled back as Ladd picked himself up and without making a sound or shedding a tear, moved on toward the other drawing room. Carrie smiled when Ladd, spotting his father, rushed forward and threw his short arms around Douglas's trousered leg.

Without interrupting the conversation, Douglas looked down, grinned, laid a hand on Ladd's head and pressed his son's cheek to his thigh. Carrie could hear Ladd's bubbling laughter from where she sat. She was, she realized fully, the luckiest of women.

Upstairs, the tense drama continued.

The hour of 5:00 p.m. was fast approaching when finally, at long last, Miss Laurette Taylor Howard announced her arrival with a loud resounding cry. His heart hammering in his chest, T.H. burst into the room and saw Delia carefully cleaning the red, squalling infant. He hurried to his exhausted wife and kissed her.

"Are you all right, my love?" he asked, looking from her to Dr. Ledette who nodded his gray head.

"I'm fine," Marion said, "but I've failed you, darling. You wanted a son, but we have a girl."

"And I'm so glad we do," he assured her. "What could be sweeter than a little girl just like you? Our Laurette."

Delia, cooing to the squirming infant now swathed in a soft white blanket, came to the bed to place the child in its mother's arms. The parents gazed at their newborn in wonder. "T.H.," said Dr. Ledette, "why don't you go now and give Marion a chance to get a little rest?"

"Yes, of course," replied the smiling father, who kissed both his wife and daughter and then rose to his feet. Turning to the doctor, he asked, "After Marion has rested, could I bring a few friends up to see our daughter?"

Dr. Ledette looked from T.H. to Marion. She smiled and shook her head, knowing how much it meant to her husband to show off his child.

"Wait at least half an hour," warned Dr. Ledette. "Then, bring only one or two at a time and let them stay no longer than five minutes. After an hour of showing off Laurette, you must send everyone home and let Marion get a nice, long night's sleep."

"You have my word," said the beaming T.H.

Taking the stairs two at a time, he rushed downstairs, stopped squarely in the center of the foyer between the two crowded drawing rooms and proudly announced, "My wife has just delivered a perfect daughter whom we've named Laurette Taylor!"

Cheers and shouts went up and T.H. opened one of his most expensive boxes of cigars to pass out to the gentlemen. Laughter filled the big house. Champagne corks popped and toasts were made to little Laurette. A half hour into the celebration, T.H. raised his hands to make yet another announcement.

"You may all have a quick look at my dear daughter, but you must come up two at a time, no more." He glanced at Carrie Dasheroon who was holding her son, Ladd, on her lap. T.H. motioned to her, indicating that she and her husband were to be the very first to see his daughter.

The Dasheroons followed T.H. up the grand staircase. Inside the master suite, Carrie warned her son to be very quiet. Cautiously, she lowered him to the floor. Little Ladd Dasheroon didn't waste a second. He ran across the room to the satin-draped bassinet, rose on tiptoe and reached chubby hands up to grip the cradle's top edge. But he was too tiny to see inside. Frustrated, he squealed and attempted to pull himself up.

"No, Ladd, sweetheart," warned his mother, pulling him away from the bassinet. "You must be quiet and not wake the baby."

"Baby!" declared the little boy loudly, wanting to have a look at the sleeping child.

"Yes, a beautiful baby girl," said his smiling mother who lifted Ladd back up into her arms and showed him the infant. "Now be quiet, sweetheart."

"Baby, baby," Ladd kept repeating, squirming to get down as his mother and father joined T.H. at Marion's bedside.

Marion was radiant and smiling, despite her exhausting labor. The grown-ups talked for a few minutes, then Carrie said, "The others are dying to come up. We'll be over tomorrow. Is there anything we can do for you?"

"No," Marion replied, sighing with happiness as she glanced up at her husband, "I have everything I've ever wanted."

Douglas Dasheroon smiled and leaned down to press a kiss to Marion's forehead. Then he shook hands with T.H. and congratulated him again before moving with Carrie toward the door.

"No, Ladd!" his mother had to once again scold him to keep him from disturbing the baby.

Putting up a fuss, which was not like him, Ladd kept straining against her, an arm outstretched over her shoulder, his fingers vainly reaching for the white bassinet.

"Carrie," said Marion with a laugh, "It's okay. Take him back over there. It won't hurt anything. Dr. Ledette said she'll soon be waking to nurse."

"You sure?" Carrie asked.

"Yes, let Ladd have a good long look at Laurette."

While Douglas Dasheroon, his arms crossed over his chest, waited at the door, Carrie took Ladd back to the bassinet. Lowering him to his feet, she said, "You may touch her lightly, Ladd, but you must be very careful not to squeeze or hurt her.'' Carrie slid a footstool forward and helped Ladd up onto it.

For a long moment the little boy stared at the pink-faced baby as if he were trying to figure out what she was. Then very carefully, very slowly—with his alert mother monitoring his every move—he reached out a tiny brown hand and laid it ever so gently atop the baby's downy head. She slept peacefully on.

''Baby,'' he whispered and, at his mother's request, reluctantly took his hand away.

Laurette Taylor Howard held a great fascination for Ladd Dasheroon.

And would for the rest of his life.

Two

It was inevitable that Ladd Dasheroon and Laurette Howard would become good friends. Not only did they live directly across Dauphin from each other, their backgrounds were similar. Both families were wealthy and privileged—from Mobile's Old Guard.

Ladd's father, thirty-four-year-old Douglas Dasheroon was a successful planter who owned, through inheritance and marriage, outlying sugar and cotton plantations as far away as the Georgia border.

Douglas was an imposing, dark-haired man with piercing blue eyes, a ready smile, an easy charm and a great zest for life. He was a West Point graduate who had turned his back on a promising military career after meeting and marrying Carrie Lynn Crawford, a raven-haired belle from a monied Southern family.

Without a second thought, Douglas had resigned his commission and built his bride a handsome home in the heart of Mobile's Silk Stocking row. The Greek Revival style house featured a curved stairway from the center of the lower level to the upper floor. Galleries with square pillars formed a pedimented portico across the large home's front.

The double entrance doors opened into a large, wide hall that extended the length of the house. Crystal-and-brass chandeliers hung from the high ceilings and lush Oriental rugs covered the heart pine flooring in the spacious parlor. Marble mantels and pier mirrors graced many of the home's twenty rooms.

Upstairs, in the center of the house, was a room especially designed to be a reception room or ballroom. Thirty feet square with eighteen-foot ceilings, its walls were adorned with applied pilasters. Huge double doors opened out onto a wide front balcony on both sides of the great hall.

A platoon of servants dressed in fitted black uniforms with white aprons and lace caps saw to it that the home's many rooms were kept sparkling clean and that the Dasheroon household ran smoothly.

The mansion of successful cotton and sugar broker T.H. Howard and his wife Marion was no less grand. The large, white dwelling with its two-story porch framed by eight Ionic columns was an architectural masterpiece. All the windows were floor length and the lower sashes raised above head height into the wall for circulation. Kashmir rugs covered the pine floors in the double parlors and priceless art adorned the walls. Mirrored mantels graced both rooms and a wide curving staircase ascended from the nine foot wide, thirty foot long front hallway to the upper floor.

Chippendale furniture had been imported from Europe and in the sunny music room was an ornately carved piano of gleaming mahogany, which had been made in Baltimore especially for the musically inclined mistress of the mansion.

In T.H.'s library, where four hundred leather-bound first editions filled the tall shelves, was a round gaming table with a checkerboard top. It was his pride and joy.

Both stately homes boasted manicured grounds and lush gardens and sculptured marble statuary. Scattered throughout both terraced estates, iron lace benches and settees and chaise longues afforded the homes' occupants and their guests the pleasure of enjoying the outdoors in the welcome warmth of springtime and the pleasing cool of early autumn.

Spaced uniformly along both sides of Dauphin Street were huge, ancient oaks dripping Spanish moss and generously shading the quiet residential boulevard. The district was known as Dauphin Way and it was a sheltered, peaceful, highly desirable area of the city.

Life was good for those who were fortunate enough to live there.

Carrie Dasheroon kept her promise.

As soon as Douglas left for one of his many plantations the morning after the Howard child was born, Carrie went to visit Marion and the new baby, Laurette. She took Ladd with her, but before they went she reminded him over and over that, when they were in the room with the new baby, he would have to be very quiet and still. Ladd had smiled and bobbed his dark head.

Carrie sighed. "You don't really have any idea what I'm talking about, do you?" Again a wide smile and a bob of his head. His mother laughed then, charmed by him as always. Sinking down onto her heels and clasping his small waist, she said, "We are going to see the new baby and I want you to mind me while we are there. Will you?"

This time she received a puzzled frown.

Carrie gave him a motherly kiss, came to her feet and taking his hand in hers, said, "Let's go." The pair started through the grand hall, but before they reached the double front doors, Carrie stopped abruptly. "Wait, sweetheart," she said, "I almost forgot, Mattie baked a delicious chocolate cake for us to take to the Howards. You stay right here!" she commanded, shaking a finger in his face.

She turned and hurried back through the house toward the kitchen. The minute she was out of sight, Ladd raced for the open front doors and dashed outside. Laughing now, he hurriedly crossed the wide, shaded veranda.

When he reached the steep front steps, he sat on the top step and scooted down, pushing off with his hands. He gave a sharp squeal of triumph when he had successfully navigated the final step and reached the flagstone-bordered front walk. At once he was running as fast as his short legs would carry him.

Ladd was almost to the front gate and freedom when Carrie burst out of the mansion, shouting his name. He stopped running and turned to face her.

Carrie set the freshly baked cake down on the veranda and stalked after her disobedient son. Ladd frowned as she bore down on him.

Her hands went to her hips and she scolded him soundly. "Young man, you know better than to go out of this house alone! How many times do I have to tell you?" Ladd crossed his short arms over his chest and hung his head. "You look at me!" Carrie demanded. Sheepishly, Ladd looked up at her. She said firmly, her jaw set, "You did not mind me, Ladd Dasheroon. I told you not to move and you didn't obey. You have been bad and must be punished."

Ladd, not really understanding, gave her a questioning look.

She said, "Since you didn't behave, you will not go with me to see the new baby."

"Baby!" Ladd said forcefully, pointing in the direction of the tall white columns across Dauphin. "Baby."

"No, you're not going to see the baby. Instead you will…"

Bright tears instantly sprang to Ladd's large blue eyes. He manfully attempted to sniff them back. Carrie stopped speaking. Apparently he understood that he was not going to see the baby and he was terribly disappointed. He stood there biting his lower lip. His tiny chin was quivering. Carrie shook her head, defeated. She was a pushover for this sweet little boy of hers. He was so small and bright and cute and lovable. How could she stay angry with him?

Carrie began to smile. "You really want to see the baby, don't you?" she asked softly.

Ladd nodded vigorously. "Baby, baby," he declared.

"Oh, all right, you may go with me. But if you misbehave while we are the Howards', you're coming straight home. Do you understand?" Again he nodded. "Fine. Now, I am going back up to the veranda to get the cake. If you move one inch from where you are standing, you will be sent right back into the house."

Ladd did not move.

Carrie and Ladd were welcomed into the Howard home by the Howards' uniformed butler, the white-haired, good-natured Abraham.

"Miz Marion is expecting you," he said, taking the cake from Carrie and winking at Ladd. Ladd stared at him, puzzled. "Go right on up," instructed the beaming Abraham.

"What on earth are you doing out of bed?" Carrie asked when they entered the spacious master suite to find Marion seated in a winged chair that had been pulled up beside the bassinet.

"Carrie. I'm so glad you came," said Marion, smiling and starting to rise.

"Don't get up," Carrie said, holding out a hand, palm up, "unless you want me to help you back into the bed."

"I don't. I want to sit here and gaze at my exquisite daughter forever," said the glowing Marion. She looked past Carrie to Ladd, who was hanging back, suddenly shy, a finger in his mouth. She said, "Ladd, would you like to come over here and see the baby?"

Ladd looked to his mother. She shook her head and said, "Yes. Go ahead."

Ladd eagerly crossed the lush Aubusson carpet. When he reached the bassinet, Marion picked him up and sat him on her knees. Eyes only for the sleeping infant, Ladd leaned close, curled his short fingers around the crib's top edge and stared, entranced. When Laurette squirmed and yawned, he giggled with delight.

But when, abruptly, she awakened and instantly began to cry, Ladd frowned at her. He put his hands over his ears and made a face.

Marion laughed, gave his smooth cheek a quick kiss and lowered him to the floor. Ladd made a beeline for the door, his intent to get away from the crying, red-faced creature. But a sharp look from his mother stopped him dead in his tracks.

Marion moved to the rocking chair while Carrie lifted the crying Laurette from the crib and placed her gently in her mother's arms. Already the child seemed to know who held her. The minute Marion's arms closed around Laurette and she rocked once back and forth, Laurette's loud wailing softened to an intermittent, jerking sob. Soon she was quiet and still. Totally content.

Since she was no longer putting up such a terrible racket, Ladd ventured closer. He stood beside the rocking chair, hands clasped behind his back, carefully studying Laurette.

* * *

The new baby enticed many visitors to the Howards' Dauphin Way mansion. Martha Ivy came frequently to coo over the darling baby girl. Melba Adair and her shy daughter, Lydia, were regular visitors, invariably bringing huge bouquets of exotic blooms from Melba's lush gardens. Lena Parlange came often, declaring that being allowed to hold the gurgling Laurette was the next best thing to holding her own twin granddaughters, Juliette and Johanna, who were far away in South Carolina. Dozens of friends called at the mansion to get a glimpse of the new mistress.

Carrie and Ladd Dasheroon visited every day. Ladd's fascination with Laurette never waned. He wanted to look at her, to touch her, to pat her soft cheeks.

By the time Laurette was six months old, Marion allowed Ladd to hold her. Carrie anxiously watched as Marion, once again as slim and beautiful as ever, instructed Ladd to climb up into the rocking chair. With a little help he scrambled up, quickly turning about to sit down.

"Now, Laddie," Marion said sincerely, "you'll be holding my most precious possession, so be very, very careful not to let her squirm out of your arms. She's stronger than she looks."

Ladd smiled and held his arms open wide. Marion laughed and very carefully placed her bright-eyed daughter on Ladd's lap, gently leaning Laurette back against his narrow chest. Ladd's short arms came around Laurette and he held her as if she were a rare work of art. Which, of course, she was. To her mother's delight, Laurette did not cry or attempt to wiggle free. Instead she lay there, staring up at Ladd, gurgling.

Both young mothers, standing protectively close, smiled and exchanged looks. Wordlessly they agreed that seeing the dark-haired, olive-skinned eighteen-month-old Ladd tenderly holding the fair-complected, blond-haired six-month-old Laurette was a wondrous sight to behold.

A treasured vision never to be forgotten.

Three

"He's the sweetest little boy," everyone agreed any time Ladd Dasheroon's name was mentioned. "Just the sweetest little boy I've ever known."

Ladd *was* a sweet child. Happy, mischievous and full of energy, he was, at the same time, thoughtful, mannerly and respectful of others. Naturally outgoing and affectionate, he loved everyone and wasn't embarrassed to let them know it.

But he was sweetest of all to the feisty, golden-haired charmer who lived across Dauphin. From the time she started walking at the ripe old age of ten months, Laurette Howard followed Ladd around as if he were the Pied Piper, stamping her small feet and squealing her displeasure if he got too far ahead of her.

Reminded, often, by his mother to "look after" Laurette, Ladd was happy to do so. In his mind, Laurette was more or less his own living play toy. She belonged to him, had been put on earth for his amusement and benefit. She was his and he liked watching over her, liked having her at his elbow, looking up at him.

The two quickly became inseparable. If Ladd was

not at Laurette's home, she was at his. He was patient with her and extremely protective. If she stumbled and fell, he picked her up, dusted her off and soothed her. If she was cranky and fussy, he softly reasoned with her until she became placid and calm. If she was sleepy, he rocked her, humming and singing to her. If she cried, he made funny faces and teased her until he got her to laugh.

Laurette Howard, although a happy, lovable child, was a handful from the very beginning. As a baby she was bright-eyed and inquisitive, regularly attempting to climb out of her crib. As a child, she was antsy, energetic and full of curiosity. Everything and everyone intrigued her. And, if there was something she didn't know, couldn't figure out, she asked Ladd, assuming that he was the authority. Laurette idolized Ladd and wanted to play the kind of games he liked. Games boys played.

By the time Laurette was six years old, she was unquestionably a tomboy, thanks in part to her close friendship with Ladd. Ladd Dasheroon was all boy. He liked the rough-and-tumble, didn't mind getting his clothes dirty. He liked to climb trees and take chances, was never afraid of getting hurt.

Laurette was not to be outdone.

Anything Ladd challenged her to do, she did. Like him, she loved running, jumping, climbing, shouting, wrestling and executing neat handstands.

Just like Ladd had taught her.

On one such occasion, Laurette's mother came out of the mansion just as Laurette was perfectly balanced on her dirty little hands, slippered feet high in the air, white ruffled pantalets showing for all the world to see.

Marion was horrified. As soon as her daughter's feet hit the ground, she called the puzzled Laurette inside, stopping Ladd when he followed.

"No, Ladd, dear," Marion said, gently, "you two have played enough for today. It's time for Laurette's afternoon nap."

Ladd shrugged, nodded and backed away, while Marion, holding her daughter's thin arm none too gently, ushered Laurette inside and directly up the stairs to her room. There Marion lectured her daughter. And not for the first time.

Once again she informed Laurette that it was not proper for a young lady to be turning cartwheels and doing handstands. She was to be more prudent in the future. She was *never* to allow her underclothing to show—not even to Ladd—it was not decent. Marion firmly reminded Laurette that she was a girl, not a boy like Ladd. She couldn't do everything Ladd did and she would do well to remember it.

But to no avail.

Together constantly, the pair were two peas in a pod. They never thought of each other as being of the opposite sex. They were friends, playmates, pals. They got along famously, but they also argued with regularity. The fiery, hot-tempered Laurette had the calm, well-brought-up Ladd at a disadvantage. While he was not averse to shouting at her and occasionally shoving her away, he would never have laid a hand on her in anger.

Instinctively, Laurette knew it.

So, once when she was really angry with him, she doubled up her fist and socked him squarely in the nose.

Blood spurted.

The minute she saw the bright red blood, Laurette was sorry for what she had done.

"Oh, Ladd, Ladd, forgive me," she began to beg. "I didn't mean to hurt you, I didn't. Please, please forgive me."

Pinching the bridge of his nose and holding his head back, Ladd turned away. He shrugged her hand off when she laid it on his shoulder. She had no right to hit him. She was a spoiled, selfish brat. Angry, Ladd withheld his forgiveness for as long as possible.

Which hadn't been very long.

Laurette, her big, dark eyes filled with genuine remorse, danced nervously around him, saying, "Oh, Ladd, if you'll just forgive me, I promise I'll never, ever hurt you again as long as I live!"

She gave him a hopeful little smile and handed him the lace handkerchief her personal servant, Ruby Lee, had tucked into the sash of her dress. Ladd took it and dabbed at his nose and made a point to ignore her worried pleading. But hard as he tried, he couldn't stay angry. Not with Laurette. She was, after all, his best friend, always had been and always would be. Besides, she was great fun and she was cute with her snaggletoothed smile and wild blond hair and dirty white dress. And she always seemed to know how to jolly him back into a good mood.

Astute, Laurette sensed that Ladd was already softening and she gave a great sigh of relief. Then reached out, took his hand, led him around the mansion to the vast terraced back lawn, and straight to an iron lace settee resting beneath a huge shade-giving oak.

"You sit here and I'll run inside and get a wet cloth," she instructed.

Ladd nodded. She raced away and was back in minutes, carrying a tray with two frosty glasses of lemonade and a clean damp cloth. Ladd lounged back on the settee while Laurette painstakingly cleaned his bloodied nose.

"There," she said when she was finished. "All better." Then she frowned and asked, "We're still best friends, aren't we, Ladd Dasheroon?"

"I suppose," he said, then added, "but you have to do everything I ask you to do for a full week."

"I will," she promised. "What shall I do first?"

Ladd finally grinned. "Hand me a lemonade."

She hurried to obey.

"Now what?" she asked.

"It's hot out here," he said, leaning lazily back, stretching his legs out before him. "Fan me, Lollie."

Frowning, Laurette looked anxiously about, but could not find anything to use as a fan. So she impulsively yanked up her dress and vigorously fanned him with her full skirts while he drank his lemonade.

* * *

"But, Mother," said an unhappy seven-year-old Laurette, "I don't want to take piano lessons. Please don't make me."

Marion Howard sighed heavily. "Laurette, I had hoped that by now you'd be eager to take lessons. I was when I was your age." Marion shook her head, thoughtfully. "How can you be my daughter and not be musically inclined?"

Mother and daughter stood in the sun-filled music room before the ornately carved piano. Waiting in one of the double parlors was Miss Jillian Foster, Mobile's highly acclaimed music teacher. Miss Foster taught piano and voice to a select number of the city's upper crust. A prim lady in her midtwenties who loved music and children in that order, she immensely enjoyed teaching piano and voice to young people and nothing thrilled her more than to discover a pupil who was truly talented.

With those gifted few, she cheerfully spent additional time at no extra charge. Jillian Foster was, like Marion Howard, confident that young Laurette would prove to be one of those who possessed musical talent. Why shouldn't she? Marion Howard played the piano beautifully.

Smiling at the pleasant prospect of tutoring a naturally gifted pupil, Miss Foster had no idea that an argument was going on between mother and daughter.

"I will take piano lessons only if Ladd does, too!" stated Laurette emphatically, her face screwed up into a frown of unhappiness.

"Ladd is a boy!" Marion said, annoyed. "And he

is not *my* boy. He doesn't have to take lessons. You do.''

''Yes, he does, if I do,'' Laurette reasoned. ''It isn't fair for him to—''

''Laurette Taylor Howard, I've had just about enough of your foolishness,'' her mother interrupted. ''*You* are taking piano lessons and that is final. Now I am going to bring Miss Foster in here and you will do exactly as you are told.''

''Yes, ma'am,'' said a sullen Laurette, head sagging on her chest. Then she immediately brightened and asked, ''If I can get Ladd to agree to take lessons with me, will you say yes?''

Marion hesitated. ''I suppose so, but I don't think he will....''

''Yes, he will,'' said Laurette and, smiling now, daintily took a seat on the piano bench.

''No, no, Lollie,'' Ladd gently scolded, shaking his dark head and taking a seat beside her on the piano bench. ''It goes like this.''

He brushed her hands away and settled his long, slim fingers on the ivory piano keys. He began to play a familiar and hauntingly beautiful polonaise by Frédéric Chopin. Laurette sat silent, listening, awed. Ladd played the difficult musical masterpiece from beginning to end without striking a single false note. It was perfect. It was divine. It was inspiring.

The ten-year-old Laurette sighed, defeated.

For three years she and Ladd had been taking piano lessons—two afternoons a week—from the patient

Miss Foster. Within weeks of beginning their lessons, an amazed Miss Foster was praising Ladd, declaring that he had natural talent. A prodigious talent. If, she pointed out, he would faithfully practice each day as she advised, he could, perhaps, become the most accomplished of all the gifted students she'd had the pleasure of teaching.

But, much to Miss Foster's dismay, Ladd's only response had been—and still was—a flippant wink and a teasing smile. He wouldn't come right out and tell her, but he wasn't about to spend his afternoons practicing the piano when he could be outdoors doing the things he loved.

And he had absolutely no interest in learning to play the piano. He had reluctantly agreed to the lessons only because Laurette had pleaded and cajoled and begged and solemnly promised that she'd be ever so nice to him if he would do her this "one little favor."

Now, as the eleven-year-old Ladd sat in the Howards' music room and effortlessly played Chopin's polonaise with Laurette seated beside him and Miss Foster standing nearby, he smiled as he saw the humor of the situation.

With little practice, he could, Ladd realized, play quite well. Laurette, bless her, despite the hours of torturous practice demanded by her mother, couldn't compete. They had been working on this same composition for several months and Laurette still could not execute it correctly.

Ladd finished and Miss Foster opened her eyes and beamed proudly at him.

"Bravo, bravo," the pleased music teacher praised.

"Now, you try it again, Lollie," said Ladd. "You'll get it this time."

Nervous, Laurette nodded, took a deep breath and began to play. Halfway through the piece she was biting her lower lip and her forehead was perspiring. She struck several false, ear-punishing chords. Miss Foster made a face and cast her eyes skyward. Ladd shook his head and rose from the bench.

"I have to go," he announced, giving Laurette's blond hair a playful tug.

Laurette immediately stopped playing. She twisted around on the bench and said, "Wait, I'm going with you."

"You can't, you haven't finished with your lesson," he said. "Besides, we're having company this afternoon."

"Who's coming?"

"His name is Tigart. A Mister Darcy Tigart," Ladd said. "That's all I know. We haven't met him yet."

"Why would you invite a stranger to visit?"

"Father's been hunting for a new overseer for River Plantation since Brady left unexpectedly. Yesterday, Colonel Ivy told him about Darcy Tigart."

"So? What does that have to do with you?" asked Laurette, ignoring Miss Foster's stern look and gestures for her to resume playing.

"Mr. Tigart has a son about my age. He's coming along and I want to meet him," Ladd explained. He yawned suddenly, stretched, rose up on tiptoe with his arms raised above his head. Laurette jumped up from the piano bench and tugged on Ladd's shirtfront. He came back down on his heels.

"I want to meet him, too!" Laurette exclaimed.

"I'm sure you will," Ladd replied, freeing his shirt from her clutches, "but not this afternoon. I think you'd better spend more time practicing. Don't you agree, Miss Foster?"

"I most certainly do," said the exasperated music teacher.

Laurette frowned meanly at Ladd. He laughed and said, "Better be careful, Lollie, your face might freeze like that."

Four

The thin, sallow-skinned Darcy Tigart and his tall, sandy-haired thirteen-year-old son, Jimmy, arrived at the Dasheroon home on Dauphin Street at four o'clock that balmy March afternoon.

Young Jimmy, his hazel eyes wide with awe at the mansion's size and splendor, nervously lifted the heavy brass door knocker. He gave it a couple of heavy thunks, then stood back and waited.

Inside, Ladd shouted to Delson, the Dasheroon's smartly uniformed butler, "I'll get it, Delson!" Ladd raced through the house, yanked both double doors open wide and graciously offered his hand to the pair standing on the shaded veranda. "Mr. Tigart, Jimmy, welcome to Mobile." Both nodded. "I'm Ladd Dasheroon," Ladd said, eyeing Jimmy Tigart, sizing him up, noting with no small degree of disappointment that Jimmy was a good half a head taller than he. "Won't you please come inside? Father is waiting in the library."

The Tigarts followed Ladd into the richly paneled library—Darcy Tigart nervously twisting his battered hat in his gnarled hands, Jimmy eagerly taking everything in.

"Father," Ladd said as they stepped into the library, "This is Mr. Darcy Tigart and his son, Jimmy."

Douglas Dasheroon, seated behind his mahogany desk, immediately rose to his feet, came around the desk and offered an outstretched hand to the elder Tigart.

"Douglas Dasheroon, Mr. Tigart," he said with a smile and firm handshake. "Thank you both for coming."

"Thanks for inviting us," said Darcy Tigart, looking tense and uneasy.

Douglas's attention swiftly shifted to the sandy-haired youth standing beside his father. "Welcome to our home, Jimmy," he said, and shook the boy's hand.

"Thank you, Sir," Jimmy replied shyly.

"Ladd," said Douglas, releasing the boy's hand and turning to his own son, "why don't you and Jimmy get acquainted while Mr. Tigart and I have a talk?"

Ladd looked at Jimmy. "Want to go outside?"

Jimmy nodded almost imperceptibly. He and Ladd exited into the long, wide corridor, fell into step and walked unhurriedly through the mansion. Jimmy managed to appropriately utter yes or no to each question Ladd asked, but he was not really listening. He was far too distracted by the grandeur of his surroundings. Never in all his life had he been inside such a magnificent mansion and he was overwhelmed by what he saw. The high, frescoed ceilings. The deep, lush carpets. The heavy, handsome furniture.

Jimmy had only enough time for quick, appraising glances at the spacious rooms they passed. But he saw enough to realize that the Dasheroon family lived very differently from his own.

He envied this gangly, talkative boy walking beside him and wondered why he couldn't have been born into the great wealth and lofty status that this Ladd Dasheroon likely took for granted. Jimmy gritted his teeth and his hazel eyes narrowed at the unfairness of fate.

When the boys stepped out onto the wide back veranda and walked down the steps, Jimmy gazed at the rolling green lawns and well-tended gardens and tall oak trees. It was easy to imagine himself living here, playing croquet with guests, sipping lemonade from crystal tumblers, strolling arm-in-arm through the grounds with a beautiful, wealthy young girl.

"...and if your father, Mr. Tigart, should become our overseer, you'll live less than a mile away," Ladd said, intruding into Jimmy's pleasant daydreams.

Jimmy smiled, nodded and sat down on a bench. "That would be nice," he said.

Jimmy generally didn't have anything to do with someone younger than he. He felt older than his thirteen years and preferred the company of fifteen- and sixteen-year-olds. But this was different. Ladd Dasheroon had the kind of life—and probably the kind of friends—Jimmy wanted to have.

"And perhaps I could come here to your home to

visit you now and then?'' Jimmy suggested, with a disarming smile.

"Of course, you could," Ladd was enthusiastic, flattered that the older boy would want to be his friend. "We'll be at school together, too, and I can introduce you to everyone. Next time you're here, you'll meet my friend, Laurette Howard. She's a girl who lives just across Dauphin." Explaining that he felt obligated to keep a eye on Laurette, Ladd grinned and admitted, "She's a pest sometimes, but she's like a little sister to me, so I have to look after her."

"I have nothing against girls," said Jimmy. "Especially if they're pretty."

Ladd shrugged narrow shoulders. "She's pretty, I guess. I never noticed."

"You, my love," said Carrie Dasheroon to her husband, "are an exceptionally kind, compassionate man."

Douglas Dasheroon smiled boyishly. "You are just now learning that?"

"No, I've always known it," said Carrie, as she stepped closer, and put her arms around her husband's neck. "That's why I love you so much."

It was nearing midnight and the pair were finally alone in their upstairs bedchamber, preparing to retire for the evening. Earlier in the day, Douglas had told his wife that, after verifying several references, he had offered the overseer's position to Darcy Tigart. Tigart had eagerly accepted.

Carrie had briefly met the man and had known right

away—as Douglas surely had—that Darcy Tigart was not well. He was not strong and robust as a plantation overseer should be. He was, obviously, in failing health.

Who but her dear, noble, tenderhearted husband would have given Darcy Tigart the overseer's position at River Plantation? No one. Carrie smiled now as her big, handsome husband felt the need to continue to explain his dubious decision to hire Tigart.

"I suppose I could have found someone better suited to the job," Douglas said, as he kissed Carrie's temple, then disengaged himself from her, "but the poor fellow came to Mobile from Kentucky believing he had a position at the Battersly paper mill. The Colonel told me that when Tigart arrived, he found there was no job for him." Unbuttoning his shirt, Douglas sat down on the bed and began removing his shoes as he spoke. "As you well know, I need someone right away. And young Jimmy can be of assistance."

"Yes, of course," Carrie said, nodding. She sat down beside her husband.

"Darcy Tigart can start as early as tomorrow, and that is certainly in his favor," Douglas pointed out. "Brady's been gone little more than a week, but the place is already going to seed. I need a man out there to…"

Douglas continued to rationalize his choice while Carrie listened, smiling fondly with affection. She was fully aware of which man was getting the better end of the bargain. It wasn't Douglas. And it wasn't the first time. The caring, benevolent Douglas often overruled the shrewd, business-minded Douglas.

Darcy Tigart would receive a small salary and a generous bonus on crops at harvest time. And he and his family, a wife, whom they'd not yet met, and their thirteen-year-old son, would live, rent free, in the fully furnished eight-room overseer's house at River Plantation. They would have at their disposal a buggy and several horses and they would enjoy an abundance of fresh fruits and vegetables from the plantation's orchard and garden, as well as meat and eggs from the farm.

The entrance to River Plantation was less than a mile north of the city proper. The Tigarts' son could easily walk back and forth to Hillcrest School.

"...and if I spend a few days out there getting him started," Douglas was saying, "we could have the operation running smoothly again in no time at all." He stopped speaking, looked at his smiling wife, his brows knitted. "What? What's so amusing?"

"You," she said, and laid a soft hand on his chest where his shirt was open. "You're absolutely precious when you're defending yourself."

"Is that what I'm doing?"

"It is and it's totally unnecessary, although I find it tremendously appealing." She moved her hand farther inside the unbuttoned shirt, raked her nails through the crisp dark hair.

"You're poking fun at me," he accused.

"No, I'm not, Douglas," she said softly. "There is nothing quite so attractive as watching a big, strong, virile man demonstrate his innate compassion and gentleness. It touches me.'' She impulsively bent her dark head and brushed a kiss across his exposed chest. ''It excites me.''

Douglas lifted his muscular arms around his wife. Carrie raised her dark head and looked into his eyes. She saw the quick flare of passion in their blue depths and sighed with pleasure. She laughed low in her throat when he urged her up off the bed and turned her to stand between his knees, facing him. She helpfully lifted her arms when he eased her nightgown up her slender body. When the gossamer negligee was bunched up beneath her throat, Douglas released his hold on it, leaned forward and kissed her round right breast.

Trembling now, Carrie slid the gown up over her head, dropped it to the thick carpet and eagerly took a seat on her husband's left knee. If his empathy and tenderness excited her, she knew what most excited him.

So she cupped his face in her hands, kissed him, then whispered, ''Know what I want you to do to me?''

Douglas swallowed hard. ''Tell me, angel girl.''

She did.

Carrie Dasheroon, looking directly into her husband's eyes, said something shockingly scandalous, boldly using the most graphic language.

That's all it took.

Douglas could feel himself stir. To hear his exquisitely beautiful, sweetly demure wife saying such erotic, forbidden words caused him to instantly harden against her bare, soft bottom.

Carrie felt the swift, physical response and, covering his face with kisses, continued to murmur—in explicit, obscene terms—exactly what she wanted him to do to her.

He loved it.

And she loved exciting him.

Years ago when they had first married, Douglas had teasingly suggested she say a taboo word. The refined, sheltered Carrie had been shocked to the roots of her dark hair at such an appalling request. She had haughtily demurred, stating emphatically that she would never allow such filth to pass her lips. But in time, she had relented.

They had agreed that their risqué banter would always remain strictly between the two of them and would only be spoken in the total privacy of their bedroom. Nowhere else. After much gentle coaxing and flirtatious teasing, he had finally gotten her to say the kind of coarse, crude words to him that would have made even the most foulmouthed sailor blush.

The married lovers used the explicit profanity on random nights—or lazy afternoons—when the two of them were especially aroused, when they had been wanting each other all day long and were ready and eager to play bawdy games.

When Carrie had come to fully realize just how much the game excited her husband, she knew that she could arouse him any time she chose. Armed with that knowledge, she had, a few times, leaned over while they were out in public—at the theater, or a restaurant, at a party—and wickedly whispered, so softly that only he could hear, one of his favorite words.

On each of those occasions, Douglas had swiftly made their apologies to their hosts, rushed his thrillingly naughty wife home and straight up the stairs to their big four-poster.

Now tonight, in the total privacy of their bedroom, while the big mansion slept, a naked, laughing Carrie sat on her husband's knee and teased him in the manner he most liked to be teased. She squealed with pleasure when he abruptly rose to his feet with her in his arms, turned about and dropped her onto the middle of the soft, silk-sheeted mattress.

She watched as he hastily undressed. Letting his clothes lay where they fell, he was naked in seconds and anxiously joined her on the bed. He urged her slender legs apart, made a place for himself between them and said, "Know what I'm going to do to you, you brazen, wicked wench?"

"I have no idea, you vile, unscrupulous seducer," she whispered playfully. "You'll have to tell me."

He told her.

And then he took her.

Five

The minute Ladd introduced Laurette to Jimmy Tigart, she got the sinking feeling that nothing would ever be quite the same again. It wasn't that she didn't like Jimmy. She liked him well enough. He was friendly and pleasant and his teasing was good-natured and he was fun, but she missed being Ladd's only best friend. For as long as she could remember it had been Ladd and her. Now Ladd and Jimmy were frequently together and Ladd no longer paid her as much attention.

For a year the three of them all attended the Hillcrest School together, but Laurette was, sadly, often left out of their after-school adventures. A fact that secretly pleased her mother. Marion felt it was high time her daughter's friends were girls, not boys. To ensure that the willful Laurette made friends of her own sex, Marion enrolled her daughter in the prestigious Hunnicutt Academy for Young Ladies in the autumn of 1855 after Laurette turned eleven.

Laurette was outraged. She protested angrily, but calmed somewhat when Ladd told her that he and Jimmy would no longer be at Hillcrest, either. Both were to attend the private military academy located at the corner of Claiborne and St. Michael. Jimmy was attending as a scholarship student.

Ladd and Laurette remained close, but she missed him. Fortunately, just as her mother had hoped, Laurette met new friends at Miss Hunnicutt's academy. Girlfriends. There were several young ladies she liked immediately. Missy Tyler and Belinda Vance and Paula Gentry were all very nice.

But her best friends quickly became the Parlange twins, Juliette and Johanna. After losing both their parents in a tragic riverboat explosion more than a year ago, the twins, who were two months older than Laurette, had come to Mobile to live with their paternal grandparents, Judge Noble and Lena Parlange.

The twins were almost identical in appearance: raven-black hair, pale, porcelain skin, large emerald eyes and full, wide mouths. But the pretty young twins were as different as night and day in temperament. Juliette was quiet, demure and studious while Johanna, like Laurette, was fiery, boisterous and outspoken. Laurette liked them both and they liked her. She visited them at the Parlanges' Springhill home and the twins came often to the Dauphin Street mansion.

Soon after meeting them, Laurette introduced the twins to Ladd and Jimmy Tigart. When the boys had left, the frank Johanna had innocently commented that while both Ladd and Jimmy were both nice looking, Ladd was downright adorable. Laurette's dark eyes immediately blazed.

"Johanna Parlagne," the firm-jawed Laurette stated, "Ladd Dasheroon belongs to me."

Johanna laughed uproariously. "Don't be silly, Laurette."

"I'm not being silly," Laurette snapped. "Ladd is mine and always has been. I intend to marry him when I'm old enough."

Again Johanna laughed, but promised she'd never use her abundant charms to dazzle Ladd.

The trio spent many an hour in Laurette's bedroom, Laurette and Johanna gossiping and screeching with laughter, while the calm Juliette smiled with amusement.

The friendship between Ladd and Jimmy Tigart seemed solid, but it became even more firmly cemented one hot summer afternoon when the boys, now thirteen and fifteen years old respectively, slipped down to Pirate's Cove for a swim. The secluded inlet was a favorite swimming spot.

Far, far out in the bay, a buoy bobbed. There was a definite chop to the water as a warm wind blew steadily in from the open seas to the south. The two boys had often talked about swimming out to the distant buoy, but had never seriously considered doing it.

Still, on this particular sultry summer afternoon, Jimmy felt adventurous. Smiling, pushing his damp sandy hair back off his face, he challenged Ladd.

"I bet I can swim all the way out to that buoy."

Ladd grinned. "Is that a dare?"

"It is."

"Let's go," said Ladd, rising to his feet.

Laughing and shouting, the boys raced each other across the sand and into the water. A relentless August sun beat down from a cloudless sky, turning the lapping waves into thousands of blinding mirrors of light.

Halfway to the buoy Ladd could feel his arms and legs begin to knot and ache, but he wasn't about to admit it. He continued to slice through the steadily roughening waters, ignoring the burning of his lungs, the aching of his limbs.

Minutes later, terror seized him when he realized that he was not going to make it. He was tired, so paralyzingly tired, he could no longer fight the strong current.

He was about to go down when Jimmy, glancing over his shoulder, saw that Ladd was in deep distress. Jimmy immediately turned and swam back. Ladd's head was just disappearing beneath the surface when Jimmy reached him and pulled him up.

"I've got you, Laddie," Jimmy said, "I'll get you back to shore."

And he did.

When Ladd told his parents of Jimmy's selfless heroics, explaining how his friend had saved his life, Carrie and Douglas were tremendously grateful to their landseer's son. They assured him they would never forget what he had done. Douglas proved it. A West Point graduate, he used his considerable influ-

ence to get Jimmy a much coveted appointment to the
military academy.

And, when Darcy Tigart passed away in the winter
of 1857, Douglas allowed Jimmy and his mother to
stay on in a summer cottage at River Plantation.

In the early autumn of 1858, Ladd, Laurette, their
parents, the Parlange twins and a host of other well-
wishers were at the busy downtown levee to see
Jimmy off to West Point, New York. There was
laughter and high spirits and, when the time came for
Jimmy to board the waiting riverboat, a lot of back-
slapping and hugging.

When Jimmy turned to Laurette, she noticed a
strange look come into his hazel eyes. And when he
enfolded her in his arms, she felt his heart race against
her soft bosom as he briefly pressed her closely to
him.

Swiftly he released her and she wondered if she
had imagined the whole thing. But she knew that she
had not. Jimmy had regularly jested and flattered and
flirted with her, but she had always assumed it had
been nothing more than harmless teasing. Now she
was not so sure.

Troubled, she watched as he grabbed the laughing
Johanna Parlange and gave her a big bear hug, then
turned to the quieter Juliette, causing Juliette to blush
profusely when he planted a kiss on her pale cheek.

Lastly, he embraced Ladd. The two boys clung to
each other for a long moment.

And then Jimmy was gone.

* * *

Laurette felt guilty.

She couldn't help it, she was glad Jimmy had gone away. At long last she had Ladd to herself again. In Jimmy's absence, Ladd spent more time with her, but to her dismay, he continued to treat her as he always had. Like a little sister or a member of the same sex. Couldn't he see that she was growing up? Didn't he realize that they were no longer children?

No matter how hard Laurette tried to entice Ladd, intrigue him, make him see that she was turning into a woman, Ladd seemed not to notice.

In despair, she told her best friends, the Parlange twins, that she was convinced Ladd, whom she adored, would never look on her as anything other than a friend. A sister.

Until, one day, abruptly, without warning, everything changed.

Not for Laurette.

But for Ladd.

It was the winter after Jimmy had gone to the Point. Ladd had turned fifteen the summer past, Laurette fourteen. On a gray December day, Laurette, at his mother Carrie's invitation, had come over to help decorate the tall, fragrant evergreen tree that stood in the parlor.

When Laurette arrived, Ladd answered the door.

In that instant, Ladd Dasheroon saw Laurette Howard in a totally new and different light.

"Hi!" she said cheerily.

"Hello," Ladd managed to reply, after nervously clearing his throat.

He stared at her, hypnotized. Her large, dark eyes were sparkling with life and her lips were full, pink and soft looking. She wore a hooded cape of scarlet velvet and her chilled cheeks were almost as red as the luxurious wrap.

Ladd realized, with no small degree of surprise, that his little Laurette was rapidly changing. Had changed before his very eyes. She was growing up. She was no longer a child. She was a very pretty girl. He wondered when it had happened. And why he hadn't noticed. It was as if he were seeing her—meeting her—for the first time.

And he was utterly enchanted.

From that memorable moment when she stood there on the cold, windswept veranda swathed in flaming red velvet, Ladd never again thought of Laurette Howard as a playmate. Or even as a little sister.

Now, whenever he held her hand as they crossed the street, or climbed the church steps together on Sunday morning, or went for a walk along the river, the touch of her soft fingers laced through his own gave him an indescribable thrill.

No matter that he was only fifteen, she fourteen, Ladd Dasheroon was in love with Laurette Howard. He didn't dare tell her. He knew her too well. She'd just laugh in his face if he told her. So he kept it from her, pretended nothing had changed, went out of his way to treat her just as he always had. But it was far from easy. Every time he saw her his heart skipped several beats, his palms grew moist and his knees became disturbingly weak.

He couldn't tell her, but he had to tell someone. So he wrote a letter to Jimmy, exclaiming his newfound love for Laurette and swearing Jimmy to secrecy.

Never dreaming that Jimmy secretly wanted the blossoming Laurette for himself.

And that he intended to have her.

Six

Saturday the twenty-third of July, 1859.

Laurette Howard's fifteenth birthday.

Ladd Dasheroon's sixteenth birthday.

Engraved vellum invitations, banded in gold, had gone out two weeks ago. A twenty-piece orchestra from New Orleans had been engaged. An expansive menu had been planned by a trio of Mobile's most sought after chefs. Melba Adair, as usual, had insisted on providing bowers of fragrant flowers from her famous gardens.

This gala in Dauphin Way—the combined birthday celebration—had become legendary. The festivities had been an annual affair since the summer of '45 when Ladd Dasheroon had turned two years old and Laurette Howard had reached her first birthday.

On this balmy Saturday evening the formal event was hosted by the Dasheroons. As darkness descended, the brass-and-crystal chandeliers blazed in every room of the big red mansion. Downstairs, in the spacious dining room, a sumptuous buffet, fit for royalty, was laid out on the long linen-draped table.

Upstairs, the ballroom was beautifully decorated with hundreds of prized white roses, camellias and gardenias. A half-dozen chandeliers, suspended from the eight-foot ceiling, cast a soft, mellow glow on the polished parquet dance floor below. Gilt chairs lined the walls in deference to the older guests who preferred to sit and watch rather than dance.

The matching double doors—a set at each side of the ballroom—were thrown open onto a wide balcony that spanned the entire front of the grand house. An unseasonably cooling breeze wafted through the open doors, stirring the brocade curtains in the giant ballroom and keeping the dancers from becoming too warm.

Guests had begun arriving as soon as the sun had gone down. The younger set was well represented. Dozens of Ladd's and Laurette's school chums eagerly hurried up the stairs and into the ballroom. Tall, shy, fresh-faced boys laughed and flirted with pretty young girls in shimmering summer dresses.

The older crowd turned out as well. Colonel and Mrs. Ivy. The Adairs. Judge Noble and Lena Parlange. Miss Foster, their dear music teacher. The Faradays. The Pirrilliats. A cortege of carriages, transporting the city's formally attired elite, came in a steady stream up the graveled front drive. Gentlemen in dark, well-cut evening attire escorted jewel-bedecked ladies in colorful silks and satins.

All were ready for a delightful evening.

And across Dauphin Street, inside the Howard home, Laurette was still in her camisole and petticoats as full darkness fell over the city. The Parlange twins, beautifully gowned in shimmering blue silk, were anxiously waiting for Laurette to get dressed.

"For heaven sake, Laurette, make up your mind!" said Johanna with annoyance. "The dancing's already begun. I can hear the music from here."

"I know, I know," said Laurette, frowning with indecision.

On Laurette's lavender-canopied four-poster bed lay a half-dozen ball gowns. Tried on and quickly discarded. Laurette's personal maid, the usually indulgent Ruby Lee, balled fists on her hips, stood shaking her head.

"Laurette Taylor Howard," said Ruby Lee, "you are going to be late to your own birthday party and that is mighty rude, if you ask me!"

"I didn't ask you," said an upset Laurette. "Oh, what am I going to do? I have nothing to wear! Nothing!"

Ruby Lee harumphed loudly, turned and waddled into Laurette's large dressing room. There she rifled through dozens of lovely dresses, many of which had never been worn. Finally she chose a frothy rose chiffon ball gown, tossed it over her arm and went back to Laurette.

Ruby Lee held out the garment, "Let's try this one, honey lamb. You've never worn it and the color would look real nice with your hair."

"Yes!" Laurette agreed, enthusiastically, "Exactly what I've been looking for! Something grown-up and alluring. I simply have to look my best tonight!"

Ruby Lee chuckled. "You say that every time you

go out." She lifted the dress over Laurette's head, muffling Laurette's reply. When the dress fell into place on Laurette's slender body, Ruby Lee immediately began fastening the tiny little self-covered buttons in back. "What did you say?"

"I said, tonight is different."

"And why is that?" asked Johanna, a well-arched eyebrow lifted.

Laurette spun around to face her inquisitive friend. "Because I intend to make Ladd Dasheroon realize that I am no longer a child."

Ruby Lee chuckled. "You're both still children and as far as I can see..."

"You may go now, Ruby Lee," Laurette cut her off.

"I'm going, I'm going," said Ruby Lee, wagging her head and muttering to herself as she left.

Laurette turned about several times in front of the free-standing mirror, checking to make sure the skirts of the rose chiffon dress would swirl out prettily when she danced. They did. She pinched her cheeks, bit her lips and then, grinning naughtily, urged the bodice of her tight-waisted ball gown down a half inch lower than it was supposed to be worn.

She checked the gentle swell of her pale bosom that rose subtly above the low-cut bodice. Oh, yes. Surely, Ladd would notice. Jimmy, home on summer furlough from West Point, would be sure to see, and to let her know that he had. But it wasn't Jimmy's attention she wanted. It was Ladd's. She wanted Ladd to notice. She had to make him notice. She had to make him start seeing her as the woman she now was.

Laurette exhaled with frustration.

"What's wrong now?" asked Johanna, motioning to Juliette as she took Laurette's arm and began propelling her toward the bedroom door.

"Nothing's wrong, Johanna," Laurette said sharply.

But it was. She had, in the past few months, tried her best to captivate Ladd, to intrigue him, to make him aware that she no longer thought of him as a big brother. And that she didn't want him to think of her as a little sister.

What, she wondered, would she have to do to make Ladd love her as she loved him?

Directly across Dauphin, Ladd was still in his bedroom at the front of grand Dasheroon mansion. He was not yet dressed. He could hear the music, the talking and laughter. He knew it was getting late. Knew he should be with his mother and father, greeting arriving guests.

His valet, Lucas, had laid out a pair of perfectly pressed evening trousers along with a matching frock coat, white pleated shirt and black cravat.

But if he wore the dark suit, Ladd reasoned, he would look exactly like every other male present. He didn't want that. He wanted to stand out. He wanted Laurette to walk into the ballroom and immediately spot him in the crowd. He wanted her eyes to cling to him, her pulse to quicken, her heart to flutter a little.

Wearing only his white linen underwear, Ladd stalked into his cedar-paneled dressing room. From an extensive wardrobe, he decisively took down a handsomely tailored white dinner jacket, slipped his long arms inside and looked at himself in the free-standing pier glass. He liked what he saw well enough. He had spent time out in the sun, helping out at River Plantation and taking swims in the bay. His deeply tanned skin was accentuated by the stark contrast of the snowy-white dinner jacket.

Ladd felt that he had to look his very best tonight. He had decided he would wait no longer to tell Laurette he loved her. Tonight was to be the most important night of his whole life and he wanted everything to be perfect.

Dressed at last, Ladd gave himself one last quick appraising glance in the mirror. He grimaced in annoyance. A lock of unruly raven hair fell forward onto his forehead. He impatiently brushed it back, but it wouldn't stay in place. There was nothing he could do about it.

Sweeping the rebellious lock back again, Ladd left his room. He hurried toward the ballroom. His heart racing with excitement, he paused in the arched doorway, looked around and entered the crowded hall.

And immediately felt his heart stop, then squeeze painfully in his chest when he spotted his slender, golden-haired angel dancing in the arms of his best friend Jimmy Tigart.

Laurette was smiling and her eyes were shining and she appeared to be having a wonderful time. Jimmy was holding her intimately close and bending to whisper something in her ear. She laughed, turned her head and saw Ladd. But before she could make eye contact, he was gone.

Miserable, Ladd turned and fled the crowded ballroom. He anxiously exited the open double doors onto the moonlit balcony and raced down the curving steps. He hurried around the house and sprinted all the way out into the far back gardens to be alone.

Laurette could hardly wait for the dance to end.

An innocent dance with Jimmy Tigart had done what she'd been trying to do for months. It had made Ladd notice her in a way he never had before. Ladd had walked into the ballroom, seen her in Jimmy's arms and had suffered a bout of jealousy.

She was elated.

He wouldn't be jealous if he didn't care. Although there was no need to be jealous of Jimmy. She loved only Ladd. Jimmy was quite dashing in his dress gray uniform, but she thought of him only as a friend. She belonged, heart and soul, to Ladd and always would.

And, oh, how handsome he looked tonight. One quick glance had taken her breath away. His black hair had gleamed in the light of the chandeliers and an unruly lock had fallen appealingly low on his forehead. His smooth olive complexion made a striking contrast to the spotless white jacket he wore. His incredible indigo eyes were broodingly beautiful and his perfectly sculpted, full-lipped mouth was set. He was tall and trim and he stood out from the crowd.

And Laurette knew that he would stand out from the crowd for the rest of his life. For the rest of hers.

The waltz finally ended.

Laurette started to step out of Jimmy's arms, but he held her fast. "One dance is not enough, sweetheart. Give me another."

She shook her head decisively. "Sorry, Jimmy." She skillfully disengaged herself. "I can't. Not right now."

She started backing away. He followed.

"Of course, you can," he coaxed. "Come here to me, birthday girl."

"I said *no*," she told him firmly and, eyes flashing with determination, she turned and left him.

Outside on the balcony, Laurette lifted the full skirts of her ball gown, descended the steps and went in search of Ladd. Forgetting, momentarily, that she was now a young lady, she yanked her billowing skirts up to her knees, raced around the house and hurried out onto the estate's manicured grounds.

She found Ladd out beyond the last terrace at the far edge of the gardens where the camellia and azalea bushes gave way to a row of banana trees bordering the estate. He was standing with his back to her, arms crossed over his chest. Laurette didn't speak his name or call out to him. She walked directly up to him, stopped and waited until he sensed her presence and turned to face her.

At last he did.

Slowly he turned, looked squarely at her, and the misery written on his boyishly handsome face and in his azure eyes touched her heart as nothing had before.

Laurette didn't hesitate.

She stepped closer, put her slender arms around Ladd's trim waist, guilelessly looked up at him and said softly, "Ladd, do you know that I love you?"

"And I love you, Lollie," he replied, afraid to make too much of her confession.

"No, no, I don't mean that way," she eagerly set him straight. "Not like when we were children. I am in love with you, Ladd, and if you don't love me back, I will die of a broken heart."

So relieved that he wanted to shout with joy, Ladd started to grin as his nervous arms went around the young girl he adored. Swallowing anxiously, he said, "Lollie, I do love you. Oh, I do. I love you, I've always loved you. I will never love anyone else."

"Nor will I," Laurette declared, then affectionately pressed her cheek against his chest. "You are the only one I will ever love," she promised. She lifted her head, smiled up at him and repeated, "The only one, ever, I swear it."

Ladd was dazzled. By what she was saying and by the sight of the summer moonlight silvering her long, pale hair and the unmistakable look of love shining out of her beautiful dark eyes. His arms tightened around her.

His knees trembling now, he asked, "May I…kiss you?"

"Yes." She was quick to give permission. Then, brows knitting, added candidly, "But I don't know how to kiss."

"I don't, either," he admitted, "but we can learn together."

"Yes," she said, "we can. We will. Kiss me, Ladd. Kiss me."

Ladd gently drew Laurette up on tiptoe, lowered his head and timidly pressed his closed lips against hers. It was a sweet, brief, innocent caress, but thoroughly pleasing to the young pair involved. Laurette loved the feel of Ladd's smooth, warm mouth covering her own and Ladd immensely enjoyed tasting Laurette's soft, sweet lips.

At the conclusion of that first kiss, the couple stood in the moonlight, silent and unmoving, hearts beating as one, gazing at each other in wonder and adoration. Abruptly, they became aware that their bodies were touching from torso to knees.

It was a brand-new sensation for them both. Laurette thrilled to the feel of the hard, sculpted muscles of Ladd's chest gently crushing her sensitive breasts. And the touch of his flat, washboard belly pressed against her nervously fluttering stomach. And the long, granite bones of his thighs intimately brushing hers through the folds of her full chiffon skirts.

If it was exciting to Laurette to stand in Ladd's close embrace, it was heaven on earth for Ladd. Her soft, full breasts pressing into his chest made him shiver with pleasure and the feel of her pale thighs rubbing against his own through the barrier of their clothes was nearly too sweet to be endured.

Ladd kissed Laurette again.

And yet again.

Their birthday party forgotten, Ladd and Laurette continued to stay there in the moon-silvered garden for another half hour, kissing, touching, sighing.

And making vows.

"Promise me you'll never let anyone else kiss you, Lollie," Ladd whispered against her temple.

"I promise," Laurette murmured dreamily. "Yours are the only lips that will ever touch mine."

"You'll remember your promise when I'm far away at West Point?"

"I will," she said, "besides, we have a whole year before you leave."

"Yes," he said, smiling, "we can do a lot of kissing in a year."

Laurette laughed merrily. "Yes, we can. We will. But now, we have a duty to our guests. We'd better get back, don't you think?"

"I'd totally forgotten about the party," Ladd happily admitted and kissed her one more time.

Seven

Ladd and Laurette's sweet, innocent romance began that warm summer evening in the fragrant gardens of the Dasheroon estate. In love, happy, Laurette and Ladd were content to be alone together. To kiss and kiss until their lips were puffy and tender and their hearts were racing with excitement.

They didn't immediately tell their parents that they had fallen madly in love. They were afraid that if their parents knew how they really felt about each other, they wouldn't be allowed to spend so much time alone.

But, with Laurette's permission, Ladd did tell Jimmy. The very next day after the big birthday party, Ladd confided in his friend.

"She loves me!" Ladd joyously declared. "Laurette loves me as much as I love her."

"How do you know?" asked Jimmy, brows knitting. "I thought you were going to wait. Weren't going to tell her yet."

"I didn't. She told me!" Ladd was ecstatic.

"I don't quite follow."

"Last night Laurette came out to the garden, walked right up to me and told me that she loved me and wanted me to love her back. And I do love her, so I told her so and that I wanted to marry her.''

''I'm happy for you both,'' said Jimmy Tigart with a smile that didn't quite reach his eyes.

By the Thanksgiving holiday the couple could no longer keep their secret. Over roasted turkey and corn bread dressing served in the spacious dining room of the Howard mansion, Ladd announced that he and Laurette had fallen in love and intended to marry and spend their lives together.

Both sets of parents were fully approving of the match. The Howards couldn't have asked for a finer young man to be their spirited daughter's beau. They trusted Ladd implicitly, knew they could count on him to behave properly with the naive Laurette. The Dasheroons realized just how much Ladd cared for Laurette and were thrilled with the prospect of having her for their daughter-in-law.

Douglas Dasheroon, with T. H. Howard nodding his agreement as he accepted a second piece of pumpkin pie, reminded his smitten son and the girl he loved that Ladd was expected to follow in the family tradition and go to West Point.

''I know,'' said Ladd. ''Laurette understands.'' He looked at her and smiled.

''I'm sure she does,'' said her father, T.H., ''but do both of you realize that the growing rift between the North and South could lead to…to war?''

''T.H.!'' Marion scolded her husband, ''this is a holiday.''

"T.H. is right," said Douglas, looking somber. "The recent violence at Harper's Ferry is only the beginning. The South is a powder keg, ready to explode. And, should war come..."

"I would serve in the Confederacy," Ladd interrupted, unworried.

"And I would wait for his return," stated Laurette.

"Let's hope that won't be necessary," said Carrie, shooting her husband a silencing look. She smiled at Ladd and Laurette and said, "All we ask, children, is that you wait to marry until Ladd has completed his education." The other parents nodded their unanimity.

The sweethearts agreed.

And then gave silent thanks that they had an advantage over most young couples who were in love. It appeared that their fears had been unfounded, that they would continue to be allowed the luxury of being alone whenever they chose without censure from either set of parents.

They were right.

Neither the Howards nor the Dasheroons worried about Ladd and Laurette spending so much time together. After all, the children had grown up together, had spent their lives together. It would be senseless to try to keep them apart now. Besides, they had complete trust in both Ladd and Laurette, just as they'd always had.

Laurette and Ladd were acutely aware of that trust and truly wanted to be worthy of it. Neither wanted to do anything that would hurt or disappoint their parents. Both were honorable and responsible, had been raised to respect their elders and to abide by the dictates and restrictions of courtly society.

But they were so desperately in love that they yearned to share more than just kisses. Their fevered, fully clothed bodies strained and ached with their growing need. Their eager hands grew ever more bold, nervous fingers anxiously exploring the wondrous configuration of their very different bodies.

Ladd's gentle hands frequently found their way to Laurette's soft, full breasts and she hadn't the will to make him stop. She squirmed and sighed and trembled as he tenderly caressed her through the fabric of her clothes.

On a foggy Friday night in early January, the embracing pair sat in the darkness of a parked carriage directly in front of Laurette's house. The Dasheroon's driver, the easygoing Moses, sat atop the brougham's box patiently waiting for them to get out.

But they lingered, reluctant to say good-night. Kissing, sighing, the embracing pair couldn't get enough of each other. Each time they were alone now, the burning desire blazed ever hotter, their need for each other so intense it was painful. All their good intentions to remain pure and virginal were beginning to melt away in the burning heat that constantly enveloped them.

After yet another prolonged kiss that left both Ladd and Laurette weak with wanting, Laurette gasped softly with shocked pleasure when Ladd's hand drifted down to her flat belly, then moved lower still. She gazed into Ladd's smoldering blue eyes as he tenderly caressed her where she had never been touched before. His long, tanned fingers seemed to burn their way right through her full woolen skirts and silk underwear.

It felt good.

So good.

"Oh, Ladd," she breathed, excited, disturbed, "you must stop. Please stop."

"I know," Ladd said, quickly withdrawing his hand. "I'm sorry, Lollie, forgive me."

He gritted his teeth and silently cursed himself. His passion for her had become a constant driving force in him, causing him to lose sleep, torturing him almost beyond endurance. At the same time he loved her so much he wanted to safeguard and protect her, even from himself.

"Let's go in," he said, reaching for her hand. "It's getting late."

Laurette nodded, but stayed as she was. "I'm sorry, Ladd. Don't be angry with me."

He managed a weak smile. "I could never be angry with you, Lollie. It's just…oh, sweetheart…I can't help it, I want you so much, it…it…hurts. *I* hurt."

"I know," she whispered, understanding completely, and then caused Ladd to lose his breath when, to his astonishment, she placed her hand on his groin. Her warm, soft palm and slender fingers settled possessively on the hard flesh straining the confines of his tight buff trousers. She said truthfully, "I love you, Ladd. I'd do anything for you. I don't want you to hurt. I don't want you to *ever* hurt." Her fingers awkwardly stroked. "Let me take this hurt away."

His breath shallow and ragged, Ladd managed, "I—I promised your father I'd have you inside by ten."

"I know." She nodded and sighed.

"It's almost ten."

"There's always tomorrow and..." her words trailed away and she looked into his eyes, her hand remaining on his rigid flesh.

"Yes! Tomorrow," he said, excitedly. "Tomorrow's Saturday. We can spend the entire day together."

"We can," she agreed. "As I'm sure you know, our mothers are going out to Spring Hill to attend a luncheon at Marie Lassat's."

Ladd nodded. "I heard mother talking about it. Something to do with the Mardi Gras."

"Exactly," said Laurette. "Marie Lassat is having a Twelfth Day get-together to celebrate the start of Mardi Gras."

"Something our mothers wouldn't dare miss," Ladd said with a smile.

"Not for anything."

It was the winter social season in Mobile and Marion Howard and Carrie Dasheroon were very much a part of the city's elite Mardi Gras society. They were instrumental in helping to plan the Camellia Ball as well as a number of the other galas. The important luncheon they were to attend was at the luxurious

Spring Hill mansion of the blue-blooded Marie Lassat, a woman who proudly claimed that her roots went back to the beginning of the eighteenth century when her family came over with Bienville on the first ship of French colonists to arrive in Mobile. Only the cream of Mobile's aristocracy would be present. And that privileged Old Guard included Carrie Dasheroon and Marion Howard.

"They'll be gone most of the day," Laurette said simply.

"I'm sure they will."

Both fell silent, planning, considering what they would tell their parents and where they would go to be safe and alone and assured of total privacy. Ladd came up with the solution. "Let's go across the bay to Spanish Fort," he eagerly suggested. "There are dozens of remote places over there in the dense woods beyond the village. We'll find a spot where no one's ever been."

"Yes!" Laurette was quick to agree. "We'll tell our parents that we're going over to the eastern shore to have a picnic and that we might spend the day."

"I'll get Moses to drive us down to the harbor."

"I'll have Hannah pack a lunch and I'll bring a blanket."

"Pick you up at ten?"

"Yes," she said, "Oh, yes. I'll be ready, Ladd."

He considered the import of what they were intending, of what she was saying. He looked at her for a long time, then said, "Are you sure, Lollie?"

"I'm very sure," she said as she leaned up and

brushed a kiss to his mouth. Against his lips, she whispered, "I love you with all my heart and soul and I want to belong to you completely."

They couldn't believe it.

They had aroused no suspicions when they'd told their parents of their day-long plans.

"A picnic in January?" was Carrie Dasheroon's response. "Ladd, it could be quite cold tomorrow."

"If it is too cold, you and Laurette can picnic here at the house," said a smiling Douglas Dasheroon.

"Oh, good," Marion Howard had said when Laurette told her and T.H. "I hated to leave you here alone all day. I have that luncheon I simply must attend and your father has business in town."

"Why go so far just to have a picnic?" inquired T. H. Howard. "You know it may be too cold to be outdoors."

That was it.

Nothing more was said.

Now, on Saturday morning, as the carriage rolled down Dauphin Street toward the waterfront, Laurette and Ladd held hands and said little, their thoughts on what was going to happen today and of how it could change their lives. They were not nervous, just reflective, quiet.

Fate had been kind, the weather was near perfect. One of those warm, sunny Alabama days that can occasionally occur in mid-January. The sky was a bright cobalt blue overhead. The still, heavy air was balmy. It might have been May, so warm and perfect was the morning.

Laurette sighed with contentment. The subtropical climate was one of the things she most loved about her Mobile home. That and the broad avenues shaded by rows of majestic oaks. Beyond the oaks, thick Saint Augustine grass lawns sprawled before stately, pillared mansions, neat white Creole cottages with green shutters and raised Gulf Coast bungalows. Intricate balconies graced many of the houses and decorative iron fences, fountains and lampposts were everywhere.

It was a beautiful, romantic city—the place she wanted to live in for the rest of her life. And, seated beside her in the moving carriage, was the handsome, loving boy with whom she wanted to spend all the rest of her days.

And nights.

Laurette looked at Ladd and smiled. He squeezed her hand, smiled back and said, "We're almost to the levee."

She nodded. The carriage was approaching downtown's lush Bienville Square where towering live oaks with long gray beards of Spanish moss shaded the many lacy iron benches below. There friends congregated in warm weather to visit and gossip and enjoy band concerts. Just ahead was old Fort Conde and, beyond, the calm waters of Mobile Bay. South of the bay were the sugary white beaches of the Gulf Coast and the mighty ocean beyond.

When the carriage rolled to a stop at the busy

docks, Ladd said to Moses, "You'll pick us up at 4:00 p.m.?"

Moses grinned, nodded and said, "I'll be right here waiting. You children enjoy your day."

"We will," they replied in unison.

"Thanks, Moses," Ladd said, grabbing up the picnic hamper and blanket.

Waving goodbye to the beaming black man, Ladd and Laurette hurried down to the levee. Rushing up the gangplank, they eagerly boarded the waiting ferry, *Cloverleaf,* for the short ride across the bay. The ferry was crowded with people heading for the various settlements along the eastern shore: Spanish Fort, Daphne and Fairhope. And the lavish resort at Point Clear where Mobile's elite, including the Howards and Dasheroons, spent at least four or five weeks each year escaping Mobile's humid summer heat.

Once underway, Laurette pointed, directing Ladd's attention as a host of white pelicans riding a warm air current circled an invisible tower before heading back out to the open Gulf. Midway across the calm bay, the pair turned their backs to the railing and gazed at the bustling city they were leaving behind.

It was nearing eleven when the *Cloverleaf* pulled into the wooden docks at Spanish Fort. Ladd and Laurette were the only passengers who got off. That suited them fine. They didn't want to be going where everyone else was going. They wanted to be alone.

The sleepy shoreside fishing village was high above on the timbered bluffs. A rickety wooden staircase led to the top. The young, healthy pair raced up the steep steps without effort. When they reached the top, they stopped and once again looked back out over the water at Mobile in the distance.

Holding hands and laughing they walked into Spanish Fort. They didn't stop. They didn't slow down. They passed directly through the tiny settlement and were soon on a narrow, dirt road bordered by tall oaks and fragrant pines and dense undergrowth. The trail led directly east, into a thick, dark forest.

Less than a mile from Spanish Fort, Ladd stopped, took Laurette's hand and led her off the dusty trail and into the timbered wilderness.

"Do you know where we're going, Ladd?" Laurette asked, holding his hand as they negotiated the uneven ground and picked their way through thick underbrush.

"I'll know when we get there," he said and flashed her a boyish smile.

They moved through the woods, ducking low limbs, squinting in the deep shadow, going single file when necessary. Swallowed up by the deep-green forest, they walked a good half mile before emerging into a small clearing where a carpet of soft green grass covered the level ground, and at its edge a cold, clear stream rushed over the rocks toward the bay far below.

The couple stopped abruptly, looked around, looked at each other and smiled, knowing they had found just the right place. Ladd lowered the hamper and the blanket to the ground.

Suddenly shy and tense, Laurette sank to her knees and began busily spreading the blanket on the grass. When she had finished, she sat down and impulsively took off her kid slippers and white cotton stockings. She wiggled her toes before rising back up onto her knees.

Ladd followed suit. He bent over from the waist, took off his shoes and stockings, then straightened as she smiled, kissed her fingertips and brushed them across his bare right instep.

He stood above, watching her, wanting her, wishing that he were not so ignorant about the art of lovemaking. He wanted so much to please her, to give her pleasure. He wasn't confident that he could. He didn't know nearly enough about her body. Or even his own.

Remaining on her knees on the neatly spread blanket, Laurette slowly raised her head, looked up at Ladd and caught the worried expression on his smooth, handsome face.

She, too, was totally ignorant to the ways of lovemaking, but she was intuitive enough to know what was going through his mind. She reached out and circled the back of his knee with her hand, laid her cheek against his thigh and looking up at him, said, "It doesn't have to be perfect, Ladd. We've the rest of our lives to learn how to make love."

Ladd exhaled with relief, thankful that the girl he loved was so perceptive and understanding. He put a hand to the back of her head, urged her face up and slowly sank to his knees to face her.

"If I live to be a hundred," he said as his arms encircled her, "I will never love you more than I do at this minute."

Laurette gripped his trim waist, pressed her face into the curve of his neck, kissed his tanned throat and said prophetically, "Yes, you will. By the end of this day, you'll love me even more."

Eight

For a long, tense moment the pair stayed there on their knees, unmoving, excitement and expectation now slightly tempered with rising apprehension. Ladd was afraid he would do something wrong, would ruin what should be beautiful. He was reluctant to undress. The sight of his naked body might shock and repulse her. She might change her mind about him, beg him to take her home at once.

"Aren't you going to kiss me?" Laurette finally asked, looking to him for guidance.

Ladd managed a weak smile, raised his shaking hands, cupped her pale cheeks and said, "Yes, I am, sweetheart. And if you decide that kissing is all you want, just let me know."

"I will," she said.

Her head fell back, her eyes met his and she shivered at the look of love in his beautiful blue eyes. His long arm encircled her waist and he drew her closer. He lowered his dark head, paused when his lips were a mere scant inch from hers, then kissed her.

He kissed her as he had never kissed her before. He held nothing back. All his love, all his passion, all his need was in that slow burning, totally commanding caress. Laurette sighed and melted against him, surrendering completely to the power and potency of that devastating kiss.

When at last Ladd's heated lips left hers and he lifted his head, Laurette sagged weakly against him, her feverish cheek resting against his. Their hearts beating as one, their breath rapid and ragged, both shuddered with a mixture of anxiety and exhilaration. Ladd's hand cradled Laurette's head, then slid down the side of her throat to her shoulder.

Gently he sat her back and, looking directly into her eyes, urged the gathered sleeve of her square-necked, blue merino wool dress off her shoulder. Then he leaned forward, brushed a kiss to the pale flesh he had bared and began unbuttoning her dress. Laurette bit her bottom lip, but didn't protest. Within seconds, he was taking her dress off, laying it aside.

Again Ladd kissed Laurette and as his lips moved provocatively on hers and his tongue stroked the sensitive insides of her mouth, his nimble fingers undid the hooks of her white batiste camisole. When all the tiny hooks were undone, his lips released hers. He hesitated for only an instant before sweeping the open camisole apart. Laurette heard his sharp intake of air and saw the muscles in his tanned throat move with his nervous swallowing.

"Oh, Ladd," she murmured as he pushed the camisole's lace straps down her arms and the wispy garment fell to the blanket.

Laurette's first impulse was to quickly lift her arms and cover herself. She didn't do it. Instead, almost immediately, she thrust her chest forward as Ladd's burning eyes consumed her bared breasts with such blazing fire she believed she could feel their heat. Her soft, satiny nipples tightened in response and stood out in taut twin crests.

"You're...perfect," Ladd said huskily. "So incredibly beautiful."

Laurette could tell by the shaky timbre of his voice that he was awed and pleased by the sight her. Which made her giddily happy. She wanted to be pretty for him. She held her breath when he lifted a lean hand and gently cupped her right breast. When his thumb brushed back and forth across the sensitive nipple, she exhaled anxiously.

Ladd's hand left her and she watched as he hurriedly unbuttoned his white shirt, yanked the long tails free of his trousers and took it off. Laurette had only a second to examine his naked torso before he put his arms around her and drew her into his close embrace. Both sighed as their flesh made initial contact.

The feel of her bare, soft breasts resting against the flat, hard muscles of his chest was extremely pleasurable to them both. So much so, they sighed and sensuously rubbed against each other, enjoying the tingling sensation of Laurette's diamond-hard nipples against Ladd's firm chest with its smattering of dark, crisp hair.

Like children with a brand-new toy, they played for several thrilling moments until Ladd said against

Laurette's temple, "Let's take off the rest of our clothes, sweetheart."

He didn't wait for her permission. He urged her up to her feet, lifted his hands to the tape of her full white petticoats. They came open and he hastily swept them down and off. Laurette, blushing now, stood before him wearing only her white, lace-trimmed pantalets. She started to sink back to her knees.

He stopped her.

"No, Lollie," Ladd said softly, "Not yet."

Laurette swallowed hard, nodded and then tensed when he slowly eased the lacy underwear down her wildly fluttering belly, over her flaring hips and past her dimpled knees. When the snowy-white pantalets pooled at her feet, Laurette put her hands on Ladd's bare shoulders and stepped out of them. She closed her eyes.

Expecting him to come to his feet, she waited. He didn't move. Finally she opened her eyes. And felt her bare belly contract sharply as he remained on his knees before her, his eyes focused squarely on the triangle of blond curls between her pale thighs. She felt a stirring low in her belly, a clenching of muscles, the feeling that his hands as well as his eyes were touching her there. Her face afire, she started to lower her hands and shield herself.

"No, sweetheart," he said, and caught her wrists. "Let me look at you. All of you. Just for a minute."

He released her hands and moved his own to gently clasp the curve of her hips. He exhaled heavily, then impulsively pulled her to him and pressed his hot cheek against her bare stomach. His silky hair ruffled against her, tickling her, thrilling her, causing her to tremble. And she knew that his beautiful blue eyes were closed because she could feel the restless flutter of his long dark lashes against her sensitive skin.

"My sweet love," he whispered, his breath a hot flame. He turned his face inward, kissed her naval and lifted his head to look up at her.

"Ladd," she murmured breathlessly.

He came to his feet before her, drew her into his arms and kissed her hungrily. With his burning lips devouring hers, Laurette could tell by the rapid, heavy beating of his heart against her naked breasts that he was excited. But she was far too naive to know *how* excited. The kiss deepened and as his mouth ground into hers and he pressed her to his hard, ungiving body, Laurette experienced a sudden dizziness and enveloping warmth, a new kind of hunger and need.

His broad chest felt good against her tender breasts and the fabric of his linen trousers, mildly abrasive against her bare stomach and thighs, felt somehow sensuous. Would it, she wondered, feel even better when he took off the trousers and stood naked against her?

She soon found out.

With his mouth still masterfully possessing hers, Ladd put his hands between them, swiftly flipped open the buttons of his tight trousers and gave both them and his white linen underwear a decisive shove. Her lips still clinging to his, Laurette gasped into his mouth as his clothes fell away and his freed flesh

surged hotly against her. Stepping free of the garments and kicking them aside, Ladd wrapped his
hands around Laurette's thighs and pressed her closer.

She winced with wonder and surprise and finally
tore her lips from his. Reeling, she clasped her wrists
behind his head and clung to him, her innate sexuality
swiftly emerging. She sighed and sensuously undulated her slender naked body against his tall lanky
frame. Ladd groaned in response and thrust his slim
hips forward, letting her feel the effect of his fully
formed erection.

Laurette was at once dazzled and frightened by the
potent male power throbbing against her belly. Instinctively, she knew that Ladd's lean male body
could give a female great pleasure. At the same time
she felt certain they were not going to fit together.
She didn't believe that the hot, heavy flesh pulsing
forcefully against her could possibly go inside her.
That would, she feared, be absolutely impossible.

"Oh, Ladd, it…it isn't going to work for us," she
whispered against his throat.

"What isn't going to work, sweetheart?"

She lifted her head, looked up at him sorrowfully.
"Making love. We can't."

Ladd's heart thudded with disappointment, but he
said calmly, "You know how much I love you, how
much I want you, Laurette. But if you don't want to
make love, then we won't."

"It isn't that, I want it as much as you, but…
but…"

"But what? What's wrong, Lollie? Tell me."

Laurette hesitated, her face flushing. She shook her head. She couldn't tell him, she couldn't say it out loud.

He gently coaxed, "It's Ladd, Lollie. *Your* Ladd. You can tell me anything, you know that."

Finally, she nodded. "I—I just…I know that I'm too small to…ah…that is my—my body can't…oh, Ladd, you're too big to go inside me!"

He didn't laugh or make fun of her. He wasn't even certain that she wasn't right. He said, softly, his voice low and caressing, "That could well be, sweetheart. But we won't know until we try." He spread his hand across the cleft of her rounded bottom, pressed her closer and said, "If you don't want to try, we don't have to. I'll be content just to lie beside you all afternoon."

"Could we do that?" she asked, wary, worried.

Ladd took a long, deep breath. "Yes, of course. Let's lie down. Want to?"

Nine

Laurette nodded.

He released her and took a step back. She stared curiously at his naked body. Just as she had done earlier when he had examined at her, Ladd started to cover his groin.

"No," she protested, quickly closing the space between them and taking hold of his hands to move them away. His face now scarlet, Ladd stood vulnerable before his innocent sweetheart while she inspected him, her lips parted, her eyes wide with curiosity.

Forgetting her own nakedness, Laurette gazed upon the boy she loved. Never in her life had she seen a man totally nude. She'd heard her friends at the Hunnicutt Academy for Young Ladies whisper how they had been told that men's bodies were hard and hairy and ugly, downright disgusting. They had giggled and said that when they got married, they'd allow their husbands to make love to them only in the darkness of the night.

Her friends were wrong.

There was nothing ugly or disgusting about Ladd. He stood there in the dappled shade with his bare feet slightly apart, tall and tan and appealingly masculine. Laurette's heart swelled with pride. He was nothing short of beautiful. All six feet two inches of him. A young, slim Adonis with coal-black hair and smooth olive skin. She noted, with genuine delight, that even the parts of his body that were usually covered with clothing and untouched by the sun were as dark as the rest of him.

Embarrassed by her unblinking scrutiny, Ladd sank to his knees on the blanket and held out his hand to her. She took it and came down before him. He put a stiffened arm behind him and, bringing her with him, stretched out.

Again he assured her, "We will just lie here and hold each other. That's enough for me."

Pressed against the naked length of him, knowing how much he wanted her, Laurette whispered, "No, Ladd, I love you, I belong to you. Let's try to make love."

"Oh, sweetheart," he murmured and urged her over onto her back.

He lay on his stomach beside her, his bare torso partially covering hers. More afraid than he'd ever been in his life, he began kissing her and as they kissed his hand cupped her warm, soft breasts and his fingertips gently plucked at the taut nipples.

He was just as virginal and unschooled in the ways of love as Laurette. Afraid that she might be right, that he couldn't possibly fit inside her, he wondered how he was supposed to know in advance. And how was he to know when she was ready for him. With him it was obvious, but with a female…?

Breathless, hot and cold at once, Laurette clung to Ladd, excited by his kisses, stirred by the touch of his gentle hands on her tingling flesh and by the heavy hardness surging against her hip.

When finally his lips left hers and Ladd raised his dark head, Laurette whispered honestly, "Ladd, I—I don't know what I am supposed to do. Will you show me?"

"Lollie, I'm a virgin just like you are."

"I know and I'm glad."

"Me, too, but I don't know how to love you as you should be loved."

She smiled reassuringly at him and said, "We'll learn to make love just as we learned to kiss."

"Yes, we will," he whispered, kissed her again and laid his spread hand on her stomach.

Led by passion and instinct, he swept his hand down over her flat belly and put it between her legs. Gently, carefully he pressed his long middle finger against her sensitive flesh and felt a fiery wetness. He dipped the tip of his finger into that wetness and gently pushed it upward. Laurette gasped, arched her back, then thrust her pelvis up off the blanket.

"Ladd, Ladd," she breathed.

"I know," he whispered and continued to caress her, to arouse her, to prepare her body to accept his.

But she had other ideas. "I—I want to touch you the way you're touching me," she said.

"No," he was quick to protest. "No."

"Why not?"

Terrified that if she touched him he would explode in involuntary climax, he said, "Because I...it would...you can't..."

"Yes, I can," she said as she rolled up into a sitting position and reached for him. He flinched, then bit the inside of his jaw when her soft, slender fingers closed possessively around him. "Lie down," she urged and, surrendering, his chest heaving, he stretched out on his back.

Ladd watched through tortured hooded eyes as she played, toying with his aching masculinity, her gentle fingers awkwardly holding him as though she were holding a stick of dynamite. *And,* he thought, *if she doesn't soon stop what she is doing, that dynamite is going to detonate.*

Ladd tore her hand away, rolled up off the blanket and swiftly pressed her down onto her back. He positioned himself between her legs and gently urged her pale thighs apart. He checked to be sure the hot liquid was still flowing from her and, knowing he couldn't last much longer said, "If it hurts too much, I'll stop." With that he thrust swiftly into her.

Ladd felt Laurette's entire body recoil, heard her cry out with shock and pain, felt her hands pushing frantically on his chest and her pelvis attempting, in vain, to dislodge him. His loving heart wanted to stop immediately, to spare her any further pain. But his aroused body did not agree with his heart. It wanted her at any cost. The hard throbbing flesh buried deep inside her had a mind of its own. Totally selfish and uncaring, it callously ignored the tears spilling down Laurette's cheeks and her obvious discomfort. It ignored his silent command to let her go, to inflict no more pain.

Ladd couldn't stop.

He had no idea how to control his body. So he pumped forcefully into her, his pleasure so intense he moaned with ecstasy until he felt himself coming. He couldn't stop that, either. He thrust deeper, faster and quickly exploded in a shuddering orgasm.

Her tear-filled eyes open, Laurette watched as his handsome face contorted, the veins standing out in his throat, and she wondered if he was in pain, too. Maybe she was hurting him as much as he was hurting her.

Ladd collapsed atop her. He pulled out, fell over onto his back and closed his eyes, his breath coming in loud labored pants, his face shiny with perspiration.

"Ladd," she whispered, staring at him, "are you all right?"

"Oh, sweetheart," his eyes opened and he immediately took her in his arms and began apologizing. "I'm so sorry I hurt you, I never will again. I'll become a better lover. I'll learn how to give you the kind of pleasure you gave me."

Her brief pain already forgotten, Laurette snuggled close, kissed his chest and said, "My pleasure is being held like this in your arms. I need nothing more."

His long arms tightened around her and he said, "You're so sweet, so loving, I want to make you happy more than anything in the world. Next time will be better, I swear it.''

She smiled and sighed and for a time they lay relaxed and entwined on the blanket, in no hurry to do anything.

Finally, Ladd said, ''Do you suppose that stream is so cold we'd freeze if we took a bath in it?''

Her blond head shot up and the sassy Laurette he so adored smiled and asked, ''Is that a challenge, Mr. Ladd Winston Dasheroon?''

He grinned. ''It is, Miss Laurette Taylor Howard.''

In a flash they were up off the blanket, laughing and racing each other down to the stream. She squealed and he gasped as they stepped off the smooth grassy banks into the cold, clear stream. Knowing that the only way they could stand it was to completely submerge themselves in the frigid waters, they did just that. Laughing and whooping, they sank down on the rocky bottom of the shallow stream, Laurette holding her long hair atop her head, Ladd holding her. He drew Laurette's slender legs around his back, pulled her close and kissed her smiling face.

Her teeth chattering, she asked, ''You cold?''

''No.''

''Liar,'' she accused and he laughed.

He put his hands beneath her rounded bottom and rose to his feet, holding her in his arms. She wrapped her legs around him and clung to his neck as he stepped up onto the bank and carried her to the blanket. Freeing one hand, he reached down, yanked the blanket up and swirled it around them.

Shivering, laughing, kissing, they awkwardly dried each other, then dropped the damp blanket back to the ground and, teeth chattering, hastily dressed. Soon they were completely dressed and warm and dry.

And hungry.

They heartily ate the tempting foods Hannah had packed for them. When every last bite was gone, they sighed, rubbed their full bellies and again stretched out on the blanket. Happy, content, they fell asleep and napped peacefully in the dappled shade.

An hour later Laurette awakened with a start. The sun had completely gone. The slices of sky she could see through the trees were no longer bright cobalt blue. They were a dark, depressing gray. The balmy weather had changed with the sky. It was no longer a warm, springlike day. It was cold and getting colder.

Laurette shivered violently, her sense of well-being gone with the sun.

Her sudden movement awakened Ladd. He rolled up into a sitting position and saw immediately the stricken look on her beautiful face. He felt his heart hammer with fear. "What is it?"

Laurette shook her head, said nothing. Trembling, she lunged into Ladd's arms and clasped him tightly to her. She was frightened, but she didn't know why.

Ladd held her, rubbed her slender back and asked, "Is something wrong, sweetheart?" He could feel the fierce, rapid beating of her heart, the shaking of her slender body. "Is there something you want to tell me?"

In the shelter of his arms, Laurette began to calm.

She hugged him and finally said, "No, nothing. Just that...I love you so much it...sometimes it frightens me."

He pressed her golden head to his shoulder, felt her beginning to relax against him, and said, "I know exactly what you mean." He smiled then and told her, "You know something, Lollie, you were absolutely right."

She lifted her head, looked at him. "Right? About what?"

"This morning you said that before this day was over, I would love you even more. And I do."

"Oh, Ladd, Ladd, hold me. Don't ever let me go."

Ten

Ominous rumblings of approaching war had begun to inflame the passions of the South. As the winter of 1860 turned to spring, conversation among the gentlemen at every social gathering was dominated by loud, heated discussions of the gathering tempest and bold vows were made to put the meddling North in its place.

If precious blood had to be shed to ensure the sanctity of state rights, then so be it. The brave sons of the South would fight until the last Yankee was in his grave!

Like everyone else in Alabama, Ladd and Laurette heard many of those impassioned diatribes. But they paid little attention. Neither believed that there was even a remote possibility of a war between the states. Something that horrible could never happen in civilized America.

Besides, they had little time for thoughts of anything or anyone except each other. While the constant war talk lodged somewhere in the backs of their minds, they didn't let it interfere with their happiness or plans for the future.

They were so much in love, so mad about each

other, they could hardly hide their intimacy. They realized that they had to be discreet, but it was far from easy. They seized any and every chance to be alone, even if only for a few short minutes.

With the chill, damp winter giving way to an early spring it was easier for them. While the cold and rain had often kept them trapped indoors where their parents could keep a watchful eye, the warmth and mildness of the Alabama spring offered ample opportunities to spend time outdoors where they could be alone.

Happy as they'd never been before, they were ingenious at finding locations where they could make love. They were not always the most romantic of spots, but the young lovers didn't mind. Barely able to keep their hands off each other in the presence of others, they anxiously shed their clothes the minute they were alone.

They made love in the Dasheroon carriage house on the supple leather seat of the parked brougham. And on the soft grass in the moonlight beneath the leafy banana trees at the back edge of the estate. In the vine-covered gazebo on the distant eastern border of the Howards' sprawling property. Wherever and whenever. Each time was urgent and hurried and they were always afraid of being caught, but the stolen moments of intimacy were worth the risks.

Like the fading of a fragile rose, spring was quickly gone and summertime, with its endless sunny days, punctuated with fierce afternoon lightning and thunderstorms, was upon them. A hot, muggy heat quickly blanketed Mobile, making it hard to get a breath, much less do much of anything.

The wilting heat and high humidity worked to Ladd and Laurette's advantage. It was so miserable in the city that the Dasheroons and the Howards decided to spend both July and August across the bay at the Grand Hotel in Point Clear.

The eastern shore's Grand provided an incredibly romantic setting for lovers of any age. The elegant suites were large and airy with long, wide balconies that overlooked the water. The hotel's luxury and comfort could be taken for granted, but the individual attention each guest received set the fabulous Grand apart.

The illustrious clientele were catered to by a small efficient army of tactful, resourceful and patient hotel employees. The concierge, the maitres d'hotel, sommeliers, bartenders, headwaiters, activity directors and housekeepers were all intent on making their guests enjoy their stay at the Grand, be it for a week or a year.

Each day a myriad of activities was planned for those who wished to participate: sailing, fishing, picnicking, horseback riding, croquet, treasure hunts, treks in the woods, card games, chess, whisk, fashion shows and band concerts.

Those who did not care to exert themselves sat contentedly on the hotel's front veranda in white rocking chairs, watching people come and go and enjoying the cooling breeze off the bay.

The hotel's range and quality of cuisine and cellar were unequaled. In the ornate dining hall sumptuous seven-course meals accompanied by the finest wines were served by handsome white-jacketed, white-gloved waiters. After dinner each evening an orchestra played in the giant ballroom and guests turned about on the floor beneath sparkling chandeliers.

Stewards passed among them carrying silver trays with crystal flutes of chilled champagne to quench the dancers' thirst. Laughter and gaiety were the norm at the Grand and the ladies were delighted that their husbands temporarily forgot about business and became more like the romantic young gentlemen they had once been.

For Ladd and Laurette, the long stay at the Grand Hotel on the eastern shore was a treasured interlude in paradise. A magical summer of undiluted pleasure and one they would never forget. The long, sunny days were perfect. The balmy moonlit nights intoxicating. While they good-naturedly joined in many of the hotel's planned activities, they managed to find ample time to be alone. And when they were alone, they made the most of it.

It was, of course, necessary to exercise great caution because they knew many of the guests staying at the Grand. A mix of wealthy Easterners and old family friends were in residence. In fact, they dined regularly with Colonel George Ivy and his wife, Martha, from the Oakleigh Garden district.

Paul and Melba Adair and their spinster daughter, Lydia, were at the Grand. Laurette's best friends, the

Parlange twins, were there with their aging grandmother, Lena. Their grandfather, Judge Noble Parlange, had passed away in the winter. The placid Juliette was content to sit on the sunny veranda and
read, but the lively Johanna, always in search of fun
and adventure, was frequently at Laurette's elbow.
Other young girls from Miss Hunnicutt's and boys
who had attended the military academy with Ladd
were also staying at the hotel.

Minding their manners, the starry-eyed Ladd and
Laurette were unfailingly gracious and friendly, but
even as they dined with family and friends or turned
about on the crowded dance floor, they were counting
the minutes until they could slip away to be alone.

On one such evening in mid-August the pair were
at a gathering on the hotel's sprawling northern lawn.
At the velvety green lawn's center, a raised, white-
latticed dance pavilion was crowded with youthful
dancers. The music drifted out over the water. The
silver moon was high and full. The night air was
sweetly perfumed with the seductive scent of gardenias.

Laurette, looking young and fresh in a low-cut
dress of snowy-white organza with billowing skirts,
stood below the pavilion beside the tall, handsome
Ladd, her hand enclosed in his. They had danced.
They had drunk glasses of chilled fruit punch. They
had socialized with the other guests. Johanna, who
they hadn't been able to shake all evening, had just
accepted a dance with a tall young man from Georgia.
Finally, the lovers stood there alone.

It was nearing eleven. Laurette had to be inside the hotel no later than midnight.

Ladd slowly turned his head and glanced down at her. She looked so incredibly innocent and pretty that at the mere sight of her his heart skipped a couple of beats and he felt sensations that would not be denied.

"Let's go," he said, leaning close. Laurette nodded.

Together they slowly sank back away from the crowd, being careful to attract no attention. When they were several yards away, they turned and ran. Laughing and out of breath, they raced across the sprawling lawn. When the hotel and the lighted dance pavilion had been left far behind, they picked their way down the bluffs, not stopping until they were almost to the water.

"Do you know how long it's been since I kissed you?" Ladd asked as they carefully stepped out of the trees and onto a large, flat boulder jutting out some twenty feet above the calm waters of the bay.

"Five and a half hours," she said, recalling the afternoon's last sweet kiss before they had returned to the hotel.

"Well, that's too long," he said, taking her into his arms and kissing her.

With the moonlight washing over them and the romantic music from the dance pavilion softly drifting down over the bluffs, they made hurried love, only half undressing. Afterward they adjusted their clothing, climbed to the top of the bluff and dashed across the manicured hotel grounds. They hurried up the steps of the Grand with only three minutes to spare.

As they passed the gentlemen's lounge with its oak-and-damask walls and constant haze of blue cigar smoke wafting out into the hallway, they heard loud voices.

Curious, they paused to listen.

"...and you, sir, are an ill-informed fool if you think the South will ever back down!" They recognized the deep, strong voice of Ladd's father, Douglas Dasheroon.

"I'm sure you won't," replied a man whose accent was distinctly northern. "You're all so spoiled and pigheaded down here, you won't be happy until there is a war. A war which the South will most certainly lose!"

At that arrogant statement a host of voices raised as shouting matches erupted between the visiting Easterners and native Southerners. Most of the gentlemen had imbibed too much Kentucky bourbon or sparkling champagne and emotions were running high.

Listening in horror, Laurette clung to Ladd's hand, a worried frown on her face. It was becoming increasingly difficult to ignore the very real possibility of approaching war. The prospect of such an occurrence chilled her blood.

Ladd, the love of her life, was now seventeen years old and would leave for West Point early next month. If war came, he would surely be called on to fight.

* * *

Their cherished time together, their perfect, carefree summer, had ended. Bright and early tomorrow morning, Ladd would leave for West Point.

It was his last night in Mobile.

His last night with Laurette.

The Dasheroons were hosting a big going-away gala for their only son. The party—food, drinks, music—was held on the smooth grassy banks of the Mobile River downtown. At least two hundred guests were in attendance. Everyone who had been invited was there.

Wishing they could spend this last night alone, knowing that they could not, Ladd and Laurette laughed and talked and pretended they were having a marvelous time sharing the sumptuous spread with old friends and family.

After the meal, all the gentlemen were eager to talk with Ladd, to give him advice and to wish him well. Laurette sat quietly by with the Parlange twins. But she hardly heard what Johanna was saying. She was watching Ladd with pride, straining to hear what he was saying, longing to be in his arms.

Her heart began to pound when finally she heard Ladd say, "Father, Mister Howard, gentlemen, with your permission, I'd like to take Laurette for a walk in the moonlight."

The young lovers were barely out of sight before they were kissing, holding each other, declaring that they were going to miss each other terribly.

"I want you so much, Lollie," Ladd murmured as

they clung to each other and fought for breath. "Let me make love to you one last time."

Her heart racing, wits scattered, she breathlessly protested, "Ladd, we can't, you know we can't."

"Yes, we can," he said as he gripped her hand and anxiously led her farther away from the laughter and the music.

In minutes they were ducking into a dark, willow-enclosed spot along the river where even the full harvest moon could not penetrate. Blackness enveloped them. The kind of absolute darkness where you could not see your hand before your face.

"Ladd," Laurette whispered, "I can't see you."

"But you'll be able to feel me," he said as he took her in his arms and kissed her.

When his heated lips left hers, Laurette sighed, "Yes, oh yes."

Without another word they anxiously undressed, and when they were naked Ladd drew Laurette up against his tall, lean body.

"Feel that?" he asked as he thrust his pelvis forward against her, his erection pressing insistently against her belly.

"Yes," she whispered, "I feel it, I feel you. I want it. I want you."

She sighed softly when he turned her about so that she was facing away from him. He leaned her back against him. He wrapped his arms around her, bent his head, kissed the curve of her neck and shoulder and murmured, "You taste good."

She replied, "You smell good."

He raised a suntanned hand, placed the tip of his forefinger against her soft lips and said, "Lick my finger, Lollie."

She put out her tongue, licked his finger, then sucked it when he popped it into her mouth. When he removed the moistened finger, she told him, "You taste good, too."

"Mmm," Ladd murmured as he lifted her soft, rounded breasts in his hands. She squirmed against him. "Feel good?" he asked as his wet forefinger circled, teased and gently plucked at her nipples.

"Like heaven," she sighed and asked no questions when the forefinger of his other hand came up to touch her lips. She automatically licked and sucked on it.

And seconds later, in the thick, black darkness that concealed them, she felt that dampened finger touching her between her legs, toying, arousing, setting her on fire. She sighed and writhed and became so incredibly hot she knew that if he didn't stop she was going to climax.

As if he'd read her thoughts—or perhaps her responsive body—Ladd quickly turned her about to face him and, bending his knees slightly, wrapped his fingers around his hard pulsing flesh and placed just the smooth tip up inside her. He then lifted her off the ground, clasped his wrists beneath her bottom and coaxed, "Get comfortable with it, then slide all the way down onto it, sweetheart."

Laurette did just that. Clinging to his wide shoulders, she slowly, surely, impaled herself upon him.

Both gasped with pleasure at the completion. And then they made love. It was the strangest, most seductive, most satisfying lovemaking they had ever experienced.

While the party in his honor was in full swing a few short yards away, Ladd stood with his bare feet apart, his hard male member buried deep inside Laurette, the twin cheeks of his brown buttocks flexing as he thrust rhythmically into her. Laurette's slender legs were wrapped around Ladd's back, her arms around his dark head. His mouth was at her breasts, licking, nibbling, sucking.

In total darkness they made hot, desperate love of a kind that was brand-new to them. Incredibly arousing. Totally abandoned. Shamelessly animalistic. And the sensational experience was made all the more thrilling because they could not see each other, could only hear and smell and taste and feel.

When their shared release came, Ladd had to quickly cover Laurette's mouth in a silencing kiss so that everyone at the riverside party wouldn't know what they were doing.

After the totally fulfilling loving, the two of them sank weakly to the grass and struggled to catch their breath. When their heartbeats had slowed and the perspiration had began to dry on their naked bodies, Laurette clung to Ladd and said, "Don't go, Ladd. Don't go off to West Point tomorrow. There's a war coming, you know there is. If you go to the academy, I will never see you again."

Ladd's arms tightened around her. "Of course,

you'll see me again," he reassured her, "war or no war. We're getting married, remember. We'll spend the rest of our lives together."

"But what if you—?"

He interrupted her. "I won't get killed, I promise you." He kissed the crown of her golden head.

"Then what if you forget me," she asked, "find another girl and—?"

"Lollie, Lollie," he said, calling her by the name only he ever used, "I could never love anyone but you. Never. I wouldn't want to live if I couldn't have you. Even when we are apart, you'll still be with me. You are always in my heart."

"Oh, Ladd, I love you so much."

"And I love you. Just promise me that no matter what happens, you will wait for me."

"I promise," she vowed, kissed his chest and added, "I'll wait forever for you, Ladd."

"I know you will, sweetheart," he said. "We'd best get back to the party."

"Yes," she agreed, then said once again, "I will wait forever."

Eleven

On Friday, the twenty-first day of September, 1860, seventeen-year-old Ladd Winston Dasheroon arrived at West Point on the Hudson.

Shading his eyes against the strong morning sunlight, Ladd stood at the railing of the slow-moving steamer as it approached the levee, thoroughly awed by his first glimpse of the United States Military Academy.

His heart swelled with patriotic pride as he gazed at the buildings scattered on the lofty palisades above. Ladd was well versed in the history of the prestigious academy. He knew that some of America's finest men had graduated from West Point in its fifty-eight years of existence.

To think that he was now going to be a part of that long gray line was exciting and uplifting beyond belief. At the same time, he was anxious. His father, graduate of the class of '35, had warned him that discipline was strict and the academic courses difficult. Douglas had cautioned that Ladd would have to study hard and would have to tolerate—with equanimity—harsh treatment from some of the upperclassmen.

"Duty, honor, country," Douglas had solemnly stated. "Those words dictate what you ought to be, what you will be." He had smiled then and added, "Don't worry, Ladd, you'll make it at the Point. After all, you are *my* son."

When the steamer pulled into the landing, Ladd was overjoyed to see the smartly uniformed Jimmy Tigart standing on the wooden wharf, smiling and waving.

"Jimmy!" Ladd exclaimed excitedly as he hurried down the gangplank.

"Laddie," greeted Jimmy, holding his arms open wide.

"Lord, it's good to see you," said Ladd, grabbing Jimmy in a bear hug. "We all missed you this summer. Why didn't you come home on your furlough?"

Patting Ladd's back affectionately, Jimmy said, "I had no home to come to. Remember mother moved back to Kentucky last winter to be with her relatives. So I had no place to stay." Jimmy released Ladd and stepped back, still smiling sunnily.

"No place to...?" Ladd shook his dark head in disbelief. "For heaven sake, Jimmy, you would have stayed with us. You know you're always welcome at Dauphin Way."

"Well, that's very kind, but actually I was pretty busy this summer. A lot of things going on here."

"Oh?" Ladd's dark brows lifted quizzically. "A pretty girl perhaps?"

"Make that plural. Pretty *girls*," Jimmy corrected with a conspiratorial wink. "They've got some beautiful women in New York. I'll have to introduce you around and—"

"No, thanks," Ladd said with a negative shake of his head. "There's only one girl for me."

Jimmy Tigart waited a couple of heartbeats until he was sure his voice would hold no emotion, then asked, as casually as possible, "How is little Laurette?"

"All grown-up, Jimmy," Ladd said, "and more beautiful than ever."

Wondering how the exquisite Laurette could possibly be any prettier than the last time he'd seen her, Jimmy said, "She'll always be little Laurette to me." Then, quickly changing the subject, "Let's go. I'll show you around."

"Thanks, Jimmy," Ladd said, lifting his valise.

"At the Point, it's Cadet Lieutenant Tigart, Ladd. Not Jimmy."

Ladd smiled. "Lead the way, sir."

The two old friends started up the steep path that wound toward the flat dusty plain above. In minutes they reached the highlands upon which rested the forty-acre plateau above the Hudson. The river was now far below, making its slow, steady way between the palisades.

It was a lofty, rocky, majestic point and Ladd was immediately struck by the thought that no one could have chosen a more fitting place for the academy's location than this starkly beautiful plateau high above the Hudson.

The morning was pleasantly warm, but not hot. The sky was a deep cloudless blue. On the plain, where boy officers would soon pass in review, members of the post band were setting up their instruments and music sheets on a wooden platform. One lone trumpeter was warming up, the sound carrying on the still, clear air. Ladd felt a great sense of exhilaration, a deep pride knowing that he was to be part of this respected tradition. He would, he hoped, measure up. He wanted to be a model cadet.

Just like Jimmy.

As he and Jimmy fell into step and crossed the dusty quadrangle, Ladd commented that Jimmy should be really proud of the fact that he had excelled at the academy, was near the top of his class.

Ladd immediately noted the minute tightening of Jimmy's firm jaw as he replied, "The Point is one of the few places on earth where the standing of an individual is dependent strictly on merit."

Ladd nodded. "Yes. That's way it should be and—"

Tigart interrupted and looking Ladd in the eye said, "Here the son of the poorest and most obscure man has an equal chance to compete with the son of the most powerful and richest man in the country. Birth, avarice and connections have no effect on determining promotion or punishment at the Point."

Struck by the chilly tone of Jimmy's voice, Ladd was momentarily taken aback. He had never known Jimmy to be the least bit envious and had certainly never thought of his friend as anything other than an equal. Had Jimmy been harboring some deep-seated resentment all these years?

"Listen, Jimmy, I—" Ladd began, but again Jimmy cut him off.

"We're here," he announced, a few feet from the front door of a building.

Cadet Lieutenant Jimmy Tigart ushered Ladd into the dormitory known as Old South. On the third and top floor, Ladd was directed into a small, spartan room where two other plebes were unpacking.

When the boys saw the upperclassman, they automatically snapped to attention, chin in, chest out.

"At ease, plebes," said Cadet Lieutenant Tigart. Then to Ladd, his half-cocky, easygoing disposition back in place he added, "I'll leave you to get acquainted. You need anything, let me know."

Nodding, Ladd said, "Yes. Sure. Thanks again, Jimmy...ah, Cadet Lieutenant Tigart."

Ladd and his new roommates quickly became friends. Short, scrappy, dark-haired Thomas Little was a Nashville, Tennessee native, and the fair, blond, slim Vance Granger was from Macon, Georgia. By sunset, Ladd felt as if he had known both Thomas and Vance all his life.

As classes got underway and the three plebes became accustomed to the rules and regulations of the academy, Ladd saw little of Jimmy. He was disappointed, but not surprised, since Jimmy was an upperclassman. Still, the expression he had seen in Jimmy's hazel eyes when Jimmy had stated that a poor man's son could do as well as a rich man's here at West Point haunted Ladd. Troubled him. Stayed in the back of his mind.

Ladd was firmly resolved to be a good student. He studied long hours each evening, determined to keep up, to be in the top of his class. It was not easy. In this first year the plebes had to struggle with algebra, geometry and trigonometry, as well as history, French, Latin, literature, philosophy and chemistry. A bright boy, Ladd soon mastered his studies and he also easily adjusted to the rigors of life at West Point.

As expected, Ladd and his fellow plebes were looked down on by the upperclassmen, ordered about. They were 'animals,' 'reptiles,' 'beasts.' Most took it in their stride, knowing the derision was part of the tradition of the Point. Like most of his fellow plebes, Ladd was unbothered by the meaningless scorn and mockery.

But, from the first week he had arrived, he had continuing trouble with Gilbert LaKid, a large, ugly, sadistic upperclassmen who for some reason had singled Ladd out for rough, constant hazing.

The big, beefy upperclassman took great pleasure in causing problems for Ladd. Ladd attempted to stay out of LaKid's way, to avoid him, but often found it impossible. Every where Ladd went, LaKid showed up and immediately began ordering Ladd to drop and do a hundred push-ups. Or to stand at attention outdoors for hours on a cold, rainy night while holding a full pail of water in each hand. To reclean his room after cleaning it a half dozen times. To repress his uniform, repolish his shoes. The needless tasks sapped much of Ladd's strength and took up his precious time.

Ladd came to despise LaKid. He was dedicated and eager to prove himself, so he silently endured. He had been brought up to embrace noble values, to abhor cruelty, to fight injustice and never to whine at his lot in life.

And, he always had something to look forward to. The high point of his day was mail call and the sweet letters from Laurette which he eagerly read and re-read.

After lights out he would lie awake in the darkness, listening to the night sounds, envisioning Laurette's lovely face: her high cheekbones, pale skin, her luminous eyes. He would daydream of the time he would graduate with honor from the Point and return home in glory to marry his golden-haired angel.

Back in Mobile, that golden-haired angel was totally lost. Laurette missed Ladd so much it was like a constant physical pain. The separation was far worse than anything she had ever experienced or imagined. She had known that she was deeply in love with Ladd; now she realized that he was everything to her. Her entire universe. Without him, life would have no meaning.

As lonely as she was without him, Laurette did her best to put on a brave face around her parents. She was wise enough to know that if she revealed the true depth of her suffering, they might well suspect that she and Ladd had been too close. Had been intimate.

So she made it a point to be cheerful in their presence. She collected the mail on the way home from school and secreted Ladd's love letters away to be read when she was alone. She kept up her good grades at Miss Hunnicutt's Academy for Young Ladies. She accepted invitations to parties she didn't really want to attend. She continued her piano lessons, proudly demonstrating, to Miss Foster's delight, that she had finally mastered Chopin's polonaise. Could play it almost as well as Ladd. She successfully convinced everyone that she was still the sassy, fun-loving, adventurous girl she had always been, despite the fact that Ladd was gone.

But when she was alone, when bedtime came and she could flee to the privacy of her room, Laurette let down her guard. There she would read and reread Ladd's letters, press them to her breasts and allow the hot tears of loneliness to slip down her cheeks.

Many late nights, long after everyone was asleep, she would sit on the wide front windowsill, knees drawn up, arms hugging them, gazing out at the lights of Mobile and the darkened bay beyond.

Thinking about Ladd.

Missing him.

Wanting him.

Her heart would pound as she recalled the ecstasy of being held in his arms and loved by him. She could almost feel his hot, bare body pressed against her own sensitive flesh, his lips feasting on hers. She shivered at the vivid recollection of the last time they had made love.

The two of them naked and enveloped in hot, shielding darkness while only few short yards away their unsuspecting parents, along with a host of friends, laughed and talked. Ladd standing with his bare feet apart, holding her in his arms.

On one such late, sultry night, Laurette's flat stomach contracted at the vivid memory. Her nipples tightened and she exhaled heavily. Her nightgown was suddenly uncomfortably warm and tight. It clung to her sensitive flesh. She was perspiring. She was miserable.

Laurette leaned forward and looked out and checked to make sure no one could see in. Satisfied her solitary perch on the tall windowsill was safely in the concealing darkness, Laurette got up and stripped off her nightgown, tossed it to the carpeted floor. Naked, she climbed back onto the windowsill and sat there as before, with her knees bent and raised, bare feet on the sill.

Oh, Ladd, Ladd, she sighed in her yearning.

She closed her eyes and touched a bare breast with a tentative hand. Pretending that it was Ladd who was touching her, she toyed with a sensitive nipple and recalled how sweet it felt to have his warm, wet mouth enclosing it.

Shamed by her burning desire, but desperately in need of some small measure of relief, Laurette soon allowed her hand to slowly slip down from her breast to settle on her flat stomach. For a time she rubbed her bare belly, breathed through her mouth and finally gave in to her relentless need. Slowly, she allowed her bent knees to fall apart. Eyes closed, breasts aching, Laurette licked her fore and middle fingers, briefly touched her pebble-hard left nipple, then slipped her moistened fingers between her legs and touched herself. Awkwardly, anxiously, she rubbed the pulsing flesh and within a matter of minutes had to viciously bite the back of her hand to keep from crying out in her sudden release.

Immediately ashamed of herself, Laurette leaped down from the windowsill, dashed on weakened legs into her bathroom and washed thoroughly. When she came back into the bedroom, she snatched up the discarded nightgown and anxiously slipped it on, hoping that she hadn't committed some terrible sin for which she would be direly punished.

Admittedly more relaxed than she'd been in ages, Laurette climbed back onto the windowsill, sighed, and turned her thoughts to the things she and Ladd had done together, of all the good times they had shared through the years. And she told herself that before she knew it, it would be summertime and he would get his first furlough and come home.

Home to her.

Laurette smiled, closed her eyes and attempted to envision the glorious scene: a warm, perfect day beneath a cloudless, blue Alabama sky. She would be in her prettiest summer dress. He'd be wearing his snappy dress uniform. She'd be at the levee to meet him, waving madly. He'd race down the gangplank to her and she'd fly straight into his outstretched arms.

Laurette's smile faded and finally disappeared. Her eyes slowly opened and a wistful expression came into them. Her brows knitted and she frowned. A clear vision of the happy occasion refused to appear.

She could not see it.

She shuddered.

Twelve

Without warning the serious disquiet that had been brewing between the North and the South exploded into all-out war when a group of Citadel cadets opened fire on a Northern ship attempting to deliver supplies to the garrison at Fort Sumter.

The first shot was fired from Fort Johnson at 4:30 a.m. on April 12, 1861. After thirty-three hours of bombardment, the Sumter flag went down. Charleston bragged of victory. Headlines in the North used the word *war*. And young men, from both the North and the South, began flocking to the banners.

At West Point, the cadets were almost evenly divided between the Union and the Confederacy. Great, good friends now found themselves on opposite sides in the coming conflict. Cadet Lieutenant James Tigart, a native Kentuckian, chose to remain with the Union. Ladd, a true son of the South, opted to leave the academy at once and ride down to Virginia to join General Robert E. Lee's army.

Before going their separate ways, Ladd sought out Jimmy to bid him farewell. On the historic old plain,

the childhood friends met and said a strained goodbye
as clouds overhead threatened rain.

"I must and will be loyal to the Union," Jimmy
stated emphatically, a hand gripping Ladd's shoulder.

"I understand," Ladd replied. "Just as I must be
loyal to the Confederacy." Jimmy nodded. Ladd continued, "You will never be the enemy to me,
Jimmy."

"Always comrades, Laddie," Jimmy replied.

Attempting to lighten the mood, Ladd said, smiling,
"If I run into you on the battlefield, I promise not to
take a shot."

Jimmy laughed, shook his head. "Same here, my
friend. We'll meet again, I'm sure of it. You take
care, you hear?"

"Will do. See you after this is over."

Jimmy gave no reply. The two young men embraced, then turned and went in opposite directions.

Neither looked back.

Mobile was up in arms.

In every household in the city, men, young and old,
were saying goodbye to wives, sweethearts and families before going off to war. The Confederacy, they
declared with heartfelt patriotism, needed every able-
bodied man.

At the mansion on Dauphin, T. H. Howard was
preparing to leave, while Marion, eyes bright with
unshed tears, helped him pack.

"Now, dear," said Marion, "I'm putting in two
pairs of your nice silk pajamas so that—"

"Marion," he cut in, smiling indulgently, "where my command is going, I won't be needing silk pajamas."

"No, of course not," she said. She removed the pajamas, pressed them to her breasts and finally began to cry.

"Oh, darling," her husband soothed, taking her in his arms. "I won't be gone long. This will all be over soon. We'll easily lick the Yankees," he promised. T.H. brushed a kiss to her forehead, and released her. He turned, closed the valise, picked it up and said, "It's time for me to go, dearest."

Marion nodded, sniffed back her tears and went downstairs with him where a distraught Laurette waited. T.H. placed the valise on the foyer floor, took his only daughter in his arms and said softly, "Sweetheart, I know you're worried about Ladd, but he'll be fine. He's a brave, smart, resourceful young man, and after a year at the Point he'll surely make a superb soldier."

Unconvinced, Laurette said, "Oh, Father, I have the most terrible feeling that I will never see Ladd again."

"Foolish girl," he said, hugging her close, "this war will be over before you know it. Ladd will be back in Mobile by summertime and so will I."

"I hope you're right," Laurette managed to reply.

"I am. Count on it."

On the south side of Dauphin, a similar scene was being played out in one of the double parlors of the

Dasheroon mansion. Douglas Dasheroon was preparing to leave Mobile. He would reclaim his command and get into the war. Carrie Dasheroon was weeping, her slender shoulders shaking. And she was bitterly protesting the fates.

"It is not fair," she sobbed as she watched her big, handsome husband calmly prepare to leave her. "Am I to give up my son *and* my husband? This Confederacy is asking too much. Ladd's just a baby, not even eighteen. Oh, Douglas, go find him, bring him home now."

Douglas Dasheroon exhaled wearily, turned, clasped his wife's shaking shoulders. "My love, please pull yourself together and be strong. We must all make sacrifices, but this upside-down world will right itself again, you'll see. Ladd and I will be back home with you before Ladd turns eighteen."

Eight months at West Point had not prepared Ladd for the horrors of war. The fighting was fierce and he was frightened. Death and destruction were his constant companions. He lived with both each moment of every day and night. The sights, sounds and smells were nightmarish. But Ladd carefully kept his fear to himself so that it could never be said that he was a coward.

The bloody skirmishes were continuous and Ladd realized, at the very beginning of the war, that any hopes he had entertained of going home to see Laurette come summer had been duty-dashed.

A good officer, he doggedly fought the enemy with

the fervent pride and passion of a true Southerner. And any time he got the opportunity, when there was a blessed lull in the bombardment, he sat down on the ground and wrote to his beloved Laurette, never knowing if she got his letters.

Summer, 1863

The war continued. Even the proud Southerners had come to face the sad truth: they were not going to whip the better armed, better trained Yankees as easily as they had thought.

After two years on the front lines, Ladd was a tough, seasoned captain. He had managed to lead his troops through battle after battle with only close calls and minor losses.

And then one hot still day in May, his luck ran out.

The Battle of Chancellorsville was a prolonged battle in which General Lee brilliantly outmaneuvered the enemy. However, the Union Army's rifled firepower extracted such heavy casualties, the victory yielded no decisive advantage for the South.

In the thick of it and temporarily cut off from Jackson's mighty Rebel force, Captain Dasheroon was trapped. "Stay close behind me and I'll do my best to get you through this alive," he calmly commanded his soldiers.

It was not to be.

When the ferocious battle ended, Ladd was the sole survivor of his small command. Badly wounded, but alive, he had taken a minié ball in the right side and was bleeding profusely. He lay in the warm Virginia sun amid the dead, anguished that he had let his men down, had lost them all. But fully accepting of the fact that, like his fallen men, this was likely to be his last day on earth. He was having difficulty breathing, could feel the very life ebbing out of him. His thoughts turned to his beloved Laurette. A faint smile touched his chapped lips as in his mind's eyes he saw the impetuous, cute as a button, six-year-old Laurette turn somersaults on the lawn. Then the precocious child faded and the lovely sixteen-year-old Laurette took her place.

Grimacing with pain, the wounded Ladd pressed a hand to his bloodied, shattered ribs and swallowed hard, recalling, with vivid clarity, his last night in Mobile.

"Lollie," Ladd mouthed her name without sound. "Dearest Lollie."

The high, bright sun began to dim. The distant sounds of gunfire began to fade. Ladd gave a sigh of resignation as blessed darkness enveloped him.

Winter, 1863

Gone now were the snappily uniformed, bright-eyed West Point cadets with their daredevil perform-ances, their youthful elegance, their respect for duty and honor, their gleaming white smiles, sleek muscles and chiseled jaws, and courage of a sort rarely seen.

Those young, brave, proud cadets from both the North and the South were now either hardened vet-erans engaged in bloody battle, dead and buried where they fell, or incarcerated in military prisons.

Prisons with romantic names like Belle's Isle, Cas-tle Thunder, Hope Slater, Governors Island, Myrtle Street and Point Lookout.

Ladd Dasheroon was in such a prison.

A prison with a romantic name—Devil's Castle.

Captured by the advancing Union soldiers that May day at Chancellorsville, the near-dead Ladd had been immediately shipped to Devil's Castle. The old stone fortress with its thick, high walls was located on a small rocky island in Chesapeake Bay, just off the Maryland shore.

Built as a fort more than a hundred years earlier, then used as a penitentiary until it was considered too inhumane for even hardened criminals, it had been deserted for decades. Now it overflowed with sick, starving, dead and dying Confederate prisoners. Eighteen hundred men in a facility meant to contain five hundred.

As soon as the prison's chief surgeon released Ladd from the hospital, he was tossed—literally—into the large, overcrowded common room that held hundreds of men. He landed atop a couple of startled prisoners: Captain Andrew Scott, 5th N. Carolina regiment, who was a cadaverously thin, thirty-eight-year-old who had lost an arm in battle; and Private Duncan Cain, 3rd Alabama regiment, a young boy of twenty.

The gaunt Captain Scott wrapped his one arm around Ladd—who was freezing cold despite the stifling heat—lifted him gently and said, "Don't worry, we'll take care of you." Scott glanced at Duncan Cain. "Won't we, Duncan?"

The boy nodded, took the thin, folded blanket he was sitting on and carefully spread it over the shivering, ashen-faced Ladd. "Sorry there's no pillow," said Duncan.

Ladd managed a weak smile, thanked the two men with his eyes and fell asleep.

Andrew Scott and Duncan Cain worked tirelessly for the next several days to nurse Ladd back to health. The three became good friends. They looked out for each other. They stayed close in the overcrowded common room. They talked together of home and family and happier days. Each worked to keep the others' spirits up.

But life inside the old stone prison was harsh and cold. The big common room where they were confined had only four small-size windows at each end that admitted a limited amount of light. At the room's center, it was too dark for reading, even in daytime.

But that didn't matter. There was nothing to read. Letter writing or receiving was strictly prohibited. As were newspapers. Every channel of communication was cut off, leaving the poor souls inside to wonder what was going on in the war and how their families were faring back home.

At Devil's Castle, there was never enough to eat, and what was served was often unappetizing, even spoiled. Hunger gnawed constantly and Ladd, like his fellow prisoners, quickly became emaciated and weak. But no matter how sick or weak a prisoner became, he had no cot to stretch out on, no pillow on which to lay his weary head. Except for a couple of stoves, there was no furniture in the room. The prisoners sat and slept on the cold stone floor, many with no blankets to keep them warm.

All that, Ladd could easily have endured.

But he was called on to endure much more.

Thirteen

Gilbert LaKid, the upperclassman who had caused Ladd so much grief at West Point, was Captain of the Guards at Devil's Castle. LaKid, who'd lost an eye, but gained thirty plus pounds during the war, encouraged his guards to inflict punishment and show contempt to the prisoners.

Especially to Ladd Dasheroon.

LaKid's fleshy face, when it twisted into an evil smile, was the face of a monster. And that nasty smile appeared any time he caught sight of Ladd.

Prisoners were punished only for insulting prison officials, for trying to bribe guards, for fighting, for stealing and for attempting to escape.

Ladd was guilty of none of those transgressions, but he was often punished as if he were the worst offender at Devil's Castle. Any time he saw the beefy, one-eyed LaKid swagger into the prison's common room, he was immediately filled with dread. Still weak and tired, Ladd would sit on the crowded stone floor between Captain Scott and Private Cain, hugging his knees, slumping, attempting to make himself invisible in the mass of humanity.

It never worked.

LaKid always spotted Ladd. And when he did, he tromped forward into the sea of hovering men, knocking them out of his way, stepping on those who didn't move quickly enough. His smile became broader, nastier, the closer he got to Ladd.

As the sadistic bully approached, Ladd purposely stiffened his spine. As his side began to slowly heal and he regained his strength, he assured himself that he could withstand any punishment LaKid had planned for him. He would no longer allow the evil Captain of the Guards to break him. He was a whole man now, and he had been hardened by two and half years on the battlefield. He could and would take whatever LaKid meted out without complaint.

On one such occasion, a miserably cold, gray December afternoon near Christmas of 1863, LaKid came looking for Ladd. When the guard's big, booted feet stopped directly before him, Ladd raised his head and met his tormenter's one-eyed gaze.

With a nasty grin, LaKid inquired, "How is our sickly little Alabama boy feeling this afternoon?"

"How kind of you to inquire," Ladd replied sarcastically, as was now his habit. "While many of the guests in this fine luxury hotel of yours seem to be dying, I myself feel tip-top, thank you very much." Ladd flashed a wide smile at the frowning LaKid as the admiring prisoners within earshot silently applauded Ladd's unshakable nerve.

"Get to your feet, you uppity southern son of a bitch!" snarled LaKid.

"My pleasure," said Ladd, using all of his will-power to rise without the use of his hands. "Anything else?"

LaKid's one eye narrowed. "It has been called to my attention that you mocked a night guard. We don't tolerate that kind of behavior at Devil's Castle. You will be punished."

Ladd didn't bother disagreeing. He had insulted no one and LaKid knew it. LaKid was constantly trumping up bogus charges against Ladd in order to torture him. This time, like all the others, Ladd resolutely followed the stocky guard out of the room while his friends Andrew and Duncan shook their heads, knowing that he was in for it again. They were puzzled that Dasheroon and a few others were regularly singled out for punishment for no apparent reason.

All of the prisoners were aware, however, that the officers and men of the regiment guarding them were spiteful devils—there was nothing too mean or low or insulting for them to say and do. The fearful prisoners were surrounded by bayonets and artillery, guarded by soldiers who cursed, swore and fired among them when they pleased. And it was whispered that on occasion those guards, specifically LaKid, had resorted to ball, chains and dungeons for the slightest offense.

All eyes clung to Ladd's thin frame as he walked out of the room as if he were off on a Sunday stroll, his back as straight as the proudest West Point cadet. Outside, it was bitterly cold and Ladd wore only a tattered cotton shirt and a pair of cotton trousers. No shoes. No underwear. His teeth began to chatter as he was flanked by two more prison guards and marched across the muddy quadrangle beneath a gray, leaden sky.

Forty yards from the prison's main building, he was ordered to halt directly beneath a crossbar.

"Raise your arms, Reb," commanded the grinning LaKid. Ladd obeyed. "Now stretch up onto your tip-toes and reach as high as you can," ordered LaKid. Again Ladd complied.

He was then suspended by his thumbs and left dangling there for several hours in the freezing December weather. It was dark when he was finally let down and dragged back inside, fully conscious but sick from the cold. Ladd's friends were seated close to the door, anxiously watching and waiting for Ladd's return. When LaKid shoved Ladd inside, Andrew and Duncan shot to their feet and went to the fallen man.

"Oh, God," Andrew said, gathering the faint, freezing Ladd against him, "they're trying to kill you, the bastards."

Ladd attempted a smile. "Well, it won't work," he said, shivering. "I'd never give them the satisfaction."

Duncan wrapped his threadbare blanket around Ladd's thin shoulders, and asked, "What did they do to you this time?"

"Nothing much," Ladd replied, but his worried friends saw his bloodied thumbs and knew. Everyone at Devil's Castle had heard of the various forms of punishment, including that of suspending a prisoner by his thumbs.

Some, it was said, were left dangling until their thumbs burst and they fell to the ground.

* * *

Ladd's thumbs were just about healed when LaKid came for him again. This time he was bucked and gagged.

Ladd was ordered to sit down on the cold, muddy ground. A stick was tied across his open mouth, his wrists were tied together and slipped over his drawn-up knees. Then, a longer stick was wedged beneath his knees and across his forearms. He was left to sit in that position for eight long hours while a chilly January rain fell down upon him.

When LaKid and his minions, laughing and enjoying themselves, came to untie Ladd, they expected to find a fearful, beaten man. The chuckling LaKid took the stick from Ladd's split lips and, seeing Ladd's wet face and rain-clumped lashes, teased, "What have we here? You crying for your mommy?"

"Kiss my skinny Confederate ass!" said Ladd and spat in the big man's ugly face.

Infuriated, LaKid instantly struck Ladd with the butt of his rifle. Blood splattered. Pain exploded inside Ladd's head. He hardly felt it. He did not regret his impulsive action. It had been worth it. He had wanted to spit in Gilbert LaKid's repulsive face since his days at West Point and, now that he had nothing more to lose, he had done it.

"Take this piece of Southern white trash inside and see to it he gets no supper tonight!"

The next time Ladd was escorted outside by the guards, he was introduced to yet another ingenious form of punishment called "on the chines." He was forced to stand and balance himself on the top edges of a flour barrel—which had the head knocked out—for a long period of time.

And he had on no shoes.

While straddling the barrel, he was handed a heavy log to cradle in his arms. If he refused to take the log, or if he later dropped it, he was to be immediately shot by the guards.

Ladd prayed to the Almighty to give him strength as the soles of his bare feet became red and raw and his arms grew so weak they began shaking. He told himself repeatedly that he could do it, that they couldn't best him. He had too much to live for. This war would end one day and he'd go home. Home to his sweet Laurette. So he'd be damned if he would die here in this pesthole surrounded by a bunch of laughing Yankee animals.

Ladd wet his lips, called on all his reserves of fortitude and began to whistle a snappy tune as if he didn't have a care in the world.

Frustrated and determined to break him, the Captain of the Guards stepped up Ladd's torture. Almost every day Ladd was called on to withstand some form of punishment. More than once he was handcuffed to a high pole and flogged, given as many as one hundred lashes at a time. He was secured in heavy balls and chains. He was bolted to the walls or floors. Nothing seemed to work.

Then, finally, LaKid had an inspiration.

As excited as a child at Christmas, LaKid had his guards herd all the prisoners outdoors into the bitter cold and raw February winds. Warned that they would be shot should they try to escape, the shivering men stood gathered around a small fire that had been built in a stone pit at the center of the prison yard.

Ladd, like his fellow prisoners, had no idea what the fire was for or what was going to happen.

Not even when his name was called.

Ladd exchanged glances with Andrew and Duncan.

"Hell, let's make a run for it," whispered Andrew.

"No," said Ladd, "they'd kill us all, there's a Gatling atop the south wall."

Ladd took a deep breath and began making his way through the crowd. When he reached the opening where a dozen guards stood around the fire in a semi-circle, rifles at the ready, he walked directly up to Gilbert LaKid and said, "So what's it to be today? Burned at the stake?"

The Captain of the Guards laughed heartily and replied, "Not a bad idea, Reb, but in case you've failed to notice, we are civilized here at Devil's Castle."

Grinning, he ordered Ladd to turn with his back to the prisoners, drop his tattered trousers, bend over and grip his knees.

"No, I don't think I'll do that," Ladd stated calmly as he crossed his arms over his chest and flashed the guard a grin.

LaKid jerked his head in a silent command and two guards swiftly stepped forward, turned Ladd about and roughly stripped his tattered trousers down. Then they trussed him with strong ropes, shoved on his back and, bending him over, exposed his bare buttocks to the cold February air.

The prisoners watched in rising horror. A guard

reached into the fire pit and handed Gilbert LaKid a glowing hot branding iron. Enjoying the prisoners' fear and apprehension, LaKid thrust it back into the pit of the fire.

He held it there for several heartbeats.

Then with great relish LaKid withdrew the glowing, white-hot iron and pressed it to the bony left buttock of Ladd Dasheroon. Ladd clenched his teeth and tried very hard not to make a sound.

He failed.

With smoke from the wound choking him and the stench of his own searing flesh strong in his nostrils, he emitted a strangled sound of distress. The heat of the sizzling imprint swiftly spread throughout his thin frame. He was instantly hot all over, in pain and burning from head to toe.

Victorious, Gilbert LaKid gave a great shout of triumph as Ladd sank weakly to his knees and slumped, chin on chest. The conquering Captain of the Guards lifted a heavy booted foot and viciously kicked the bound, kneeling prisoner. Ladd crumpled like a rag doll and fell over onto his face.

He made no attempt to move.

Suffering in silence now, he lay still and quiet. Finally he smiled faintly as he felt the comforting cloak of unconsciousness close over him, liberating him, carrying him away from this hell on earth to a safe, sunny place.

Fourteen

In the middle of a cold February night in 1864, Laurette awakened with a strangled cry. She bolted up in bed, trembling, her heart pounding. She'd had a terrible nightmare—one that had been so incredibly real, it had left her distraught, terrified.

She drew her knees up to her chest and hugged them tightly, attempting to stop the violent shaking of her body. Her breath came in shallow, choking gasps and she felt as if she were suffocating. She told herself it had only been a dream, a very bad dream.

The dream had started out so pleasant, so very sweet. It was summertime and there was no such thing as a war and she and Ladd were together down at the river landing. They were strolling along the levee, hand in hand, watching the large cumulus clouds building out over the gulf.

The bright sun was shining on the river and the clouds seemed to glow from within. A flock of gulls swooped low, whooping and giving their shrieking cries, then circled and winged out toward open waters.

It was midsummer thunderstorm season and just like clockwork, at three in the afternoon, the sun disappeared. Minutes later, the first huge raindrops began to fall. She and Ladd laughed and ran for cover.

And magically, as often happens in dreams, they found themselves no longer in downtown Mobile on the riverfront, but across the bay on the eastern shore in the Dasheroons' empty bayside cottage.

They were on the thatch-covered veranda of the secluded cottage, watching the storm build over the bay, inhaling deeply of the clean scent of rain. Thunder rumbled and lightning streaked across the darkening sky.

Wordlessly they turned to each other. They kissed and undressed right there on the rain-peppered veranda. Naked they stood embracing, the wind-driven rain wetting their feverish bodies and pressing their hair to their heads.

Kissing and clinging to each other, they sank weakly to their knees, excited, aroused. When Ladd's gleaming lips finally left Laurette's, he asked, "Do you want to go inside, to the bed?"

"No," she decisively replied, tightening her arms around his neck, "Love me right here in the rain."

And so he did.

While the violent thunderstorm intensified and the rain came down in torrents they made love, unworried that they might be seen. Their privacy was assured by the blinding sheets of rain as well as the thick, tropical growth of oleander, oak leaf hydrangea, mimosa, banana trees and tall sago palms that surrounded the cliffside cottage.

Their bodies wet with rain, they slipped and slid

sensuously against each other and Laurette could feel Ladd filling her, stretching her, making her his own. They moved together with near perfect precision. Giving to the other and taking for themselves. They were learning more about lovemaking every time they were together.

Lost in the building pleasure, Laurette gazed at Ladd's handsome face just above hers, taut with passion. His sculpted shoulders were wide, his arms—the arms that held her—were muscled and strong. His body was lean, toned, beautiful. He was young and virile and possessed plenty of potent strength to love her as often and as long as she wanted.

And then—all at once—as he thrust into her with the kind of seeking force that gave her incredible ecstasy, he began to change before her frightened eyes. His deep tan quickly faded to a sickly pallor. His wide, muscled shoulders became painfully thin and bony beneath her hands. He sagged wearily against her and the hard masculine flesh that was buried deep inside her became limp and lifeless.

"I'm no use to you anymore," he lamented, his gaunt, hollow-cheeked face moving away. "They're killing me, Lollie. I'm dying."

"Who?" she had screamed, struggling to hold on to him. "What is happening, Ladd?"

But he was already leaving her, floating away, his sallow face becoming a grotesque mask.

"Ladd! Ladd!" she sobbed and awakened with a start, weeping.

* * *

Now, as she sat in the chill February darkness, Laurette was overcome with fear that the ghastly nightmare held meaning. Was something terrible happening to Ladd? Was he suffering? Was he dead or dying? She hadn't heard from him in over a year, had no idea where he was or even if he was still alive. She lived in agony, fearing the worst, expecting to hear that he had been killed in battle.

Tears stinging her eyes, Laurette exhaled, lay back down and covered herself, wondering how much more she could endure. Her safe, happy, wonderful life had come crashing down around her ears and nothing would ever be the same again. Her beloved father had been killed at Gettysburg and her mother had died the following winter.

Alone now in the big, silent mansion that was once filled with life and laughter, Laurette wept for all that was forever lost. And in the cold, lonely darkness, she murmured aloud, "Ladd, please don't leave me. Wherever you are, you must keep fighting to stay alive. Please, my darling, stay alive and come home to me."

Ladd, wanting nothing more than to go home to Laurette, was doing his best to stay alive. But the misery, the hunger, the beatings, the branding and the other forms of endless torture were slowly taking their toll. His spirits were sagging, he was growing weary of the battle, losing heart. His friends, Andrew and Duncan, were worried about him. He wasn't himself. His fighting spirit was waning away.

Just as Ladd was at his lowest point, news that the Devil's Castle commandant was being replaced traveled through the prisoner community. Major Jimmy Tigart, severely wounded in battle, was being sent to take over the top position at the prison.

When Ladd heard about Jimmy, he was elated—his weariness evaporated and he was filled with relief and hope. His days of enduring torture were over! Jimmy would help him, makes things bearable. He would control LaKid and his cruelty. And, he felt certain that Jimmy would see to it that his, Ladd's, name went to the top of the prisoner exchange list. With any luck he would soon be leaving Devil's Castle!

Ladd awakened early on the day Jimmy was to take command. He looked down at his tattered clothes and groaned. He hated for his old childhood friend to see him so thin and unkempt, but there was nothing he could do.

Beside himself with excitement, Ladd waited anxiously for Jimmy's arrival. He purposely positioned himself near the common room's front doors, so that Jimmy would be sure to see him. Finally, at five minutes past noon, the heavy prison doors swung open and Ladd leaped to his feet.

A quartet of armed guards stepped inside. Directly behind them was the crisply uniformed Major Jimmy Tigart. Ladd immediately noticed that Jimmy had a limp, was using a cane to aid in his walking. Other than that, he seemed to be healthy and he sure looked good to Ladd. Major Tigart glanced around, caught sight of the smiling Ladd and his eyes widened with surprise. Ladd realized then that Jimmy had had no idea he was a prisoner at Devil's Castle.

Ladd waited impatiently while Major Tigart, leaning on his cane for support, stood a few feet from the doorway and made a brief speech to the prisoners. When the speech was ended, Major Tigart turned to Ladd and greeted him warmly.

"Walk outside with me," he said to Ladd, "where we can talk."

Waving the guards away, Major Tigart led Ladd across the prison grounds to the command building where his office and quarters were located. On the building's wide stone porch, the two men stopped, looked at each other and embraced. Each was full of questions. Neither had many answers. Jimmy told Ladd how the war was progressing. Then he asked about Laurette.

"We are not allowed to receive letters here," said Ladd. "We get no news of any kind. You've heard nothing from her?"

Tigart shook his head. The two talked and talked, Ladd confiding in Jimmy, telling him of the torture he had endured. Jimmy listened intently and assured Ladd that everything would be better now.

"And you'll put my name on the prisoner exchange list?" asked Ladd.

"At the very top. You know I will," Jimmy said. "Now you'd better go back to your quarters. But don't worry, I'll get you out of here."

"Soon?" said Ladd.

Jimmy flashed him a smile. "Consider it done."

Major Tigart stood on the stone porch in the strong March sunlight, silently watching his pitiful, cadaverously thin friend cross the prison yard. Incredibly, there was a spring to Ladd's step.

Poor devil.

Tigart went inside the command building, walked into his office, circled the desk and sat down. He propped his cane against the wall behind him, turned, put his elbows on the desk and rested his face in his hands.

He sat silently staring into space, thinking, wrestling with his conscience. His first impulse was to have Ladd immediately executed. It would be simple enough. He could easily have Ladd charged with a crime for which he would pay with his life. Or, better still, he could spread the word that he and Ladd had been boyhood friends. Then invite Ladd to dinner in his private quarters. And, at the end of the evening, report that the sickly prisoner had died.

Tigart raised his head and exhaled wearily. He couldn't do it. Much as he wanted Ladd dead, he couldn't bring himself to kill Ladd. But he could *allow* him to die.

"Captain of the Guards," Major Tigart called out after several long minutes.

Gilbert LaKid, nervous, worried about his own precious hide, immediately stepped inside the new commandant's office, expecting to be soundly reprimanded for past excesses.

Major Tigart leaned back in his chair and casually asked, "Does Devil's Castle have any dungeons?"

That was the last question LaKid had expected to hear from the new commandant and it frightened him. He knew that Major Tigart was an old friend of Ladd Dasheroon. LaKid's apprehension grew. He began to perspire.

"Yes, sir," said LaKid, reluctantly, "the dark cells. There are four underneath the main building."

"Are they occupied?"

"Only one. A political prisoner and thief by the name of—"

"So you have three empty cells?" Jimmy asked, cutting him off.

"Yes, Commandant Tigart, that is correct."

Calmly, his face showing no emotion, Major Tigart said, "You are, without delay, to throw the prisoner Ladd Dasheroon into the deepest, darkest dungeon of this prison."

Flabbergasted, but pleased, LaKid did not question his superior.

"Yes, sir," he said, turned and left Major Tigart's office.

More than eager to obey the new prison commandant's very first command, Gilbert LaKid, motioning a couple of armed guards to follow him, walked into the crowded common room of the prison and shouted Ladd's name. Ladd's heart automatically lurched. Then he remembered. No need for dread. Jimmy was now in charge. Maybe his childhood friend was already setting the wheels of his prisoner exchange in motion.

With an optimism and sense of well-being he hadn't had in ages, Ladd walked confidently toward the stout, smiling LaKid.

"Outside," LaKid ordered.

Two guards were waiting. Still Ladd was not nervous. They wouldn't dare do anything to him with Jimmy in command. Expecting to be escorted to Jimmy's office, Ladd was puzzled when, instead, he was marched to the stone building's rear.

Halting, Gilbert LaKid unlocked a solid oak cellar door set in the hard Maryland clay. Ladd, now restrained by the guards, was shoved inside. He blinked. A set of wide stone steps led downward into a dark cellar hall that was dimly lit by wall torches.

LaKid led the way down, down, down into the narrow hall. Four closed doors opened into the hallway, two on each side. LaKid passed one door, walked another twenty feet and stopped before the door on the right side of the hall, unlocked it, and motioned for the guards to throw Ladd inside. Confused and horrified, Ladd quickly found himself alone in a cell with only one high, tiny, barred window. He shouted and banged on the heavy door until he was hoarse and his fists were bloody, but no one came.

It had to be a terrible mistake. He was not supposed to be thrown into this dungeon. He was to be left alone, no longer punished. Jimmy had promised. Surely Jimmy would soon learn of this unforgivable mix-up and send someone to let him out. Of course he would. Jimmy would run this prison in a just, fair manner. Which meant that every prisoner would be accounted for at all times. The thing to do was just relax and keep calm. In a matter of hours, a day at the outside, Jimmy would hear about LaKid's actions.

Ladd sank down onto the stone floor, assuring himself that he wouldn't be down here long. Thank God.

The sun had now set and it was so dark he couldn't see his hand before his face. He considered the poor souls who had been forced to languish here for weeks at a time. He wondered if they had been able to maintain their sanity. He didn't see how anyone possibly could. He knew he couldn't. But there was no need to worry, Jimmy would get him out shortly.

An honorable man, Ladd could never have conceived of the idea that his old childhood friend might betray him. The thought never crossed his mind. The two of them had grown to manhood together. Jimmy had once saved Ladd's life, risking his own. They were like brothers.

Jimmy would never betray him.

Fifteen

When Laurette Howard turned twenty in the summer of '64, she was no longer the sassy, spirited girl she had once been. Circumstances had forced her to grow up quickly, to become sober and responsible, to literally fend for herself.

Laurette was all alone in the big Dauphin Street mansion. Both her parents were now dead. All the servants were gone. Even the faithful Ruby Lee, realizing that her young charge couldn't afford to feed the both of them, had finally moved in with relatives downtown.

Laurette's father, T. H. Howard, had lost his extensive fortune while away fighting for the Cause. There was hardly anything left, save the neglected Dauphin Street mansion. In the summer of '63, her father had been killed at Gettysburg. Distraught, her mother, Marion, not really wanting to live without him, had contracted influenza and died that winter at Christmastime.

Ladd's father, Douglas Dasheroon, had also perished. He had died in the terrible siege of Vicksburg and Ladd's grieving mother, Carrie, had sold the

Dasheroon mansion for a quarter of its value and fled to New Orleans to live with cousins.

Throughout the many tragedies and hardships, Laurette had tried very hard to keep a stiff upper lip as was the custom of well brought up Southern ladies. She kept telling herself that she could withstand anything—anything except losing Ladd. As long as she could hope for his return, she could survive.

Besides, she was not the only one whose life had been altered by the war.

Johanna Parlange had been left a widow just weeks after marrying a young soldier from Montgomery. Juliette had never married. A year ago, their stalwart grandmother, Lena, had passed away and now the twins were struggling to maintain the Springhill mansion.

Her old music teacher, Miss Foster, no longer gave piano lessons. There were no pupils. And the widowed Melba Adair, whose passion was her beautiful gardens, had been forced to sell the estate and move with her daughter, Lydia, into a cramped upstairs dwelling on Herndon Avenue where there was no ground to plant even one camellia bush.

Times were hard, but Laurette was aware that things could have been worse. The city of Mobile, with its rail and water links to the Confederate heartland, was a valuable asset to the South. The port was well-defended. On the bay's lower edge, the main entrance to the harbor was flanked, east and west, by twin masonry fortifications, Fort Gaines and Fort Morgan.

The waterway between them was largely obstructed with driven pilings and moored mines. Through the channel passed fast Confederate steamers with exports of cotton and munitions. But the blockade running trade was constantly harassed by Federal warships sitting just offshore.

Almost from the beginning of the war, the blockade and the lack of manpower to run the farms and businesses caused the citizens of Mobile to suffer from food and supply shortages. If that was not enough, tax burdens increased.

Still, the citizens took comfort in the fact that the Union army had not occupied their beloved city. All had heard how the Yankees had swept across the state's northern counties, ruthlessly burning large sections of Selma and Tuscaloosa.

Fearing the same fate would befall Mobile, Laurette had buried the family silver beneath an old oak that grew along the far border of the vast estate. Along with the heavy sterling, she had buried some sentimental treasures: an oyster shell comb decorated with semiprecious stones that had belonged to her mother; her father's gold-cased pocket watch; and last, but most precious of all, the tintype of a handsome sixteen-year-old Ladd in a heavy silver frame.

Laurette, like other worried Mobillians, kept expecting the city to fall any day.

Jimmy Tigart, who had come from modest means, had always envied Ladd Dasheroon for what he took for granted: wealth; social position; and most of all, the beautiful Laurette Howard. It all should have been his. With Ladd out of the way, perhaps it would be.

Tigart recognized this once-in-a-lifetime opportunity and seized it. Suffering nagging twinges of guilt, he nonetheless had Ladd thrown into the bowels of the prison where Ladd could no longer see or speak to anyone.

And, no one could see or speak to him, save the guards who took him meals.

Who was to know that Ladd Dasheroon was still alive? Nobody. Tigart was confident that he could concoct a serious charge—label Ladd a dangerous political prisoner—that would keep him in that dark prison dungeon long after the war was over. Some crimes carried a life sentence, war or no war. But would that be enough?

"That's it!" Tigart said aloud and snapped his fingers as a new idea came to him. He would wait a few months, then quietly have Ladd's name added to the death list and sent to Confederate graves registration.

And Ladd would stay down in that cell until he finally did die. His death would likely occur before too many years passed. No man could survive the solitude and darkness of the dungeon for long.

Tapping his fingertips together, his hazel eyes slightly narrowed, Tigart began to make plans for his own rosy future. A future that would, he sincerely hoped, include the one woman he had always desired.

Laurette Howard.

Alone in the dungeon, Ladd attempted to keep track of time. He had given up on being released from this tiny ten-by-twelve cell where very little daylight ever penetrated. LaKid had gleefully told him to abandon hope.

Ladd had.

Hope had been replaced by disbelief and then by hatred. Hatred of his old friend, Jimmy Tigart. Ladd hadn't wanted to believe the terrible truth. But he knew that a prison commandant was informed of everything that took place inside the walls. Tigart had known, from the minute it happened, that Ladd had been thrown into the dungeon.

Tigart had ordered it done.

Tigart had betrayed him.

Heartsick, Ladd cursed the friend who had so coldly forsaken him. And he trembled with fear knowing that he might never get out of this dark cell alive.

Ladd counted the days, the weeks, the months as 1864 turned to 1865. Shortly after the new year began, he lost count. With the constant isolation and near starvation, he had become confused, was no longer sure what month it was, what year. At times, he didn't even know *where* he was.

At 6:00 a.m. on August 5, 1864, under cloudy skies and with a westerly wind blowing, Admiral David Farragut ordered his fleet to steam past Fort Morgan and into Mobile Bay.

The Battle of Mobile was underway, a battle that lasted less than four hours. By 10:00 a.m. on that muggy August morning, the bombardment was over. Admiral David Farragut and his Union Navy were victorious, yet Mobile proper remained in the hands of the Confederacy almost until the war's end.

But its value to the Confederacy was gone.

Finally, in April of 1865, the long, bloody War Between the States ended with much of the defeated South lying in ruin. The citizens of Mobile counted themselves fortunate, at least in comparison to those of other Southern cities. Although many in Mobile had lost their fortunes, they were thankful that their mansions had not been occupied or burned by destructive Union soldiers.

Making the best of her lot, Laurette celebrated along with her two best friends, the Parlange twins, when they heard that the war was over. Fireworks were shot off in the harbor and there was dancing in the streets. Smiling people assured each other that life would now return to normal.

Yet in their hearts they knew that the languid, graceful, happy days so relished by the residents of the glorious Old South were forever gone.

"Jimmy! Jimmy Tigart!" Laurette exclaimed in shocked surprise when she answered a knock on the door one sunny day in the first week of May. "Is it really you? I can't believe it!"

Smiling broadly, the tall, uniformed Union officer standing on the shaded veranda, his right hand resting on a malacca walking cane, said softly, "It's me, Laurette. May I come in?"

"Of course. Where are my manners?" she said, her heart fluttering with the hope that Jimmy might know and tell her where Ladd was, when he would be coming home to her. Noting the cane and his slight limp, she said, "Oh, Jimmy, you've been wounded, you're—"

"It's nothing, really," he assured her. "I'm just fine."

"Good, good," she said nodding, and no sooner were they inside the foyer than she asked, hopefully, "Ladd? Have you heard...I keep expecting him to...to...?" Her words trailed away. She read the look in Jimmy's hazel eyes and felt herself growing faint. "No," she protested, a hand coming up to her mouth, her eyes wide with growing horror, "No...don't... I..."

"I'm so very sorry, Laurette," Jimmy said, reaching out to her. "Ladd died in Maryland's Devil's Castle prison in the fall of 1864." He shook his head sorrowfully and added, "It happened just before I was sent there as the prison's commandant. Had I arrived there in time, I would have had his name put on the prisoner exchange list." He stopped speaking, looked at her stricken face and almost changed his mind about the deception. He had never seen such naked grief in a pair of eyes.

"No," she whispered, her face totally draining of color. "No, no, no. Ladd isn't dead, he cannot be dead! I can't stand it, I won't stand it." Her chin quivered. Her eyes quickly filled with tears. Her stunned expression changed. She looked wild, as if she were about to spin out of control. She began to shudder, then to wail and scream.

Jimmy quickly enfolded her in his arms. At first she strained against him, tried to pull away, pummeled his chest with her fists. Then she finally collapsed in racking sobs. He held her while she wept, her tears wetting his uniform, her slender body jerking with her sobs. He patted her back and murmured words of solace for what seemed forever, until finally she had cried herself out.

Only then did he gently lead her into the parlor and urge her down onto the well-worn sofa. He sat beside her and talked quietly to her, soothing her, urging her to depend on him, to share her grief and troubles with him. To let him help.

Never had she been more hopeless, more vulnerable.

Ladd's death, she said, was just the last—and the worst—in a long line of unbearable tragedies that had befallen her. She told Tigart of the deaths of her father and mother. And she added that Ladd's father had also been killed in the war. She wasn't, she knew, the only one who had suffered, but she was so frightened and she couldn't bear the thought of life without Ladd. She didn't want to live. There was nothing to live for. No reason to go on.

Friends, family, finances, all were gone, sobbed a beaten Laurette, the damn bursting again and all her fears and heartaches pouring out. Jimmy, carefully hiding his relief that there was no one standing in his way, commiserated with the weeping woman.

"I'm so terribly sorry for your losses, Laurette," he said, in soft, calming tones. "Bless you dear heart, you've been through so much and you've had to face it all alone." He put an arm around her and drew her closer.

"I—I've been so—so—worried and lonely," she sobbed.

"I know, sweetheart, I know."

"I—I...kept thinking...believing...that Ladd would—would...Ladd...oh, dear God, my darling Ladd."

"Sweet little Laurette," Jimmy murmured, smoothing her golden hair, rubbing her shaking shoulders.

"I really can't live without Ladd," she choked, coughing, her face bloodred and feverish.

"I understand," he said, offering only comfort and friendship.

For now.

Major James Tigart had been sent by the Union Army to oversee reconstruction in the port city. He was to remain in the position for at least six months, possibly a year. Tigart planned to stay much longer.

He settled in into a suite in Mobile's finest downtown hotel, the Riverside. He spent his days helping solve the many problems of reconstruction. And every evening, without fail, he called on the lonely, susceptible Laurette Howard. He listened while she tearfully recalled the many happy times she'd had with Ladd. He heard her go on and on about Ladd until he thought he couldn't bear hearing Ladd's name one more time.

But he wisely concealed his feelings. And after only a month of patiently offering comfort, understanding and friendship, he managed to persuade the vulnerable, heartbroken Laurette to marry him so that he could take care of her, fight her battles, lift the burden off her slender shoulders.

"We're good friends," he reasoned, when he proposed, "good friends who both loved Ladd dearly." She nodded. He continued, "Successful marriages have been built on less, Laurette." He took her hand in his, gently squeezed it and said, "I'd never try to take Ladd's place, I know that would be impossible. But, if you'll let me, I'll honor and care for you for as long as I live."

Sixteen

On the warm, sultry evening of June 9, 1865, Jimmy and Laurette were married in the parlor of the Dauphin Street mansion. It was a private ceremony with no invited guests.

When the pastor had gone, Tigart turned to his new bride, smiled and said, "Laurette, dearest, why don't you go up first. I'll give you some time to...to..."

"Yes, all right," she said, nervously and tried to return his smile.

But as she climbed the stairs to the master suite, she was overcome with dread and apprehension. She had hoped, prayed, that Jimmy would give her a few weeks or at least a few days to get used to the idea of being his wife before they...before he...

And, perhaps, he would.

He had, since arriving in Mobile, been nothing but kind and considerate, anticipating her moods, going out of his way to be understanding.

If, when he came upstairs, she simply told him the truth, that she was anxious and not yet ready for intimacy, he would surely sympathize. He knew her true feelings. She thought of him as a good, kind friend, not as husband and lover.

There was, and always would be, only one love, only one lover for her.

A lone lamp burned in the master bedroom. The bed with the fresh sheets she had put on this afternoon was turned down. Her nightgown lay across the mattress. She bent, picked up the plain, long-sleeved, high-necked garment and thought, sadly, that this was not the kind of gown she had planned to wear on her wedding night.

For her long anticipated wedding night with Ladd she had intended to don a gossamer negligee that alluringly revealed her naked form beneath its diaphanous folds. Planning ahead, she had purchased the expensive, filmy negligee shortly after Ladd left for West Point. It was still in the box and the box rested on a high shelf in her dressing room.

It would never be worn.

Sighing, Laurette quickly undressed, slipped the modest white nightgown over her head and got into bed. She'd barely had time to fluff up the pillows at her back before Jimmy, minus his cane, limped into the room, a bottle of brandy in one hand and two crystal snifters in the other.

He smiled as he approached the bed. "Shall we drink to our marriage, Laurette?"

"By all means," she said, badly needing a stiff drink of liquor to face what might lie before her.

Jimmy poured generous portions of cognac into the snifters, handed her one, then sat down on the edge of the bed facing her.

"To us, darling girl," he said as he clinked his glass to hers, and they drank.

Laurette, as nervous as she'd ever been in her life, drank her brandy as if it were no stronger than lemonade. Jimmy immediately poured her another. By the time she finished the second, he had risen to his feet. He took her empty glass and set it on the night table. Then he bent and blew out the lamp.

In the moon's silvery light spilling through the tall open windows, Laurette tensely watched as he circled the bed, his limp more pronounced as he hurried to reach the other side. There he began to undress and Laurette quickly closed her eyes. Her heart racing, her stomach churning, she silently cursed herself for agreeing to this shameful sham of a marriage. She should have turned Jimmy down. She had been unfair to him and to herself by agreeing to be his wife. He didn't belong here in this bed with her. She didn't want him here.

Naked, Jimmy got into bed. Laurette tensed, felt as if she couldn't breathe. Jimmy slid across the mattress until he was right beside her. Supporting his weight on an elbow, he leaned down and whispered, "Can you believe we are man and wife and that I've never even kissed you?"

He gave her no time to reply. He kissed her and by the time his burning lips left hers, he had anxiously shoved the covering sheet down and had drawn her nightgown up around her waist. She was mortified and not at all aroused.

He was.

She could feel his hard flesh against her bare thigh and could hardly keep from breaking into tears and pushing him away. In seconds he was between her legs and, half apologizing for not taking more time and being more patient, he positioned himself inside her. Then she did cry, but her eyes remained dry.

The tears were in her heart.

She was clenched tight and bone dry and he was hurting her and she didn't want him and she wished it was over and she wished she was dead.

"Yes, oh yes," Jimmy was murmuring hoarsely as he pounded into her, "I've dreamed of this for years. Darling, you're so tight, so sweet. Laurette, my Laurette."

In pain, praying it wouldn't last long, Laurette disengaged her mind from her body. She was not here in bed with the naked Jimmy thrusting forcefully into her. This was not happening. She willed her mind to turn to thoughts of Ladd, to remember the sweetness of their eager, urgent lovemaking.

Silently she vowed to Ladd that in her heart she would never, ever be unfaithful to him.

Ladd lay on his thin, dirty mattress wondering what year it was. Wondering if the war was ever going to end. Wondering if he would ever see his golden-haired angel again. Wondering if she would wait for him no matter how long it took.

Laurette had solemnly promised that she would wait forever. He believed her. She would wait, he knew she would. One day this awful war would be over and he would be freed and he would go home to his beloved, faithful Laurette.

That firm belief sustained Ladd. He lay for hours and daydreamed of the happy time when he would arrive in Mobile and a laughing Laurette would run into his arms.

But in the depth of the darkest dungeon, Ladd's sustaining hope eventually faded. His faith grew dim, slipped away. He no longer bothered praying to an Almighty God who had, he firmly believed, forgotten him.

It seemed to him that he had been in this black, airless hole forever. He knew that if he didn't get out soon, he would go mad. Days and nights were all the same. Darkness. Hunger. Boredom. Loneliness.

Ladd's despair deepened with each passing minute, minutes that seemed like hours. He was tired of the struggle. He no longer wanted to live. He wanted the agony to end and he knew that could only be achieved with his death.

He thought it over as he lay in the darkness to which he had become accustomed. He was so used to the absence of light, he had become like an animal. His eyes gleamed and he could see in the blackness.

But there was nothing in the blackness to see.

Ladd quickly made up his mind. He would starve himself to death. It wouldn't take long. In his weakened condition he surely wouldn't last more than a week, if that. The prospect of deliverance from this unending horror made him feel light-headed, almost lighthearted.

He stopped eating that very night. When the unappetizing evening meal was served, he didn't touch it. He steadfastly refused the meager rations that were offered him. Soon—he didn't know how many days and nights—he would begin to feel very weak.

The end couldn't come soon enough to suit him.

The next day as the starving Ladd lay listless and despondent in his cell, the heavy iron door swung open and Gilbert LaKid announced, "Noontime, Dasheroon." He tossed a yellowed newspaper article on the cell's dirty floor directly beside Ladd.

"What is this?" Ladd asked, unmoving, blinking in the sudden brightness of the light streaming in from the hallway.

"Why it's your dinner plate," said LaKid grinning nastily, "we ran out of dishes."

As LaKid spoke, an accompanying guard forked a greasy piece of rancid meat from a platter, dropped it directly atop the newsprint. Stepping back out into the hallway, the two guards temporarily left Ladd's cell door ajar.

Staring down at the unappetizing meal, Ladd's attention was caught by the yellowed newspaper's banner. *The Mobile Press Register.* Ladd quickly rolled off his mattress, got down on his knees and anxiously read the date. June 10, 1865. Dizzy, spots dancing before his eyes, he swiped the meat aside and saw that the article was a marriage announcement.

Miss Laurette Howard became the bride of Major James Tigart on Saturday, the ninth of June, 1865, in…

Ladd finished reading the article just as the cell door was slammed shut, leaving him once again in darkness. For a long, silent time he stayed there on his knees, heartsick, his emaciated body trembling with rage and disbelief.

It all began to make sense. The terrible truth dawned and Ladd felt violently ill. Now he knew why Jimmy had ordered him thrown into the dungeon, had left him here to die. Jimmy had betrayed him in order to steal Laurette.

Laurette was as guilty as Jimmy! She had sworn that she belonged only to him, would always belong to him. Promised that she would wait forever. But it had been a lie. She hadn't waited, hadn't cared what happened to him. Hadn't bothered to find out if he was coming home. She had married Jimmy without knowing—or caring—if he was dead or alive.

Dear God in heaven! The two people he loved most had forsaken him.

Ladd, hugging his thin, trembling sides, began to rock back and forth in pain, moaning softly at first, then finally swearing at the top of his lungs. He railed and cursed those who had betrayed him until his throat was raw and his voice raspy. Burning tears stung his eyes and rolled down his sallow, sunken cheeks.

Finally, he tumbled over, laid his feverish face down on the cold stone floor and wept. He cried and cried until he was sick with despair and vomiting the bitter bile from his empty stomach.

He lay weeping like a lost child until there were no more tears left to shed. And when at last he was all cried out, he slowly lifted his aching head. Ladd looked up through the last of his tears and couldn't believe his eyes.

A beautiful butterfly—powdery purple wings banded in ebony—slowly floated down through the high, barred window. It landed in the palm of Ladd's hand. Gently he held the exquisite butterfly and stared at it, amazed that after all that had happened, there was still beauty in an ugly world. As the butterfly slowly fluttered its wings, Ladd's tearstained face hardened and he silently vowed that he would never cry again.

He vowed as well that those who had betrayed him would one day be brought to justice.

By him.

He had abided by the code of honor and had expected the same from others. That hadn't happened, so from now the rule would be *Lex Talionis*.

An eye for an eye.

He would not starve himself to death. He would start eating at once and he would survive this continuing atrocity for however long it took before he was released.

He would live!

He would live, and one day he would get out of this dark hellhole, and when he did…

Seventeen

One never-ending night as he lay sleepless, Ladd heard a noise. It seemed to be coming from the wall directly beside his bed. Turning his head to listen, Ladd detected a faint scratching sound from beyond his cell, within the earth of the prison's foundation.

He sat up abruptly. He heard it again, but decided it must be rats—the dungeon was full of rodents. He lay back down, but the tapping continued. Ladd got up, pulled his bed away from the wall and listened intently. There it was again. Excitedly, he tapped back.

Total silence.

No more tapping from the other side. Nothing. Ladd anxiously tapped again, hoping that it had been a prisoner. He was certain it had been a prisoner, because the minute he'd tapped back, the tapping from the other side had ceased. In all likelihood the prisoner had stopped, fearing a guard had heard. That's why the tapping had begun in the middle of the night. The prisoner didn't want to be heard, had waited until the only guard on duty was old Jim, the latchkey who, after a couple of snorts of liquor, seemed to fall asleep.

Ladd wished there was some way he could communicate, assure the other prisoner that he was not a spying guard. That he, too, was an inmate who was locked down here in the dungeon. Ladd frantically searched his cell, remembering the meat bone he'd cleaned and saved. Taking the bone in his hand he began to anxiously dig at the loose mortar around a heavy stone at the base of the wall. His heart hammering with exhilaration, he eagerly stabbed and scraped at the crumbling mortar. Perspiring and winded from exertion, Ladd continued to vigorously work until the first faint streaks of gray appeared in the tiny barred window high above.

Wishing he could continue his work, knowing it was too risky, he placed his bed back where it had been, covering the hole he was making in the wall. He'd hardly hidden his bone knife and stretched out on his cot before the cell door opened and the jailer brought in his breakfast.

Ladd ate the stale bread and cold meat with gusto. He was excited as he had not been in ages. He could hardly wait for night to come again so that he could move his bed and start digging.

It was the longest day of his life. The hours dragged by as he attempted to kill time. He paced the cell. He did bending and stretching exercises. He sang songs to himself. He recited poetry. He cracked his knuckles. He kept looking at the tiny barred window, for once welcoming the thick darkness that descended with the coming of night.

Ladd went to work the minute he felt it was safe.

He dug and scraped and sweated and grunted and drew the loosened stones away. And finally, his thrusting bone jabbed nothing but air. His heart thundered in his chest. He could hardly keep himself from shouting out his triumph. A narrow tunnel was now open between his and the adjoining cell.

Ladd wiped his sweat-streaked brow, laid his makeshift knife aside, sank back on his heels and took a deep breath. And jumped when from beyond the tunnel came a soft voice asking, "Who is there?"

"A lowly prisoner, like yourself," Ladd replied.

Then he laughed hysterically with joy when he saw a head with gray tufts of hair poke through the opening. The wild-eyed, emaciated little man shimmied through the opening, looked about, frowned and muttered, "Damnation, the map I so carefully drew in my mind must have been wrong! I mistook the wall of your cell for an outside wall." He stared glassy-eyed at Ladd.

Smiling, happy to see a friendly face, no matter how frightening that face was, Ladd said, "The north side of your cell is an outside wall. You tunneled south. This is just another dungeon cell."

Shaking his shaggy head in self-disgust, the little man said, "There was a time I wouldn't have made such an error." He grinned then and exclaimed, "But all is not lost. I have found a Confederate friend, have I not?"

"You have," Ladd assured him.

Then Ladd laughed with pleasure as the excited prisoner grabbed him and embraced him as though the younger man were his long-lost son. "What is your name?" he asked.

"Captain Ladd Dasheroon, and yours?"

"Major Finis Schafer, at your service, Laddie!" said the frail man dressed in tattered clothing.

"Finis Schafer," Ladd repeated the name. "You wouldn't be the same Finis Schafer who is something of a legend at West Point, now would you?"

Finis Schafer's pale eyes lighted. "You mean they still talk about me at the academy? You went to the Point?"

"I was there for a short time before the war started," said Ladd. "But I heard some fascinating tales about you."

"Ah, well, you shouldn't believe everything you hear," said Finis with a cheerful laugh.

Finis Schafer, who was as starved for company as Ladd, sat down on the stone floor and began to talk in hushed tones, to give a colorful biography of life, to reminisce about his escapades at the Point, embellishing the stories, enjoying himself for the first time in years. He talked a blue streak and Ladd learned that Finis—an orphan from Austin, Texas and a graduate of West Point some twenty years before Ladd's arrival at the academy—had been locked up in this prison dungeon for the past decade.

"You were imprisoned before the war began?" Ladd asked, baffled.

"No," said the shaggy-haired, unkempt little man, "I was captured in the summer of '63. The Yankees threw me in this pigsty and I've been here ever since.''

His eyes aglow, Ladd stared back at the man. ''But…you…you've been here for ten years?''

''That's a fact,'' replied Finis.

Frowning, confused, Ladd said, ''You're telling me it's…''

Finis nodded. ''Son, it's June, 1873.''

Shocked, disbelieving, Ladd swore, ''God in heaven! The war's still going on?''

''No, no, the war ended in the spring of 1865,'' Finis assured him. ''The Confederacy lost, sad to say.''

''If the war is over, then why am I still in prison?'' asked Ladd. ''Why are you?''

''We're political prisoners,'' Finis replied. ''I stole a shipment of Yankee gold headed for Washington.'' He shook his shaggy gray head and admitted, ''My boy, I'm afraid they've tarred you with the same brush. I heard the guards saying Secretary of War Stanton had charged both you and me with the gold theft.''

''They know better than that,'' Ladd replied. ''Besides, even if it was true, imprisoned forever? It was a war. And it was just a gold shipment.''

Finis looked sheepish as he confessed, ''The officer guarding the gold, a Major Timothy Todd, was killed during the holdup. Todd was a nephew of Mary Todd Lincoln, Abe Lincoln's wife.'' The old man ran a hand through his dirty gray hair. ''We are war criminals.''

"God almighty!" Ladd swore and, thinking back, vaguely recalled overhearing LaKid once say to one of the guards, "If Stanton has his way, Dasheroon and Schafer will never be freed."

Laurette tried to be a good wife to Jimmy. She kept the mansion clean, learned to cook and washed his clothes—tasks she had never been taught how to do. And she allowed him to make love to her when he wished. Which was far too often to suit her.

She felt that she had no grounds for refusal or complaint. She had unwisely agreed to the marriage. She would, therefore, do her best to uphold her side of the bargain. And, she had to admit that Jimmy went out of his way to try to make her happy. He loved her and he showed it in every way possible.

He had, through a stroke of good fortune, secured a well-paying position at the Planters State Bank six months after they had wed. The bank, it was rumored, had been purchased by a group of Northern investors and Laurette supposed that was the reason Jimmy had been offered employment.

He was unfailingly generous with the money he earned. He had begun the slow process of restoring the mansion, although there was still much to do. And, hardly a week went by that he didn't bring her a sentimental or personal gift: a porcelain figurine of a ballerina; a pair of delicate white kid gloves; a soft fringed shawl of white merino wool; a bejeweled comb for her hair; and, finally, a wispy black nightgown that left nothing to the imagination.

She had blushed when she opened the box. But Jimmy seemed not to notice and he had said, "We'll wait until some special occasion. I'll let you know when to wear the gown."

She had nodded, stiffly, and hoped it would be a long time before he requested that she wear it. To her genuine relief, several weeks had passed since he had given her the black nightgown and he hadn't mentioned it. Perhaps he had forgotten about the nightgown. She hoped so.

But then one unseasonably warm, sunny February noontime, Jimmy, who never came home for the midday meal, showed up unexpectedly as the chimes in the cathedral struck the hour of twelve.

"Jimmy?" Laurette looked up in surprise, her hair tied up in a snood, the hem of her faded cotton work dress wet from washing the kitchen floor. "I—I wasn't expecting you. I'm sorry I'm not more presentable."

Jimmy limped into the foyer, placed his malacca cane in the umbrella holder and said, "That's okay, Laurette." He grinned then and the light gleaming in his hazel eyes made her nervous as he added, "In minutes you are going to be more than presentable. You'll be downright desirable."

Reaching up to the take the snood from her blond hair, Laurette looked anxiously at her smiling husband and said, "I'm afraid I don't understand, Jimmy."

"You soon will," he replied, took her arm and ushered her up the stairs and into the master suite.

Anticipating his intention, Laurette protested, ''Why, James Tigart, it is the middle of the day. Decent people don't...we can't...'' Her words trailed away as he turned and went to the mirror-doored armoire, threw it open and began pulling out drawers.

''Where is it, Laurette?'' he asked impatiently. ''The black nightgown I gave you?'' He turned to face her.

She swallowed hard. ''Jimmy, surely you don't expect me to—''

''Yes, I do,'' he interrupted. ''Get the nightgown and put in on.'' He took off his frock coat, tossed it over a chair back and began unbuttoning his shirt. When she didn't move immediately, he said, his tone commanding, ''What are you waiting for?''

Laurette went to the armoire, took the revealing back gown from the lower drawer.

''Good, you found it,'' he said. ''Now go in the dressing room, put it on and come to me.''

Laurette, dismayed by the prospect of making love with him in the middle of day, tried one last time. ''Please, Jimmy, can't we wait until tonight? The sun is shining brightly and—''

''I know it is and that is exactly the way I want it,'' he said, whipping his arms out of his shirt and tossing the shirt aside. ''I've humored you long enough, Laurette. You will only agree to make love in the dark of the night so that neither of us can see the other. Well, no more foolish modesty. You're my wife and I want you to start behaving like it.'' She stood stock-still, staring at him, her heart hammering.

"Go!" he said, pointing, "and when you come back, you will allow me look at you for as long as I please."

Laurette turned and walked into the dressing room with its free-standing mirror. She placed the wispy black garment on a velvet stool and began undressing. When she was totally naked, she picked up the lace-trimmed gown and drew it down over her head. It fell over her breasts, eased down her hips and came to rest around her slender ankles.

She looked at herself in the mirror and her face turned fiery red. She may as well have been naked for all the gown concealed. The nipples of her full breasts jutted against the gossamer fabric, their size and pale wine hue perfectly clear through the black gauzy bodice. Worse, the thick blond curls of her groin were fully visible. She was totally exposed, barer than bare.

And she hated it.

"Darling, what's keeping you?" she heard the impatient Jimmy call out to her.

"Almost ready," she said, gritting her teeth, dreading what she knew was going to happen.

She always dreaded Jimmy's lovemaking. Never once had she enjoyed it. She blamed herself, not him. He had tried patiently to please her, to arouse her, but it hadn't worked. She didn't love him, didn't want him, disliked going to bed with him each night. And now she was expected to make love with him in the middle of the day!

Laurette sighed wearily, took a slow, deep breath, turned and left the dressing room.

When she stepped into the sun-filled bedroom where the tall windows were thrown open to the warmth of the February day, Jimmy was lying naked atop the sheets. Laurette quickly averted her eyes, but dutifully started toward him.

"No, Laurette," he stopped her. "Stay right where you are and let me admire you."

Laurette paused as requested and then grudgingly complied when he asked that she raise her arms and lift her long blond hair atop her head. She stood poised in that position for what seemed an eternity before Jimmy suggested she release her hair and slowly turn so that her back was to him.

She did as he asked.

He gazed at her for several long minutes before saying, "Now turn back to face me, Laurette."

Clenching her teeth so tightly her jaws ached, Laurette turned around and saw that he was now sitting on the edge of the mattress, his bare feet on the floor, his erection thrusting up between his spread legs.

"Come here, darling," he said in a husky voice.

Laurette walked to the bed. When she was a few feet away, he grabbed her, drew her between his spread knees.

"God, you are so beautiful. Every time I look at you I want to be inside you," he murmured and pressed his hot face between her soft breasts. "When I saw this gown, I envisioned you in it, knew exactly how you would look, how hot it would make me."

"Yes," was all she could manage and closed her eyes in distaste and forced herself not to flinch when he began to suckle a soft nipple through the gown's transparent black fabric, wetting it.

For the next trying hour, Laurette endured his probing kisses, his intimate touches, his eager invasion of her body while he murmured words of passion. When his sexual hunger was finally sated, he rolled, spent, over onto his back, sighed contentedly and said, "I have to get back to the bank."

"I know," Laurette agreed, experiencing a great degree of relief. Anxiously she reached down and pulled the covering sheet up over her bare body where red marks, left by Jimmy's passion, decorated her breasts and inner thighs.

She stiffened when, dressed and ready to leave, Jimmy came to the bed, picked up the discarded black nightgown, lifted it to his face, inhaled of her scent and made an animallike sound of pleasure.

Then he leaned down, brushed a kiss to her lips and said, "Darling, I can't wait to get back home to you. Promise you'll wear the gown for me again tonight."

Eighteen

Down in the dark, drafty dungeon at Devil's Castle, the two prisoners were quickly becoming friends. The long, lonely confinement and deprivation had affected them differently. Finis hadn't lost track of time. He knew what year it was, what month, what day. Even what hour. Ladd was impressed. But Finis was mortified that he had lost his sense of direction, had made such a costly miscalculation by tunneling into Ladd's cell. How could he have gotten so disoriented?

When finally Finis grew weary and said it was time he return to his own cell and get some sleep, Ladd said, "Wait, Finis. You did manage to dig a tunnel of sorts. You have tools?"

Finis nodded. "I made some for myself. I have a crowbar and a knife I fashioned from my bed rail. I dug the tunnel between us with those two tools. Twenty feet."

"My God, twenty feet?"

"Yes. It took me a long time to…" Finis hung his shaggy gray head in defeat and stated, "I realize now that escape is impossible. It is my fate to die here in this dark hell."

"No!" Ladd quickly reprimanded the older man.

"Don't give up hope. You dug one passage, why not dig another in the opposite direction? Try again?"

"Try again?" Finis looked up, frowned at Ladd as if Ladd had lost his mind. "You are insane! You don't understand, it took three years just to make the tools. Have you any idea how hard I worked, how long it took to tunnel into your cell?" Ladd shook his head. Finis continued, "Two years! For two long years I worked steadily, every night, scraping and digging at earth as solid as stone."

His wild eyes wilder than ever, Finis began to rave, waving his bony hands about, telling of how he had labored until his arms were too weak to lift and of how it had been next to impossible to dispose of the loosened rock and dirt. He had, he explained, managed to locate an abandoned drain pipe that had been barred to prevent escape, but it had afforded him a place to hide the mined earth.

Ladd listened patiently, nodding, sympathizing. And when Finis finally stopped talking, Ladd said, "But it wasn't for naught, Finis. You found me, and even if you hadn't, the project, the work itself, kept you going all those months. You had a hope of freedom, a reason to go on." Finis shrugged thin shoulders. Ladd continued, warming to his subject, "Let's dig another tunnel together. A tunnel out the north wall of your cell to freedom."

A long pause, then Finis, thoughtfully, softly, said, "It would take too long. I haven't the energy."

"I'll do the work. I have enough energy for us both."

"I don't know." Finis heaved a deep sigh and added, "You realize, it could take two, three years, perhaps longer, to complete a tunnel into the prison yard and beyond the 'deadline.'"

Smiling, Ladd quickly replied, "Is that all? With freedom possible, I could make it sitting on a straight-edged razor for a couple of years. When do we start?"

Ladd's enthusiasm rubbed off on his new companion. Finis began to smile. He said, "I'm too tired now, but if you'll come to my cell tomorrow night, we'll begin work."

That very next night the two began their tedious labor, carefully and silently. Ladd deferred to Finis, since it was his project. Finis had, in the years he had been locked up, done intensive planning, knew exactly how far to dig to get them out of the dungeon and into the prison yard.

Ladd was filled with a new sense of hope as they worked tirelessly together, night after night. They didn't work days. It was too dangerous. An alert guard might hear and expose them. But the days were not a waste of time.

Ladd was delighted to be in the company of the educated, highly intelligent Finis who dearly loved to talk and inform and was more than happy to play learned professor to Ladd's eager student. From Finis, Ladd learned more than he ever had in school or at the military academy. Finis was a fount of knowledge on a myriad of subjects: history, philosophy, art, music, the theater. Finis looked on Ladd as the son he'd never had. He spent his days cheerfully educating his young friend who was more than eager to learn. And at night, the two of them worked long and hard toward a common goal.

Freedom.

The months went by and Finis was pleasantly surprised with the progress they were making. He found that Ladd, much younger and stronger than he, could get done in one night what it would have taken Finis a week to accomplish. The tunnel moved farther and farther toward the precious liberty for which both yearned. But with the passing of time, the talkative, bright-eyed Finis began to grow weaker, thinner, more listless.

Ladd was worried about his friend. He encouraged Finis to eat even if he wasn't hungry, to get plenty of rest, to look forward to the hour when they were free. But the little man's failing health continued to worsen.

When more than a full year had passed, the tunnel was nearing completion. But Finis was seriously ill.

Both men knew that he would never leave the prison.

"You must go on alone," Finis told Ladd. "I'm not going to make it, Laddie."

"Sure you are," said Ladd, refusing to leave his friend. Instead, for the next several months, he stayed at Finis's bedside and patiently, hopefully nursed the dying man. He shared his ration of food and water with Finis. He massaged the older man's thin, aching limbs. He talked to him softly, soothingly in the long silent hours.

Finis, having no family, was grateful and impressed by Ladd's loyalty and kindness. And when he recovered enough to speak, he told Ladd he had something important to share.

"Ladd, when you get out of here, I want you to go and claim the gold," rasped Finis, his eyes rheumy, his chest rattling. "The rest of your days will be spent in splendid ease, because you will be a very, very rich man."

The next evening, a bitter cold February night in 1875, Finis Schafer died in Devil's Castle prison with Ladd at his side. When Finis took his last, shallow breath, Ladd closed the dead man's eyes, then returned to his own cell through the secret passage.

At bedtime the guards came to Finis's cell and Ladd heard one saying, "Well, I'll be damned, you win the bet. The crazy old bastard is dead."

"So he is," said the other. "Go get a shroud. We'll bury him tomorrow."

Ladd waited until the guards had put Finis in a canvas shroud. When he was sure they were gone, he returned to Finis's cell. He opened the shroud, carefully, gently took out the cold, stiff body of his dear friend and moved it into his own cell. He placed the body on his bed and positioned Finis so that he was facing the wall. Ladd covered the corpse with his thin blanket, pulling it up halfway around Finis's head and ears.

"Goodbye, my friend," he said before returning to

Finis's cell with a crude bone needle and twine. He crawled into the canvas shroud, pulled it up over his head and sewed it shut.

Then he waited.

All through the long, dark, lonely night he waited. At last the cell door opened and the burial detail came for the corpse. Ladd made his body as stiff as he possibly could. He was carried out of the prison and carted to the graveyard that was outside the deadline, the line where a prisoner would be shot if he crossed it.

There he was carelessly tossed into a shallow grave and he inwardly winced as dirt was shoveled over him. Feeling panicky and certain that he would surely suffocate, Ladd forced himself to wait until he was absolutely certain all was clear. That the guards and their snarling dogs were gone.

Only then did he cut open the shroud and struggle up out of the newly thrown sod before he made a mad dash for the nearby coastline. He leaped into the cold waters of Chesapeake Bay to avoid the prison dogs picking up his scent. He began to swim as fast as he could. But the water was frigid and he was weak and his thin arms were tired. He soon realized that he would die if he stayed in the bay.

Exhausted, Ladd paddled back toward shore, looking about to see how far he was from the prison.

Not far enough.

Beaten, he reached the slick, muddy banks, but found to his despair that he was too weak to pull himself up. He tried again and again, but he couldn't make it. The mud was too slick. He could not get purchase. He felt himself sliding back down into the icy waters. He knew he was going to die.

But he was too cold and too tired to care.

Just then a strong hand reached down, gripped his shirt collar and hauled him up onto the banks. Ladd furiously blinked away the water. The only thing he could see was a set of white crossbones.

And then he passed out.

Seconds later, Ladd came to. He looked up. Someone was crouching beside him, staring down at him. It was man, a man who looked to be of medium height, but who surely weighed a good three hundred pounds without one ounce of fat. All steely muscle.

The burly, unsmiling man was wearing black trousers, a black watch cap and a long-sleeved black-knit shirt upon which a pair of woven white crossbones stretched snugly across his gargantuan chest.

The husky man grinned down at Ladd and said, "You should save your swimming outings for summer."

"I think I will from now on," Ladd replied as he sat up and introduced himself. "Ladd Dasheroon, late of Devil's Castle prison. If you are going to take me back, do it now."

The muscular man gripped Ladd's hand firmly and said, "On the contrary, my friend, I am going to help you get away."

Relieved, surprised, Ladd said, "Then, thank you...?"

"Bones," replied his savior with a self-deprecating smile and shrug of his massive shoulders. "I'm called Bones."

He laughed then and so did Ladd.

PART TWO

Nineteen

Mobile, Alabama
Winter, 1880

"Made his fortune in rails," said one of the men.

"I heard it was gold," said another.

"Telegraph," offered someone else.

"No, no, I'm told it was running the blockade back during the war," exclaimed yet another, "he most surely made the bulk of his fortune—"

"Well, no matter," the first speaker interrupted. "I am told that he is a very wealthy man. Has tons of money."

The topic of the gentlemen's conversation was the well-heeled guest of honor who had not yet arrived at the evening's gathering. The man was an enigma to them all. Sutton Vane had recently arrived in Mobile, expressing his intention to make the port city his home.

It was rumored that the newcomer had purchased a private island off the coast near Ono where he intended to build a summer home. They knew for a fact that he had bought a magnificent mansion on Government Street in the heart of the city.

Other than that, little was known of the mysterious man who had been invited to tonight's gala by the host, Colonel George P. Ivy. The aging, silver-haired colonel had, only yesterday afternoon, played cards with Sutton Vane at the Magnolia Club. The colonel had found the much younger man to be pleasant company, if somewhat reserved, and had promptly exercised his brand of true Southern hospitality by insisting that Mr. Vane come to tonight's gathering at the Colonel's Oakleigh Garden district home.

In the Dauphin Street mansion Laurette Howard Tigart prepared to make a rare appearance at a social gathering. Laurette chose to lead a quiet, sedate life. Stung by the scandal surrounding the breakup of her marriage and the nagging rumors that her husband had been forced out of the Planters Bank amidst accusations of embezzlement, Laurette preferred the solitude and privacy of her home.

Or, of the home that had once been hers.

The title to the Dauphin Street mansion, like everything else, had been lost when her husband had defaulted on his many debts. Her beloved home was now owned by the Bay Minette Corporation. She had no idea who the owners of Bay Minette were—probably wealthy Yankees—but she was grateful that the company had graciously allowed her to remain in the house for a mere pittance a month.

Laurette had felt obligated to attend this evening's

party, since the Colonel, an old and dear family friend, had insisted that she be there. The Colonel had dropped by the Confederate Veteran's Convalescent Hospital where Laurette worked to issue his invitation.

She had started to make an excuse, but quickly changed her mind. The silver-haired Colonel's cherubic face had worn a big grin, his blue eyes had sparkled and he had acted as if he were harboring a delicious secret.

Genuinely fond of him, she had said, ''I'll be there, Colonel.''

Laurette had purposely, all during her long, unhappy marriage to Jimmy, kept her misery hidden, sharing her despair with no one, not even her best friends, Johanna and Juliette. Even when Jimmy, in the last eighteen months before he left, had openly begun seeking the company of other women, she had kept silent.

In some regards, Mobile was really a small country town and there was little doubt that the gentry had known of Jimmy's indiscretions. But Laurette had never said a word about them, either to Jimmy or to anyone else. When he came home late night after night, half-drunk and with the scent of cheap perfume clinging to his clothes, she had never once reprimanded him. She felt that she was responsible. She had never loved him and he knew it. The failure of their marriage was as much her fault as his.

Then, a year ago, when the banking scandal broke and Jimmy requested a quick divorce and promptly disappeared from Mobile, she had taken it on the chin, suffered in silence, unwilling for others to be witness to her humiliation.

And, she would never, ever have admitted to another living soul that she was glad that Jimmy was gone, was out of her life forever. She was not nearly as unhappy living alone as she had been living with him. Loneliness and boredom were, she had learned, far preferable to living a life of deceit.

And, guiltily, she admitted to herself, that not a single night had gone by since Jimmy's departure that she hadn't climbed into her big, comfortable bed and offered silent thanks that she was in it alone.

Laurette Howard Tigart, the once carefree, spoiled young belle had long ago become a sedate, responsible woman. She bore her griefs quietly and kept her own counsel. She never complained about her lot in life, but had displayed a calm acceptance of life's ups and downs.

Tired now, her back aching from lifting and bathing sick patients, Laurette nonetheless began preparing to attend the Ivys' party. The Colonel had promised to send a carriage to collect her at seven sharp.

Laurette looked through her clothes with little interest or concern. She quickly chose a plain, but well-cut ball gown of sky-blue velvet. The gown was old, but she hadn't worn it in ages. And, its matching cape would keep her warm on this chilly December evening.

Promising herself she would stay at the Colonel's only long enough to make an appearance, Laurette was already looking forward to getting back to the welcome isolation of her home.

As full darkness descended on the city of Mobile and the nightly mist rolled in off the river, Laurette stood in the spacious drawing room of the Ivys' home, talking with Melba Adair and her forty-eight-year-old daughter, Lydia.

It was common knowledge that the unfortunate Adair ladies, left poor by the war, now struggled to get by after the bulk of the money they had made from the sale of their estate had been lost when the trusting pair were persuaded to invest in bogus cotton futures by a sharpie named Jackson Tate.

A cup of mulled rum in her hand, Laurette was inquiring as to Melba's health when an abrupt stir caused her to stop speaking. Slowly, she turned. In time to see a tall, dark man, whose raven hair was liberally streaked with silver at the temples, step into the arched doorway of the drawing room. At his side was Colonel Ivy.

The stranger was impeccably dressed and strikingly handsome. The lower part of his face was covered by a neatly trimmed beard which, on him, was very appealing.

Laurette lost her train of thought. She helplessly stared at the compelling, well-groomed gentleman and an unsettling sensation washed over her. In a moment of mild distress, she put her wrist to her forehead. She suddenly felt faint. Her breath caught in her throat when she realized that the Colonel was leading the stranger directly toward her.

Colonel Ivy made the introductions, first presenting the Adairs, then turning to Laurette.

"This lovely young lady is Mrs. Laurette Howard Tigart."

Sutton Vane turned his full attention on her. She was pale, but beautiful. That flawless skin, the impressive bone structure, those dark, luminous eyes. The bodice of her light-blue velvet gown dipped just low enough to give a glimpse of her soft bosom which was, he noted, rising and falling rapidly with her anxious breaths.

He felt his heart skip a beat.

The beaming Colonel, addressing Laurette, said, "Child, may I present Mr. Sutton Vane."

"Delighted to make your acquaintance, Mrs. Tigart," said Sutton Vane in a soft, rich baritone as he reached for her hand. "I've not yet met your husband. Is he here this evening?"

Through her kid gloves, Laurette felt the heat and power of his touch. The fine hair on the nape of her neck rose, and she found herself speechless.

"Mrs. Tigart is divorced," the Colonel answered for her.

"Mr. Vane," she politely acknowledged, "welcome to Mobile."

"Thank you. I hope we'll become friends."

After a small exchange of pleasantries, Sutton Vane moved on and had no more to do with Laurette. But Laurette found that she couldn't keep her eyes off him. The mere presence of this handsome stranger had had a supremely disturbing effect on her and she found it most puzzling.

It was more than just his dark good looks, although there was no denying that he was incredibly arresting with his deep-set blue eyes, arrogant nose and full lips about which there seemed to be a permanent hardness. Sutton Vane was…different.

Gazing covertly at him, Laurette felt a shiver skip up her spine. In all his beauty and charm, there was something slightly disconcerting. A fascinating combination of grace and danger. A hint of cruelty that, paradoxically, made him all the more attractive.

Laurette was intrigued.

Sutton Vane, moving about the room, making conversation, getting acquainted, was aware of Laurette Tigart's curiosity and interest. He knew that she was—against her will—drawn to him. Knew she found him fascinating and was frightened by that strong attraction. Knew—even if she did not—that she was hoping he'd soon make his way back in her direction.

Therefore, he pointedly ignored her.

When the dancing began at shortly after nine, he spun several ladies, including a clearly pleased Johanna Parlagne Ford, around the floor.

But never Laurette.

She was secretly disappointed. And surprised at herself for being disappointed. She grew increasingly uncomfortable because the strong lure of this mysterious stranger made her feel extremely ill at ease, not herself. As soon as possible, Laurette said her good-nights and left.

She released a great sigh of relief when she reached the blessed haven of home. Shivering from the cold, she hurried to get undressed and into her bed.

Fluffing the pillows and arranging the covers, she took a book from the nightstand and began to read. Or, at least, she tried to read. She soon gave up. Her mind was not on the text. She leaned her head back, closed her eyes and saw Sutton Vane framed in the arched doorway of the Ivys' Oakleigh home.

She shuddered at the vivid recollection. The enigmatic, darkly handsome Sutton Vane was the first man to make her pulse quicken since…since…Ladd.

Twenty long years ago.

Shortly after Laurette had gone, Sutton Vane also departed. He had, all evening long, been warm and charming and outgoing, talking with everyone, dancing with the ladies, acting as if he were having a wonderful time.

But beneath that public posture roiled other, less admirable qualities: anger and distrust; idiosyncratic behavior; and dark moods. Hatreds that were more defined than likes. There was, and had been for years, a core of hollowness to his life, a self-imposed emptiness that would never go away.

The brooding Sutton was driven directly to his imposing Government Street mansion. He let himself in, walked the length of the long, wide foyer, stepped into the paneled study to find his trusted friend and lieutenant, the muscular Bones, dozing in a leather chair before the blazing fireplace.

Bones awakened, rose and immediately asked, "How did it go?"

"Exactly as planned," Sutton replied, with a cold smile of satisfaction as he dropped down into the chair just vacated by Bones.

Bones, standing just above, shook his big head and said, "Boss, where she is concerned, I wish you would give up on this quest for revenge."

Sutton Vane slowly turned his dark head, looked harshly at Bones.

"It is not revenge I seek, it is justice. *Lex Talionis.*"

Bones said no more. He nodded, left the room, locked up the big house and retired to his private quarters.

Twenty

Alone, Sutton Vane poured himself a shot glass of fine Kentucky bourbon, blew out the last lamp and sat in the shadowy darkness before the slowly dying fire.

He exhaled heavily.

Finally, it had happened.

He had seen her, been introduced to her, touched her hand, spoken with her. The beautiful, strong-willed, independent and rebellious girl whose image had tormented him for years as he lay alone in the darkness of the dungeon.

But she was no longer a girl. She was a woman. And more beautiful than ever. The golden-blond hair. The large, dark eyes. The pale, flawless skin. The slender, curvaceous body.

Sutton Vane's eyes closed and his jaw hardened until ridges stood out along the sculptured bone. But he quickly collected himself. He opened his eyes, took a generous drink of whiskey and made a face.

Tonight's brief meeting was what he'd been waiting for since the slow-moving steamer had passed Fort Morgan and plowed into the calm waters of the bay. Standing at the railing on that sunny September morning some three months ago, he had felt a heavy shadow fall across his heart.

He was, at long last, returning to Mobile. He had gazed across the mists of two decades and felt the muscles in his throat contract. And he had wondered just how he would feel when he saw her again.

Then tonight…there she was.

She didn't know him.

No one did. He was not surprised. He had changed so much during those years in prison that he hardly recognized himself. The young boy who had gone away to West Point twenty years ago had been a trusting fool who had gotten exactly what he deserved.

A sad smile touched his lips and he shook his dark head wearily. There was nothing left of that happy boy; he was gone forever.

Sutton's smile faded slightly and hatred flashed in the depths of his blue eyes as he thought of the man responsible for his long and brutal captivity.

And, of the woman who had promised to wait forever.

He downed the last of his whiskey and his sad smile was replaced with an evil one. He had vowed to himself, all those long days and nights in the dungeon, that if he ever got out, he would seek justice.

And so he had.

And would.

After he had escaped from prison and the dependable Bones had patiently nursed him back to health, they had gone in search of Finis Schafer's stolen Union gold. He'd had nothing more to go on than a very crude cloth map Finis had given him shortly before he died. The old man had claimed that he'd hidden the gold in a cave in the eastern foothills of the Appalachian mountains of Virginia.

The search had taken a full, frustrating year.

There were many small caves in the Appalachian foothills and the two men had begun to despair of ever locating the cave containing the gold. And, both had begun to wonder if there was actually any gold to be found.

Ready to give up, they had sat down to rest and drink from their canteens one chilly March morning in 1877 when Bones felt the large flat rock beneath him begin to give. Eyes wide with surprise, he shouted curse words as he and the rock crashed ten feet down into a dark hole.

"Jesus, are you hurt?" Ladd anxiously stuck his head through the hole.

"No," Bones said with a wide grin, "but I think we have found your gold."

Ladd eagerly scrambled down into the opening through which Bones had fallen. Bones was already up, dusting himself off and pointing. For several long seconds both men stood in the shadowy cave and stared in awe. Stacked neatly along the west wall of the cavern were hundreds of shiny gold bars.

He was at once a very wealthy man.

And, as only the wealthy can manage, he promptly began putting his plans in motion. Quietly, without drawing attention to himself, he had gravitated southward and had gathered several loyal men to work behind the scenes to carry out his scheme.

He, and they, had proved themselves to be masters of "the Southern way," a system of middlemen promising favors and intimidating businessmen so that they would bend to the will of the one powerful figure who carefully distanced himself from the gritty negotiations.

Through the years he had made great progress. It was he who owned the bank from which Tigart had stolen fortunes. When he'd purchased the bank he had seen to it that Jimmy was promptly promoted to president. He knew that he need only put temptation before Jimmy—he could rely on his character to do the rest.

Jimmy, proud of his position, had managed to maintain an impeccable reputation until disquieting whispers about his business practices surfaced a year into his presidency. It had been one of Vane's hand-picked foot soldiers who had started the rumors that had led to the exposure of Tigart's embezzling scheme.

Once the crime was out in the open, the disgraced bank president had been given a choice. He could go to prison for several long years or he could, after quickly divorcing his wife, flee to Europe—a one-way ticket on an ocean liner would be provided—with the understanding that he would never again set foot on American soil if he wanted to stay alive. Tigart was quietly told who had set forth the terms.

Sutton's lips twisted into a pleased smile at the recollection of just how quickly the cowardly, unprincipled Tigart had agreed to divorce Laurette. His own worthless hide was all he really cared about.

Tigart, Sutton mused, was not the only one due his special brand of justice. There was the sadistic Gilbert LaKid still to be dealt with. So far, his men had been unable to locate LaKid, but they would continue to hunt him down until they found him. And when they did, he would personally see to it that his cruel captor was properly dealt with, as befitted his sins.

But, the most significant of those yet to pay was Laurette Howard Tigart.

Sutton's blue eyes narrowed as he considered his callous, clever plan for her. He had spent many long hours considering how she was to compensate for breaking his innocent heart. What could he possibly do that would hurt her half as much as she had hurt him?

Finally he had decided.

He would—a few short weeks from now—begin courting the beautiful blond divorcée. He would purposely wait until she had almost forgotten their brief encounter at Colonel Ivy's party. He had made an impression, he knew. She had involuntarily responded to him, had become overly nervous. She would think about him for several days, wonder about him, wish they would meet once more as they had at the party.

When she finally assumed that she would not likely see him again, when she had almost forgotten about him, he would seek her out. When she was least expecting it, he would appear. He would behave the consummate gentlemen. He would ask for permission to call on her.

Permission would, he felt confident, be granted.

He would begin regularly escorting her to social

functions. He would show her great respect, he would charm her, disarm her, shower her with expensive gifts and attention.

Then he would seduce her.

He would make passionate love to the lonely destitute divorcée until her head was spinning and her body was pliant and her deceitful heart belonged to him. And, he knew that, just as she hadn't recognized him when they met, she wouldn't recognize him in bed. He was no longer the awkward, unskilled boy she remembered from the urgent, hurried lovemaking of their youth.

In the five years since his escape from prison, he had had many women: beautiful women; wealthy women; experienced women. Women eager to teach him about their bodies and his own. He had learned quickly. He knew quite well how to please and dazzle a woman.

Any woman.

He would, when the moment was right, take Laurette to bed and keep her there until she had fallen deeply in love with him. Even if it took some time, which it might. Weeks. Months. Years. No matter. He had the time.

He had nothing but time.

When she was finally his, heart and soul, then and only then would he disclose his true identity, after which, he would leave her to suffer as he had suffered while he casually took another as his blushing bride.

Christmas came to Mobile.

Holly and cedar decorated the lampposts and apple-

cheeked children in warm wraps and mufflers sang
carols in Bienville Square.

Laurette volunteered to work at the Confederate
Veteran's Convalescent Hospital on Christmas day so
that a couple of other employees could celebrate the
holiday with their families. She liked working at the
hospital. She had done some volunteer work when she
was married and Jimmy was supporting her. Now, she
was paid for her labor, thanks to the kind hospital
administrator, Gordon Hill, who was aware of her fi-
nancial situation.

She was particularly glad to be working today, both
for the money and because her best friends, the Parlange twins, were spending the holidays with distant
relatives in New Orleans. She much preferred being
here at the hospital than alone in the big, empty
house.

The weak winter sun that had appeared briefly with
the dawn had disappeared by midmorning. The skies
were now gray and bleak. Shortly after noon a cold
drizzly rain began. Walking down the hospital's
drafty hallway, Laurette looked out at the falling rain,
shook her head, shivered and drew her shawl tighter
around her slender shoulders.

When she reached the room to which she was heading, she paused, straightened her back and put a pleasant smile on her face.

"Merry Christmas to you, Mr. Cooper," she said
cheerily as she greeted the sickly Confederate veteran
who lay ashen and weak in the white bed.

Her smile became genuine when his pale eyes grew

brighter upon seeing her and he lifted a weak, gnarled hand.

Laurette went to him, took his bony hand in hers and asked, "Is there anything I can get you, Mr. Cooper? Anything at all?"

"There is," he said, and attempted to squeeze her hand. "Stay here with me for a little while."

"Why, I can do that," she said, placing his hand back on the bed.

Mr. Cooper was one of the few patients in the hospital who had no living relatives to come and visit. She imagined that he felt much like she felt on this rainy Christmas day. Lonely and yearning for those happy Christmases of his youth.

"Shall I read to you?" she asked, straightening his covers.

"I would like that," he said, "you have such a sweet, clear voice."

Laurette took a half-finished book from the bedside table, drew up a straight-backed chair, sat down and began to read.

Mr. Cooper closed his eyes to listen. She had read for only a few minutes when the frail man began to softly snore. She lowered the book and sighed. She started to rise when she heard voices in the hallway so she stayed seated.

A couple of nurses were speaking in whispers and Laurette heard one of them breathlessly say his name.

Sutton Vane.

They were talking about the man she had met at Colonel Ivy's party a couple of weeks ago. No one seemed to know why he had suddenly appeared in

Mobile. But since arriving, the handsome and wealthy Sutton Vane had been the talk of the town. Tales about him were rampant.

He had bought the city's oldest hotel, the Riverside, and planned a major refurbishing. He owned a luxury yacht. Workman had started construction on his island getaway house. Beautiful young women had been seen going in and out of his Government Street mansion as if the heavy door were a turnstile.

Laurette couldn't help herself. She was as fascinated by all the hearsay surrounding Sutton Vane as everyone else. He was, everyone agreed, like royalty in almost every sense of the word. He was treated like royalty, he lived like royalty and he had the dignified mein of royalty.

Laurette, like many others who led a quiet, rather mundane existence, lived vicariously for a moment as she listened to the nurses discuss the mysterious man's most recent exploits.

There were times when, guiltily, secretly, she found herself foolishly wishing that she were younger and prettier like the belles who found favor with Sutton Vane.

It would be exciting to share the kind of life he lived, if only for a brief, memorable time.

Twenty-One

It was a Saturday morning. The first full week of
January had passed. Laurette was on duty at the hospital when the charge nurse ask if she'd mind walking
the few blocks to the Conti Street apothecary shop.

"I wouldn't ask, Laurette," said the stout, white-
uniformed nurse, "but we're running so low on some
of the supplies that we can't possibly wait until our
next shipment arrives from Montgomery."

"Be glad to do it," said Laurette, untying the white
bibbed apron she wore over her plain, gray wool
dress. "Give me a list and I'll go right now."

Minutes later she was strolling down Old Shell
Road toward Conti. She hadn't bothered with a wrap.
It was one of those unusually warm days for midwin-
ter and Laurette noticed, with pleasure, a few scattered boughs of pale lavender azaleas, the first flower
to bloom each year in early January.

Laurette stepped into the apothecary shop and the
proprietor looked up, smiled and greeted her.

"Lovely day today, Mrs. Tigart," he said.

"Perfect," she agreed and handed him the list.

Reading the list, he said, "It'll take me a few
minutes."

"That's fine," she replied. "I can wait."

He nodded and went into the back room, leaving her alone. Laurette crossed her arms and stood idly studying the neat shelves of bandages, potions and pills.

"Excuse me, Mrs. Tigart," came a low, drawling voice.

Laurette turned quickly and looked up. Sutton Vane was standing close and smiling down at her.

"I need your help," he said, looking quite earnest now.

"My help?" she blinked in surprise.

"Yes, madam," he replied and gently took her arm. "This way," he directed her toward the apothecary shop's front door.

"No. Stop," she protested, halting. "I came here this morning to purchase emergency supplies for the hospital and I've not yet—"

"This won't take five minutes," he promised, "and I really do need your help."

Flustered, her heart fluttering, Laurette asked, "What exactly can I do for you, Mr. Vane?"

He gave no reply and she frowned, confused, when he commandingly ushered her out of the shop and into the January morning sunshine. She started to object. He shook his dark head, silencing her. And the next thing she knew, he was propelling her toward a big, black shiny brougham that was parked at the curb. He handed her up inside, then got in.

Her brow knitted and she immediately made a

move to exit the roomy coach. He stopped her with a gentle hand on her arm.

Looking directly into her suspicious dark eyes, he asked, "Are you, by any chance, free this evening, Mrs. Tigart?"

"Free?" she repeated, puzzled. "Yes, but—"

"Good," he said, and his handsome face broke into a dazzling smile. "Have dinner with me."

"Have dinner with…that's what you need with me?"

"It is, indeed. I badly need for you to break bread with me this evening."

She continued to frown. "Mr. Vane, I really don't have time for your foolishness."

"You should take the time."

"I beg your pardon."

"When did you last do something for no other reason than to enjoy yourself."

"Ah, I—I—"

"Then that's too long, Mrs. Tigart," he said with wink and a grin.

She tilted her head and her dark eyes narrowed slightly. "Mr. Vane, I know nothing about you so why on earth would I—"

"What do you want to know? Ask me."

She paused for minute, took a deep breath and said, "Just what are you doing here in Mobile? Why did you come here? Where is your home, where is your family from? Why do you want to have dinner with me?" She crossed her arms over her chest and her chin lifted defiantly.

The timbre of his voice low and mellow, he said, "I'm here because I visited Mobile on holiday and fell in love with the city. I've traveled extensively during the past few years." He looked her in the eye and said, "My last permanent address was Maryland. I resided in a big dwelling right on the bluffs of Chesapeake Bay."

"Oh, that must have been a charming place to live," she commented, envisioning his home.

His expression never changing, he said, flatly, "Unforgettable."

She began to smile. "You haven't answered my last question. Why do want to have dinner with me?"

"My dear, have you looked in the mirror of late? You are a beautiful woman and I'm told an intelligent one as well. I'd like to get to know you better. I think we might get along. Is that so hard to understand?" She shook her head. "Have dinner with me. I promise you a pleasant evening." She opened her mouth but before she could speak, he laid his long forefinger perpendicular to her lips and told her, "There's absolutely nothing to worry about, it will be quite proper. Colonel and Mrs. Ivy will be joining us. Say you'll come."

Flattered that he would find her beautiful, Laurette was tempted, but unsure. She hesitated. "I—I don't know...you see I—"

Interrupting, Sutton Vane said with cool authority, "I will send my carriage around for you at eight sharp."

"You don't know where I live," she said.

"Yes, I do," he said. "I made it a point to find out. Say yes to me, Mrs. Tigart."

Laurette swallowed hard, snared by his merciless blue eyes. Feeling the pull of his intense masculine power, she could only nod her agreement.

He took her hand in his, kissed the inside of her fragile wrist and said, "One more thing. Would you, just for me, consider wearing that becoming blue velvet gown you were wearing when we met at the Colonel's party? You looked stunning in that dress."

"I'll wear it," she said with a shy smile, thinking that she would have to wear it. It was the only decent gown she owned.

"Thank you, Mrs....thank you, Laurette. May I call you Laurette?" he asked politely.

"I wish you would, Mr. Vane."

"Sutton," he gently corrected.

"Sutton," she softly repeated, liking the sound of it, liking him.

Smiling, he pushed open the carriage door, swung agilely down into the sunlight, turned and lifted her to the ground.

"We'll dine at my home, if that is agreeable," he said, his hands lingering an extra second or two on her slender waist.

"As long as the Ivys are there."

"They'll be there."

As promised, Sutton Vane's shiny black carriage came for Laurette at eight. Inside the plush, roomy conveyance, Laurette felt a great degree of anticipation as the carriage rolled along one of the city's grandest boulevards, Government Street.

When the carriage turned into the long private drive bordered by glowing gaslight posts, Laurette was awed by her first glimpse of the majestic mansion with its huge Corinthian columns and many well-lit windows. And, she was downright astounded when Sutton Vane himself came hurrying down to the curved pebble drive to meet her.

Looking devastatingly handsome in well-tailored evening clothes, snowy-white shirt and black silk cravat, he opened the carriage door, stuck his head inside, and said, "Welcome to my home, Laurette, and thank you so much for coming."

She smiled at him. "Thank you for inviting me."

She then squealed with girlish surprise when Sutton, reaching out to help her from the carriage, swung her up into his arms and carried her, explaining, "The driveway pebbles could ruin your slippers. I'll put you down when we reach the front walk."

"Very well," she managed to say, overwhelmed by his sudden powerful closeness.

The muscles of his hard chest were pressed against her left breast and she felt as if she couldn't breathe. She didn't know what to do with her arms, her hands.

Laughing, Sutton read the indecision in her expressive eyes and told her, "You can put one hand around my neck, the other on my chest, Laurette. I don't bite."

"No, no, of course, not," she said, coloring, and draped a velvet-encased arm around his shoulders, then laid a gloved hand lightly on the white-pleated shirt covering his chest.

"Mr. Vane...Sutton, I believe we reached the front walk several steps ago," she pointed out, seconds later.

"Have we?" he said, as if in disbelief. "Could we pretend that we haven't for a minute longer?"

Yes, oh, yes! she was tempted to say and snuggle closer. But she checked herself. "Mr. Vane, you promised to put me down when—"

"So I did," he replied, good-naturedly, and then slowly, sensuously lowered her to her feet, letting her soft, slender body slide languidly down the rigid length of his, all the while looking into her eyes.

Shaken, she stepped back to put some distance between them. He took her arm and ushered her into the mansion.

Inside the opulent drawing room Colonel and Martha Ivy were waiting. Laurette was half surprised to see them. She wouldn't have been surprised if the devilishly charming Sutton Vane hadn't actually invited them, had intended to get her alone in his luxurious lair to take advantage of her.

She was immediately chagrined to realize that secretly she had half hoped he hadn't invited them. That it would be just the two of them at dinner this evening.

Mentally scolding herself, Laurette warmly greeted her old friends, the Ivys. She then glanced up at Sutton, who stood at her side, and saw bright sparks of mischief shining out of the depths of his arresting blue

eyes. *He knew! Dear lord, he knew what she was
thinking, that she had hoped they would be alone.*

Her face flushed hotly and her knees trembled. Neither the Colonel nor Martha Ivy noticed her unease.
Sutton must have because he immediately put a hand
to the small of her back and steadied her. Small talk
went on around her as Sutton, with his hand still at
her back, ushered her into the huge, candlelit dining
room and pulled out a high-backed chair of gleaming
black walnut and plush burgundy velvet.

Twenty-Two

Dinner was absolutely superb.

The tempting seven-course meal began with consommé. Next came piping hot French bread and pats of creamy butter. There were not one, but four entrees: spiced shrimp; loin of pork; ribs of prize beef; and thick sizzling steaks. Each diner was welcome to choose one—or all—of the well-prepared meats.

To compliment the entrees, there were baked and mashed potatoes, Saco corn, fried eggplant, green peas and stewed parsnips.

And, of course, fine wine served in stemmed crystal glasses accompanied each course. Everything was absolutely delicious and Laurette, unused to such an array of tempting foods, feared she was making a terrible glutton of herself, but she simply couldn't help it. It had been so long since she had enjoyed such rich, appetizing food that she sampled a little of everything.

It was between mouthfuls of tasty spiced shrimp and stewed parsnips that she noticed that her host was eating very little. With a heavy sterling fork he pushed the food around on his plate, but rarely lifted it to his mouth. She wondered why he wasn't hungry.

Dessert came and Laurette's dark eyes widened with joy: apple dumplings with cream sauce, fluffy coconut pie, coffee caramels, toasted almonds in a silver dish, lemon ice cream and huge ripe strawberries with rich whipped cream.

Over coffee and brandy which followed the desserts, the foursome discussed the changes in Mobile at length. Too soon the tall cased clock in the foyer was striking the hour of eleven.

"Oh, dear me," said Martha, "I had no idea it was getting so late." She turned to her husband, "Colonel, it's past our bedtime."

"So it is, my dear," he replied, patted his full belly, then rose and helped Martha out of her chair.

The elderly couple said their thanks and good-nights and made their slow way to the mansion's front door with Laurette and Sutton accompanying them.

"We enjoyed the evening tremendously, my boy," the Colonel said to Sutton.

"A pleasure having you," said Sutton. "Do promise to come again."

"We certainly will," said Martha Ivy.

The pair left, and the door closed behind them.

Sutton turned to Laurette. "You must be tired, too. I'll get your wrap."

"Thank you," she said and stood unmoving as he draped her blue velvet cape around her shoulders.

"My man will drive you home at once," he said, standing directly behind her, his hands gently cupping her upper arms. He paused, then added, "May I ride along with you?"

Laurette was glad she was facing away from him so that he couldn't see the foolish little smile that had come to her lips at the suggestion.

"If you like," she said as calmly as possible.

Sutton took his long black cloak from the coat tree and the two of them walked out to the waiting carriage. On the short ride in the cold night air, Sutton took one of Laurette's small hands and held it warmly in both of his own.

"I want to see you again, Laurette," he declared, his eyes flashing in the darkness. "Tell me I may."

"When?" she asked and immediately wished she could take it back so that she didn't appear so eager.

He chuckled. "Tomorrow night, my dear."

At her front door, she turned to face him, wondering if he would insist on coming inside. He did not. Nor did he try to kiss her.

He took both her hands in his and said, "I enjoyed being with you." He looked into her eyes. Then his gaze slowly lowered to her parted lips. A muscle danced in his lean jaw. "You better go inside before you catch your death."

"Yes, I...yes, it is cold tonight."

"Freezing," he replied as he leaned close and brushed a kiss to her forehead. "Good night, Laurette."

"Good night, Sutton."

The dinner engagement had proved to be a very lovely evening and it was to be the first of many. Sutton Vane, to Laurette's genuine surprise and relief, was ever the perfect gentleman. She was enchanted. She began to relax with him. A spark of her old vanity surfacing, she was pleased and flattered that such a handsome, urbane man, one who could have any woman he wanted, chose to spend so much of his time with her.

The couple quickly became the topic of much speculation. "Yes, indeed, Laurette," Johanna confirmed one afternoon, "as you might well suspect, the town gossips are busy talking about you and your questionable relationship with a man about whom none of us really know very much. They wonder just how far things have gone." Johanna raised a questioning eyebrow, hoping she might find out herself.

"Let them talk, let them wonder," Laurette said, calmly, "I don't much care."

And she didn't.

Perhaps she was being both foolish and unforgivably selfish, but she reasoned that she deserved a bit of excitement and pleasure, however fleeting it might prove to be. Hers had not been the happiest or most satisfying of lives and when she was with the magnetic, engaging Sutton Vane, she felt more alive than she'd felt since she was a young, carefree girl.

Not only was Sutton strikingly handsome and consistently entertaining, he was attentive and romantic. He listened raptly to her when she spoke, as if everything she said was of great interest to him. He made her feel that there was no one else on earth but her. And, he radiated a potent brand of dark masculinity that was electrifying.

When she was with Sutton her clothes felt uncomfortably tight and it was a struggle to keep from touching him. Often she was tempted to run a hand over his broad chest, to examine the planes and hollows with her fingertips. She caught herself wondering how he would look without his shirt, how his naked flesh would feel beneath her hands.

The innocent brush of his hard thigh against her own as they sat in the carriage, the touch of his hand on her bare shoulder was enough to make her heartbeat quicken, her breath grow short. And, when frequently she stole covert glances at his handsome face while he was unaware, she decided she could stare at him forever.

He was also a very generous man. He lavished expensive gifts on her, including exquisite ball gowns and jewelry, insisting that she accept them. He refused to heed her protests that it wasn't proper for a gentleman to give a lady such personal presents. He took her to the theater. To restaurants. To parties.

And his kisses were absolutely divine. So incredibly thrilling, he ignited a long-sleeping passion in her. Each night when he brought her home, when they stepped into the foyer, he took her in his arms and kissed her. Once. Twice. Sometimes three times or more.

The first of those incredible kisses had occurred after two full weeks of spending each and every evening together. Laurette, magnetically drawn to him, yearning for the moment when he would finally take her in his arms and kiss her, had begun to wonder if he ever intended to do so.

Then it had happened.

His warm, surprisingly soft lips closed over hers in a sweet, undemanding kiss that lasted for only a few seconds. When he'd raised his dark head, he had looked into her eyes and said, "From the moment I saw you standing before the fireplace at Colonel Ivy's party, I have wanted to kiss you."

"You—you have?"

His reply was to kiss her again, this time longer, more intimately. His arms had tightened around her and he drew her into his close embrace. He gently pressed her head back against his supportive arm and kissed her with a slow, sensual deliberation that left her weak and breathless.

Since then, he had kissed her every night. And each kiss became longer, hotter, more stirring. And, as they anxiously kissed, their tense, straining bodies pressed insistently against each other. Laurette, sighing with pleasure, molding herself to Sutton's frame, could feel her breasts flatten against the solid wall of his chest. And the steely strength of his trousered thigh would wedge persistently between her legs. She was intensely aware of his warm, searching hands as they glided caressingly up and down her back.

When at last they would tear their burning lips apart to gasp for breath, he'd say huskily, "I must go."

"Yes, yes, you must," she would hastily agree, not

wanting him to leave, not wanting him to stop kissing her, not wanting him to take his arms from around her.

Ever.

Twenty-Three

Sutton was acutely aware of what Laurette was thinking, feeling, longing for, each night when he left her. He had very carefully, very patiently woven a fine web of seduction around the unsuspecting divorcée. He knew exactly how and when to make her surrender. To make her *want* to surrender.

The time had come.

She was ready.

So, on a chilly night in early February when they'd spent an entertaining evening at the theater with the Ivys and the Parlange twins, Sutton didn't take Laurette directly home as was his custom. Instead, he took her to his own mansion, although when she realized his intent, Laurette protested.

"Sutton...no...I..." she began.

"Just for a nightcap." His tone was low, soft, but his deep blue eyes flashed with an unsaid promise of pleasure.

Afraid of what would happen if she went inside with him, Laurette tried again. "It's very late and I—I—" Snared by his heavy-lidded gaze and helplessly longing to be held in his arms, Laurette sighed and gave in. "Only one. Then I really must go."

Sutton smiled at her and said, "The very minute you're ready to leave, I'll take you home."

"Promise?"

"Promise," he said.

Once they were inside the silent mansion and the door was securely locked behind them, Sutton turned and looked at Laurette for a long, measuring moment. Then he stepped closer, took her in his arms and began kissing her. After only two or three kisses, she melted against him.

It seemed so natural, so right to be in his arms. As she savored his marvelous kisses, she was struck—and not for the first time—by the uncanny sensation that this handsome man whom she'd known for only a short time was somehow very familiar. She was comfortable in his embrace, felt as if she belonged there.

At the same time she was half afraid of him, uneasy in his strong arms. He was, after all, a stranger about whom she knew very little—a man she didn't totally trust. Yet from the moment they met, he had effortlessly exercised a powerful hold over her. She felt defenseless against his potent masculinity and had found it impossible to fight her deep attraction to him.

Sutton deepened his kiss and any lingering doubts plaguing Laurette were temporarily forgotten.

Standing directly beneath the chandelier in the center of the black-and-white marble-floored foyer, Sutton Vane began taking the final steps in his well-planned, unemotional seduction of Laurette Howard Tigart.

Overwhelmed by his smooth, slow sensual assault, Laurette felt herself losing control, knew what was going to happen if she was not careful. Suddenly, she was uneasy again. She felt as if she were in imminent danger. All at once his very image was both evil *and* erotic. Powerfully provocative. This man whose kisses she craved was, she feared, quite capable of making her lose her head, of behaving irresponsibly. Of causing her to surrender to his dark, irresistible sexuality. Should that happen, she would surely suffer for her unwise indiscretion.

She was no fool. She knew that she was not the only woman in Sutton's life. And would never be. He loved and was loved by many beautiful women.

Laurette abruptly tore her kiss-swollen lips from Sutton's and raised her hands to push on his chest. He knew she was plagued with doubt and indecision. So he wisely put her fears into words.

"My dear, you're afraid of me," he said, as if hurt by the offensive idea.

"No, no I—I'm not," she said, shaking her head.

Sutton lifted his hands, gently cupped her pale cheeks, skimmed the tips of his thumbs over her bottom lip and said, "You fear me, darling, but there's no need. You're safe here with me." He drew her closer, bent his dark head and murmured, "Kiss me. Kiss me and tell me you're not afraid."

Then his lips were on hers again, warm and smooth and persuasive while his hands slid seductively down her back and over her hips to press her closer. Laurette felt his heart beating against hers and trembled with a mixture of anxiety and elation. She wasn't safe, but she didn't want to be safe. She wanted him.

Laurette wrapped her arms around his neck and whispered, "I'm not afraid."

"Then let me make love to you, sweetheart," he murmured and kissed her again.

His kisses were always stirring, but tonight they were thrilling beyond compare. Between the probing, prolonged kisses, he teased her, brushing a kiss to the left corner of her mouth, then the right. He playfully bit and sucked on her lower lip. He ran the tip of his tongue along the inside of her upper lip.

Then he wrapped a hand around the side of her throat, tilted her head back slightly and kissed her with such passionate aggression, such intimate invasion, Laurette was left weak and half-dazed.

His lips hotly covering hers, his tongue went deep inside her mouth to possess, arouse and dazzle. As he kissed her, he slowly, deftly began undressing her. Her heart racing, wits scattered, Laurette, at the conclusion of a long, heated kiss, laid her forehead on his darkly bearded chin and said, "Sutton, the servants…"

"…are in their private quarters," he assured her, adding, "and they know better than to come out unless sent for. We're completely alone."

Laurette raised her head and nodded, wishing that they weren't. Wishing someone would rescue her from her own unforgivable weakness. Wishing she had the strength to reject the smooth advances of this dark, debonair man.

She did not.

Nobody had ever kissed her the way Sutton Vane was kissing her. And nobody had ever undressed her with such skillful dexterity. It seemed so fitting, so normal for him to be stripping her clothes away from her overwarm body. She wanted to be rid of the garments. They were hot and bothersome and she no longer wanted to wear them.

She put up no protest when Sutton lifted her free of her dress. And, she shivered deliciously when, seconds later, he tossed her chemise aside. In minutes all her clothing had magically melted away. She was totally nude. Even her shoes and stockings lay on the marble foyer floor with her discarded clothes.

Sutton took a step back, gazed unblinkingly at her and said, "God, you *are* beautiful. Have you any idea how exquisite you are?"

Pride swiftly overcoming any lingering shyness, Laurette drew in a deep breath, purposely pushing her pale breasts up and out and tightening her already flat belly. She took the combs from her hair and allowed the golden locks to spill down around her bare shoulders. She bent a knee, let her arms fall to her sides and stood there unmoving beneath the glittering chandelier, inviting his keen examination.

Blatantly Sutton studied her for several long seconds and Laurette blossomed under his heavy-lidded scrutiny. She hadn't felt pretty in years. This man made her feel beautiful.

Laurette emitted a pleased gasp of excitement when Sutton stepped forward, swung her up into his strong arms and headed for the curving marble stairway. Taking the steps two at a time, he carried Laurette down the shadowy corridor and into his spacious bedroom suite. He walked through the sitting room and into the bedroom where a lone bedside lamp burned low.

Crossing the spacious room, he went directly to the oversize bed and gently lowered Laurette down onto sheets of silver-gray satin. He stood above, still fully dressed in his dark evening attire. Again he studied the bare female body stretched out below him as if she were a divine sacrifice to her appreciative master of desire. Sutton kicked off his black patent leather shoes, got into bed beside her and began to provide ardent physical pleasure, using only his hands and his mouth.

Laurette, stretching, wiggling, sighing, couldn't believe such incredible ecstasy could be derived from lying naked with a fully clothed man. She tingled from head to toe as his talented lips pressed hot, wet kisses to her cheeks, her chin, her throat, her shoulders.

She was puzzled when, his lips tracing her collarbone, he urged an arm above her head. She shivered when he kissed the inside of her elbow. And was startled when his burning lips trailed downward and settled in the warm hollow of her underarm.

Her bottom lip now caught between her teeth, Laurette couldn't believe it when she felt his mouth open and his tongue stroke her. She would never have imagined that he would dare kiss her there. Or that it would feel so good. His silky black beard was delightfully ticklish against her sensitive skin and it was all she could do to keep from whimpering with pleasure.

His mouth left her underarm and settled on her parted lips. And, as he kissed her, he managed—she would always wonder how—to turn her over so that she was no longer on her back, but lying on her stomach. It was quite a feat because throughout the lithe maneuver, his lean hands enticingly caressed her bare flesh and his sultry lips never left hers.

Only when the turn was completed and she was lying fully on her stomach, did his mouth leave her lips. She automatically undulated when his hand swept down her back and cupped her left buttock. She shivered from his touch and from the luscious feel of the sleek, soft satin beneath her tingling breasts and belly.

"I am," he told her, "going to kiss you all over."

"The lamp...the light," she said, thrilled by the proposal, embarrassed at the idea of experiencing such intimacy in a lighted room. "Please, Sutton."

"If you'd feel more comfortable," he said as he leaned up and blew out the lamp.

He didn't mind. He could see clearly in the darkness. Years in the pitch-black dungeon had made it possible. His eyes gleamed as an animal's when he swept her long blond hair aside, leaned down and kissed the sensitive nape of her neck. Then her shoulders. Her slender arms. Her delicate hands.

He moved to her beautiful back, pressing kisses up

and down her spine. He gripped her hips lightly and teasingly kissed the twin dimples atop the beginning swell of her buttocks.

Her head turned to the side on a satin-cased pillow, eyes half-closed, Laurette was astounded when she felt the tip of his sleek tongue delve in the crevice of her bare bottom. But she didn't object. Nor did she object when his ticklish bearded face paid homage to each rounded cheek before gliding down over her thighs. She learned that the backs of her knees were highly sensitive as he kissed them and she was grateful for the darkness so that he couldn't see the foolish smile on her face.

Or so she thought.

His open mouth descended down the calves of her legs and to her slender ankles. He lifted each foot from the bed and sprinkled kisses over the soft heel, the high instep and each toe.

When at last his mouth had caressed the very last toe, he lifted his dark head and said, "Turn over, sweetheart."

Laurette felt her heart lurch. Her eyes had become adjusted to the shadowy darkness. She could see better now. The light from the sitting room was spilling into the bedroom. She considered requesting that he turn out all the lamps, but didn't. She turned onto her back and looked up to see his eyes gleaming in the shadows. His wide lips were gleaming, too, and she tensed with anticipation, eager to have that burning mouth back on her tingling flesh.

Twenty-Four

She didn't have to wait long.

Seated facing her, with an arm on either side of her body, Sutton bent his dark head and placed a kiss in the hollow of her throat. She swallowed with growing excitement. And then sighed with pleasure as he nibbled and nuzzled his way down to her breasts. His neatly clipped beard and the silky raven hair falling over his forehead were brushing her skin as he kissed her, adding to her stimulation. Flinging her arms above her head, Laurette surged against him, pushing her chest out, drawing her belly in until it was concave.

Soon she was almost sobbing with frustrated need when, pressing wet, plucking kisses all around the circumference of her left breast, Sutton mysteriously left the nipple untouched. Unkissed. Laurette bit her lip to keep from begging.

Was something wrong? Did he hold some deep-seated aversion to kissing a woman's nipples? She almost panicked at the prospect. She was highly aroused and her nipples were rigid and aching, standing up in twin points of stinging sensation.

Please, she silently entreated, twisting her body in

an attempt to position her nipple against his open lips. It didn't work. He acted as if he hadn't noticed, moving on to the other breast, kissing a path completely around it, pointedly neglecting the nipple.

Laurette clamped her teeth together to keep from moaning as his lips moved down over her rib cage and to her waist. He brushed openmouthed kisses against her prominent hipbones, to her flat, quivering stomach, to her pale thighs, her tightly closed legs. Laurette's shoulder blades lifted from the bed and she held her breath as he lingered on her lower belly, his tongue tracing the fine line of pale hair going down from her naval.

But, when he reached the triangle of golden coils below, he moved his hot face over to the outside of her thigh and began trailing his kisses down her left leg. Laurette sighed, squirmed and breathed through her mouth as he slid farther down the bed and his lips languidly kissed a path to her knees, then glided down her shins.

Her heart stopped entirely when his mouth abruptly left her flesh and he sat up. She gave him a questioning look. For an instant she was terrified that the intoxicating lovemaking was over, that he was going to leave her like this. Aroused. Yearning. Hurting. He had meticulously avoided the very places on her tense, vibrating body that most needed his healing kisses.

And then, in one, swift fluid movement Sutton lifted her left leg over his head and was sitting between her parted thighs. He then leaned down, gripped her upper arms and drew her up into a sitting position, facing him.

His eyes aglow, he said softly, his voice a low caress, "What exactly is the old maxim? 'Always save the best till last.'"

She couldn't answer, couldn't make a sound.

He slowly lowered his head and his mouth closed over and captured a pebble-hard nipple. Laurette's head fell back and all the breath left her body.

"Yes," she breathed, "oh, yes," as he kissed the nipple, circled it with his tongue, nibbled on it with his gleaming white teeth, then sucked until she could feel the fierce tugging not only at her breast, but between her legs as well.

He must have known because when he switched to the other breast, he slid a hand down her contracting belly and slipped his long fingers into the blond curls of her groin. While his lips pulled provocatively on her nipple, his middle finger parted the golden coils and lightly touched the pulsing button of glistening flesh between.

Laurette winced, then whimpered with pleasure. He continued to lick and suckle her nipple while with one dexterous finger, he slowly, gently circled the pulse point of all her raging desire.

When at last his mouth left her breast and he raised his head, Laurette began to sag weakly back to the pillows. But he stopped her.

"No," he said, his hand still between her legs, toying, caressing, "don't lie down just yet. And don't close your eyes. Watch me make love to you, sweetheart. It will increase your pleasure. And mine.''

Her breath now coming in shallow little spurts, Laurette tentatively lowered her gaze to where his hand was touching her. He was right. Seeing his lean, long-fingered hand intimately caressing her made it all the more thrilling. She watched for a long moment, then lifted her eyes to meet his.

''Would you like me to put my mouth where my hand now is?'' he asked.

Appalled, she whispered, ''Sutton, that's…indecent.''

''But do you want it?''

She gave no reply. While the suggestion shocked her, she was in such a state of high arousal, the shameful idea greatly appealed to her. She imagined that it would feel wonderful to have him kiss her there. Still, she wasn't about to say she wanted it. She wasn't that much of a shameless wanton.

''More than anything, darling,'' he said in a low, husky voice, ''I want to kiss this sweet, most feminine part of your beautiful body. I want to smell you, taste you, pleasure you.'' His gleaming eyes bore directly into hers. ''But, not unless you want it, too.'' He moved his hand from between her legs, placed it on her waist. ''Tell me, sweetheart.''

Laurette couldn't help herself. She supposed such behavior was truly depraved, perhaps even perverted. But he had her at a fever pitch. Her tense, hot body was crying out for his touch, anywhere and everywhere. She wanted what he had suggested. Wanted to

feel his burning mouth between her legs. Yes, she
wanted it. Had to have it. Couldn't live another second if he didn't do it.

Aware she was tossing pride and decency to the
wind, Laurette choked, "Yes, Sutton. Yes."

"Yes, what?" he coolly tormented her.

"You know."

"No, I don't. You must tell me what you want."

"You know what I want," she breathlessly declared.

"Then say it," he whispered, "I want to hear you
say it aloud. Tell me exactly what you want me to
do."

On a sob, she managed to reply, "I—I want you
to…kiss me."

"Where?"

More aroused than she'd ever been in her life,
Laurette told Sutton exactly where she wanted to be
kissed, and in the most graphic of terms. Never no-
ticing the cruel curl of satisfaction on his lips, she
breathed her thanks and sank back on her bent elbows
when he lowered his handsome face to her belly and
teasingly nuzzled his nose in the blond coils of her
groin. He parted the curls with his tongue and then,
before he kissed her, he opened his mouth over her
exposed flesh and exhaled a long, hot breath against
her.

It felt good.

So unbelievably good Laurette began to slowly sag
down to the mattress. Never lifting his head, Sutton

said, "No. Don't lie down. I want you to watch while
I love you. It will make your climax more intense."

Before she could reply, he was kissing her and with
the first touch of his sleek tongue on her pulsing flesh,
she began to murmur his name over and over.

"Sutton, Sutton, Sutton," she panted, the pleasure
so fantastic she couldn't believe it. "Sutton, Sutton,"
she continued to murmur and sob.

She pushed more fully up onto her elbows to
watch, just as he had suggested. Blinking in the shadowy darkness, glad now for the ambient light from
the sitting room, she could clearly see his handsome
face buried between her open thighs. What an erotic
sight it was.

His silky black beard was meshed with the pale
blond curls of her groin. His beautiful eyes were
closed, the long sooty lashes resting on his lean, dark
cheeks. He was kissing her as if he were kissing her
mouth. His hot, open lips were gently sucking, his
tongue was licking and circling that point of pure sensation where all her hot desire was centered.

Wild, immoral thoughts drifted through Laurette's
feverish brain as she watched her passionate lover
kissing her where she'd never been kissed before. She
would, she decided in that instant, keep him just
where he was for a long, long time. Perhaps all night.
She wouldn't let him up. She would demand that his
marvelous mouth stay fused to her ultrasensitive flesh
for hours and hours and hours.

But, just as those wild thoughts were running
through her sex-hazed mind, Sutton's gentle lips and

tongue became more assertive, the plucking of his lips became stronger, the licking of his tongue more aggressive.

It was pure heaven.

Laurette cried out with joy and urged him on. "Yes, yes, don't stop, don't ever stop!"

He didn't stop. He licked and lashed and loved her until the explosion that had been steadily building inside her began to erupt into an erotic crescendo.

"Oh! Oh! Oh!" she cried out and, in a sexual frenzy, reached down, grabbed the hair of his head, pressed his face closer and began to scream as the deep, powerful orgasm claimed her.

Sutton dutifully stayed with Laurette as she bucked and shrieked and quivered. After several long seconds of sexual hysteria, she had finally gotten it all out. She frantically pushed his hot face away and sank, sated and dazed, down onto her back.

Sutton raised his head and looked at her. Her eyes were closed, her face was flushed. Her breasts were moving up and down with her labored breaths, but her pale body was as limp as a rag doll's.

She made no move to cover herself. She felt no shame, only deep fulfillment. She had the look of a woman well loved and utterly content. And that was exactly how he intended to keep her.

Sutton ducked as he lifted her limp leg back up over his head and then he quickly moved up beside her. He kissed her open lips and Laurette tasted herself on his mouth. She was momentarily appalled. But then she opened her eyes and looked at his handsome face. His beautiful sculptured lips were gleaming wet with the liquid he had so skillfully coaxed from her own passion-heated body. She raised her lips to his, kissed him again, then sighed with serenity and allowed her head to fall back onto the pillow.

Laurette had no idea that Sutton was equally satisfied. Just in a different way. He had so successfully aroused and excited this lovely naked woman that he had been able to bring her to an incredible climax without so much as removing his black satin cravat and pearl stickpin. He was still fully dressed in evening attire.

He had kept his own passion carefully in check. He had, in his long prison years, learned how to control both his mind and his body. He had intended tonight's ecstasy to be hers alone. He had seen to it that she not be distracted from her own selfish pleasure.

A master at physically pleasing a woman, Sutton had silently conveyed, throughout the lovemaking, the subtle message that he enjoyed nothing more than being allowed to adore her soft, pale body in this intimate fashion.

Smiling now, he tugged a long golden lock of hair and said, ''Why don't you take a nice hot bath in my big marble tub while I retrieve your discarded clothes.''

Laurette's eyes opened. She smiled, nodded, waited until he had left the room, then went into the black marble bath and relaxed in a tub of hot sudsy water. When she got out, she wrapped herself in a big thirsty towel and came back into the bedroom wondering if Sutton would now be in the bed, naked.

She found him, still fully dressed, seated in a leather easy chair, drinking a brandy. Her clothes lay on a side table at his elbow.

"Come here," he said and she did.

When she stood before him, he offered her a drink. She took the crystal snifter, sipped and felt the brandy burn its pleasant way down into her chest and out into her arms. She flushed when Sutton reached out and casually yanked her covering towel away.

Smiling, he leaned up, put his hands to her waist and drew her down astride his lap, tucking her knees in close to his sides. Locking his wrists behind her waist, he said, "I undressed you. Now I will dress you. And I will do it sitting here in this chair with you on my lap."

Which he did.

And it was almost as exciting as when he'd undressed her.

Twenty-Five

At midmorning, Willard Gordon Keyes sat across the large mahogany desk from his boss. The heavy drapes had not yet been opened and the only light in the darkly paneled study was from a lamp atop the desk, a lamp that had a unique gunmetal-gray globe. An eerie, diffused light radiated from it, illuminating only a small portion of the desk.

In deep shadow was the face of Sutton Vane. Also in shadow were the tall, locked mahogany file cabinets directly behind him. The cabinets contained notes, letters, telegrams, newspaper clippings—each item carefully filed under one of the names on his infamous list.

Willard Keyes, who'd been known as Bones for as long as he could remember, squinted in an attempt to see the expression on the face of the man with whom he had spent the last five years. It was impossible, Sutton's face was completely concealed in shadow.

Bones remained respectfully silent as Sutton carefully read through the pages of information contained in the envelope Bones had picked up at the post office downtown. As he studied the material before him, Sutton suddenly leaned halfway up into the light, stifling a yawn. Bones knew the reason Sutton was sleepy this morning.

He was aware that his boss had stayed up very late, entertaining Laurette Howard Tigart.

Sutton had informed Bones as he was leaving last night that he was bringing Mrs. Tigart to the mansion after the opera and he wanted total privacy. Bones was to see to it that all the servants were safely in their quarters and were not to venture out for any reason.

Bones had heard the pair when they came in last night around eleven, heard the carriage roll up the pebble drive. And, later, he had awakened as Mrs. Tigart was leaving. He had glanced at the clock. It had been 2:00 a.m.

Bones frowned, wondering if Sutton's seduction of Mrs. Tigart had taken place last night. Bones didn't approve of Sutton taking advantage of the unsuspecting lady. He had met Mrs. Tigart and he had immediately liked her. He hated to see her get hurt, but when he had tried to intervene on her behalf, he had received only silence from Sutton.

In many ways Sutton was as kind and compassionate a man as Bones had ever known. But he could be calculatedly cruel to those he felt had done him wrong. Not that Bones blamed him for punishing James Tigart.

Tigart had deserved what he'd gotten and worse for having Sutton thrown into the prison dungeon so that he could steal his sweetheart. Bones had told Sutton that if he wanted Tigart dead, he'd be more than willing to do the honors. It would, he'd said, give him great satisfaction to snap Tigart's cowardly neck.

Sutton had declined the offer and Bones felt sure he knew the reason. Sutton just could not forget that Tigart had saved his life when they were young boys. He couldn't bring himself to kill Tigart.

"I want Tigart to live to be an old, old man, alone abroad, missing his home and his beautiful wife. May his days be as empty and lonely as mine were at Devil's Castle," he had explained.

Another on the list who was to suffer for his sins was the prison guard who had made Sutton's life a hell on earth—Gilbert LaKid. In Bones's opinion, LaKid deserved an even worse fate than Tigart. And he would surely get it once he was located. Sutton's men checked regularly with the authorities and made inquiries on their own, but so far the elusive LaKid had not been found. Once he was, Sutton was to be informed immediately. It would be he and no one else who meted out LaKid's punishment. Sutton had a special plan for the evil Gilbert LaKid.

And it wasn't death.

It was something far, far worse.

Gazing at his boss now, Bones thought the man a baffling paradox. As unforgiving as he was of his enemies, Sutton had a heart of gold where his friends or the downtrodden were concerned.

When Sutton had learned the sad fate of his parents, that his father had been killed in the war in '63 and that his mother, while living in New Orleans, had succumbed to yellow fever in the summer of '74, he had been in no hurry to return to Mobile.

Instead, the first thing he and Bones had done was to go in search of the two men who had befriended Sutton in prison, before he'd been tossed into the dungeon. Sutton had never forgotten the kindness and friendship of Captain Andrew Scott and Private Duncan Cain.

To Sutton's despair, he learned, when they visited the Charleston, South Carolina home of Andrew Scott, that Scott had starved to death in Devil's Castle prison in the cold winter of 1864. His tired-looking widow had remarried, to a man twice her age. Sutton had seen in her sad eyes that she'd had no choice; she couldn't have fed her three children alone.

In Birmingham, Alabama, Sutton easily found the healthy-looking Duncan Cain. Cain was shocked to see Sutton.

"We were told you died," said the blond, muscular Cain.

Sutton nodded. "They did their best, but I refused."

"Me, too!" said Duncan. "I kept seeing my red-haired sweetheart, Mary, and knew I had to get home to her. What about you, Ladd? You and Laurette married yet?"

"Not yet," said Sutton and changed the subject.

Through gentle questioning, Sutton learned that Cain was having a rough go of it, financially. He and his red-haired wife, now pregnant with their third child, were living with Cain's aged parents in a shack at the edge of the property they had once owned. Cain was doing what he could to bring in a little money, odd jobs, hiring out by the day, hunting steady employment. But he had no complaints, he was quick to point out. He was lucky and he knew it. He had lived through the war and the prettiest, sweetest girl in Alabama had been waiting when he got home.

Bones recalled with admiration how Sutton had helped young Cain without Cain's knowledge. Sutton had wasted no time. He had, using the Bay Minette Corporation, purchased the Cain property back from the carpetbaggers who had bought it. He hired Cain, at a generous salary, as the manager of the huge paper mill that was being built on a portion of the property. As the mill's manager, Cain, his wife, their children and Cain's mother and father were moved back into the old family mansion.

Yes, Sutton was a kind man and Bones knew firsthand how unselfish he could be. From the minute he'd fished the half-drowned prison escapee out of Chesapeake Bay, Sutton had shown his generosity. Trust had been established immediately between the two and not a week after they had met, the convalescing Sutton told Bones about the Yankee gold and revealed to him where it was buried. A less trusting man would never have divulged such a secret. In his weakened state, Sutton could have done nothing to stop him had Bones decided to leave him alone to die and go after the gold for himself.

When he hadn't, when he'd patiently nursed Sutton

back to health in a cheap, rented hotel room, Sutton had told him he would never regret it.

"I won't forget what you've done for me," Sutton had said. "Help me look for the gold. If we find it, your life will be one of comfort and ease."

"If we never find the gold, I'll stay with you," Bones had replied.

Bones was thirty-three years old when he'd pulled Sutton out of the bay, and he had never been more alone and lonely in his life. He'd had no purpose. No home. Nothing. He was the next thing to a derelict. And it was his fault. But he hadn't cared about anything or anyone since he'd lost the only woman he had ever loved.

He had never been able to understand how such a small, sweet-tempered, pretty girl could have actually been in love with him, a big, brawny three-hundred pound seaman. But his Amanda had loved him with all her heart and he had worshipped her. Her horrified parents had disowned her when she'd agreed to become his wife. She could have done much better, they'd said. Could have married a man of wealth and position, not some big, ugly sailor who could never give her a proper home.

It might not have been a proper one, but their rented rooms near the Maryland waterfront had been a happy home. That joy had increased when the fragile Amanda learned that she was carrying their first child. Oh, how beautiful she'd been during the pregnancy. And how happy he'd been when she'd climb up onto his lap, put her arms around his neck and declare that she was going to give him a perfect son. Those few precious months were the happiest of his entire life.

The idyll ended when Amanda, alone while he was at sea, went into an early and painful labor. A neighbor down the hall, hearing Amanda's screams, came to her aid. The neighbor sent her son to fetch the doctor, but it had done no good. After a long agonizing night of labor, Amanda delivered a perfect, tiny boy, but the infant lived for only a few short hours. Amanda died minutes later. She had forced herself to hold on for her baby's sake.

Bones had come home to an empty house and an empty life. Grief stricken, he had gone into a rage, broke every piece of furniture in the two rented rooms and crashed every dish in the cupboard. He was thrown in jail, and when he got out, he headed straight for the banks of the bay. His intent was to leap into the cold, rushing waters and end it all.

Before he could carry out his plan, he saw the thin, struggling Sutton, in danger of drowning. He saved Sutton and Sutton saved him.

Bones was brought back to the present when Sutton abruptly refolded the missive and returned it to the envelope. It, too, would go into the files under Tigart's name. Leaning forward into the light, he smiled up at Bones. The packet beneath his hands had been sent from his agent overseas—an operative who had been hired exclusively to keep a keen eye on Tigart. His job was to report any movement Tigart made, to make sure that Tigart didn't try slipping down to the docks somewhere and boarding a liner for home.

"Good news?" Bones inquired.

"The best," Sutton replied. "Tigart is out of work and without a farthing to his name. He begs on the streets of London and sleeps in the alleys." Sutton paused, tapped his fingertips together and added, "I do hope England is having a cold winter."

Bones nodded and rose. "Anything else, boss?"

"Yes," Sutton said, "there is something else."

"Name it."

"Get that look of censure off your face."

"I don't know what you're talking about."

"Yes, you do. You know what happened here last night and you don't like it."

"No, I don't like it," Bones admitted. "Mrs. Tigart has been through so much and—"

"Mrs. Tigart brought this on herself," Sutton interrupted, pushing back his chair and rising to his feet. He moved across the room and yanked open the cut-velvet drapes. For a long moment he stood looking out at the heavy gray clouds that threatened rain. His bearded jaw hardened and his blue eyes narrowed when he turned and added, "And she's been through nothing compared with what she will go through before I'm finished with her."

Twenty-Six

All day Laurette had vacillated.

One moment she was happy and starry-eyed and tingling from head to toe. The next, she was upset; filled with remorse and guilt for what she had done. As she went about her routine chores at the Confederate Veteran's Convalescent Hospital, she knew that she was alternating between blushing scarlet with shame and grinning foolishly with pleasure, but she simply couldn't help herself.

Sutton had dominated her thoughts since she'd awakened this morning. The minute she had opened her eyes, she had remembered everything that had happened between them and she had flushed hotly at the vivid recollection of his thrilling lovemaking. Scolding herself sharply for behaving like such a disgraceful wanton, she nonetheless lay in bed for a few lazy moments, drawing her knees up, savoring the sweet memory of last night's incredible bliss, stretching and purring like a satisfied feline.

And then laughing out loud with sheer, unadulterated delight.

Laurette had felt certain that what Sutton had done to her—what she had allowed him do to her, had

wanted him to do to her—was shocking and unortho-
dox. But, oh, what incredible ecstasy! She had almost
felt that moment of stunning rapture again and she'd
automatically pressed her thighs together tightly,
squeezed her eyes shut and gritted her teeth.

Finally she'd thrown back the bedcovers and sat
up. She'd swung her legs over the edge of the mattress, but still hadn't gotten up. She sat there, reluctant
to move, to do anything. She'd felt different that
morning. Not like herself. Not like she'd ever felt in
her life.

Had she looked different?

Abruptly, Laurette had risen from the bed, pulled
her nightgown off and sat back down on the mattress's edge.

She examined her naked body and shivered when
she saw that the pale flesh of her breasts, around her
nipples, was still pinkened from Sutton's burning
kisses, his sucking lips.

She had tingled with embarrassed pleasure when
she parted her legs and saw, high up on the inside of
her left thigh, a small red splotch. She touched it with
her fingertips and sighed, remembering. Sutton's
mouth had played and plucked at her thighs for a
long, lovely time and it had been pure heaven.

Laurette had drawn a quick, shallow breath at the
highly erotic vision of Sutton's handsome, bearded
face pressed between her open thighs, ardently kissing
her, lovingly licking her. Never had she felt anything
quite so pleasurable. Never had she done anything
quite so scandalous.

Suddenly embarrassed and ashamed, Laurette had grabbed her discarded nightgown, risen from the bed and, holding the gown modestly against her nude body, rushed into the dressing room to get ready for work.

Now, as her shift was ending and she was ready to leave the hospital, her thoughts remained on Sutton. Had all day. She couldn't get him out of her mind and she was already worrying and wondering when she would see him again. *If* she would see him again. If she *should* see him again. If it wouldn't be better if she never saw him again.

Who was she trying to fool? She wanted to see him more than anything in the world. She had to see him. She could hardly wait to see him.

At two o'clock sharp, Laurette stepped out the heavy front doors of the hospital. She promptly frowned. It was chilly and rainy and she dreaded the walk home. She raised her parasol, pulled the collar of her wrap up around her ears and skipped down the steep hospital steps.

She was yawning by the time she got home and strongly considering a nice, long afternoon nap. She hadn't gotten nearly enough sleep last night. Now, after a long, hard day at the hospital, she was tired, totally drained of energy.

She'd been home only long enough to hang up her wrap and build a fire in the fireplace when someone knocked on the door. Laurette sighed—the last thing she wanted on this rainy afternoon was company.

She'd bet anything that it was Johanna, bored and looking for company.

Laurette was pleasantly surprised when, pushing her hair behind her ears, she opened the door to find Sutton standing on her veranda.

"May I come in?" he asked, a bouquet of white roses in his hand.

"Please do," she said, her face growing warm.

Before he took a step inside, he turned halfway around, inclined his head and casually asked, "Who lives on the south side of Dauphin in that big red Georgian mansion?"

"The McBains," Laurette replied. "Mr. and Mrs. Ralph McBain. Their children have all grown up and left home."

"Have the McBains lived there long?"

"Yes. Sixteen years, I believe. They fled Atlanta in the war, moved down here." She extended her arm, urging him to enter. "Come on inside, it's cold out."

Sutton nodded, but stayed where he was, continuing to glance at the red mansion barely visible through the falling rain.

"Who lived in the house before the McBains bought it?" he asked, then carefully studied her face as she answered.

A hint of melancholy came into her luminous dark eyes, but with little emotion in her voice she said, "The Dasheroons. Douglas, Carrie and Ladd. Ladd was their son, a year older than I. We were playmates and best friends. We…and we…" She didn't finish the sentence.

"What happened to the Dasheroons? Did they move away?"

Laurette swallowed hard and shook her head. "They are all dead. The father and son were both killed in the war. The mother contracted yellow fever and succumbed in the summer of '74."

"I'm sorry." He came inside and, handing her the white roses, said, "I didn't mean to...don't be sad, Laurette."

"I'm not," she replied and smiled at him. "It all happened a long time ago."

Walking in front of her, his eyes narrowing slightly, he said, "And you got over it a long time ago."

"Yes, of course," she replied.

A muscle spasmed in his tight jaw at her response, but Sutton quickly regained his self-control and walked into the drawing room. Laurette followed. She put the roses in a vase and artfully arranged them.

Standing in the middle of the large room with his back to the fireplace, Sutton asked, "Where are all the servants at this early hour?"

Laurette laughed and said, "Why, I'm standing right here in front of you."

Sutton frowned with disbelief. "You mean you have no servants? None? You are all alone here in this big house?"

Before she could answer, he began to smile devilishly. He came to her, took her by the hand and led her out of the drawing room toward the staircase.

"Where are we going?" she asked.

"You'll see."

When they reached the second floor landing, he turned toward the back of the mansion. He didn't want to take her to the master suite. He didn't want to lie in the bed where she had once slept with Tigart.

Laurette stopped and said, "Sutton, my bedroom suite is the other direction. Why don't we go there and—"

"Let's not," he said and propelled her toward a little-used guest room at the very end of the hall.

When he pushed the door open and handed her inside, she turned and said, "Why are we going in here?"

"To make love," he told her and took her in his arms. Sutton kissed Laurette and as he kissed her, he reached out and yanked the covers from the bed, leaving only the sheeted mattress. The counterpane, quilt and pillows lay on the carpeted floor.

The kiss finally ended and Laurette sagged against him, her heart pounding, knees weak. His lips in her hair, she heard him say, "Do you remember how we made love last night?"

Her eyes slid closed and she murmured, "How could I ever forget?"

"Good. I don't want you to forget. I want you to remember. I want to love you like that again and again so that you will never forget." He pressed a kiss to her temple. "Only this time I want to be as naked as you. Will you help me get undressed?"

Laurette raised her head. "It will," she said with a sly grin, "be my pleasure."

She urged him down onto the edge of the bed and stood between his knees. She pushed his pale-gray frock coat off his shoulders and down his arms. "Shall I hang it up?" she inquired, as she picked up the coat and folded it over her arm.

His answer was a wink as he reached out, took the coat from her and tossed it across the room. It came to rest near the open door. Both laughed as their hands went to the buttons of his cream silk shirt. Laurette slapped his hands away.

"I've an idea," she said and her dark eyes sparkled.

"Which is?"

"You undressed me last night," she reminded him. "Now I will undress you."

"As you wish," he replied and dropped his arms to his sides. He caught himself liking the way she teased him as she unbuttoned his shirt. She let the fingertips of her right hand play in the dense hair on his exposed chest as she cupped his chin, urged his head back and kissed him, her tongue licking at his lips, her teeth nibbling. Already half-aroused, he instinctively lifted his hands to her waist.

Her lips abruptly left his and she warned, "No, don't. Allow me to fully undress you, then you may touch me if you like."

"I'll like," he said, then watched as she undid the buckle of his leather belt.

Her small hands quickly moved to the buttons of his fly. When his trousers were open, she yanked the long tails of his shirt up, pushed the sleeves down his arms, unbuttoned his cuffs and took the shirt off. She tossed it to the floor while he nodded his approval.

She paused and a look of genuine concern crossed her face. She reached out and tenderly touched the network of scars on his right side and said, "You've been badly hurt."

"Just a nasty spill off a spirited stallion," he said, making light of it. "A long time ago, long since healed."

"I'm sorry," she said softly as she sank to her knees and began brushing kisses to the scarred flesh.

Sutton gazed at the golden head bent to him and shuddered. Her soft, warm lips played on his flesh and he could feel himself stirring in response.

She finally lifted her head and Sutton drew a much needed breath. He then leaned back on stiffened arms as she knelt before him and began untying his shoelaces. In seconds both shoes and stockings had been removed and tossed aside.

"Are you cold?" she suddenly asked, "if you are we could—"

"I'm not cold," he assured her.

Nodding, Laurette stayed on her knees. She said, "I may need a little help."

"Just tell me what you want me to do."

She put her hands to the sides of the waistband of his trousers and asked him lift himself. He did. She gave the trousers a forceful yank and they slid down over his lean buttocks to his thighs. She peeled them off and dropped them, then playfully dusted her hands together as if she'd just completed a chore.

He laughed.

She did, too.

Again their eyes met. Their gazes locked and held.

He wore only his white linen underwear and he wondered if she would stop now. He assumed that she would. She was surely not seasoned enough at playing erotic games to complete the intimate task she had so coyly begun.

Her face was flushed. She was, he felt sure, not accustomed to making love in the light of day. She would be too timid to strip him naked. He was certain of it. She wouldn't dare...

At once the sobering thought flashed through his mind that he was a fool to think she was shy about anything having to do with sex. She had, after all, been married to Tigart for years, had done with Tigart all the intimate things lovers do. The realization momentarily cooled his ardor as in his mind's eye he vividly saw the two of them naked and making love. The vision sickened him.

But the image disappeared and his heart raced when Laurette gazed up at him like a naughty child reaching in the cookie jar as her fingers curled decisively around the waistband of his underwear.

"Lift up," she ordered again softly. "Let me have this. I want you naked."

He did as he was told and then found himself flushing with embarrassment when she pulled the linen underwear away from his body, releasing his rigid masculinity. He hadn't intended that to happen yet. Where was his control? Her eyes holding his, Laurette licked her lips as she slowly, teasingly peeled the underwear down his long legs. She sank back onto her heels and eased the underwear over his bare feet.

When she tossed that last garment aside, she rose up onto her knees, moved a trifle closer and asked, "Would you like me to kiss you all over just the way you kissed me last night?"

Twenty-Seven

"No, sweetheart, I don't think that—" He stopped speaking. His breath caught in his chest.

She gripped his sides and began sprinkling sweet, wet kisses over his bare, broad chest. He hadn't expected this. Didn't know if he could stand it. He didn't want it. He didn't want her to behave like this. He had to be the one in total control, not her. He was shocked by her boldness. Hadn't expected anything like this to happen. Couldn't believe that he was sitting naked with her kneeling between his legs, kissing him, torturing him.

Her tongue was presently circling his flat, brown nipple. Softly he groaned, took hold of her upper arms and gently set her back.

"Let's undress you and—"

"No," she said with calm authority. "Not yet. First I am going to love you the way you loved me."

"No, I can't...."

"Yes, you can," she interrupted and rose to her feet. "Stretch out on your stomach, Sutton."

He was torn—he *had* to keep the upper hand with this beautiful Jezebel. He could not allow himself to fall under her spell again, the way he had when he was a naive boy.

But the prospect of her soft, warm lips caressing his taut body was tempting. And the first thing he knew he was obeying her. Sutton turned and stretched out on the bed while Laurette kicked off her kid slippers.

"I wish you'd undress, too," he tried one last time.

"I will," she promised as she settled herself on the edge of the bed beside him and leaned down to press a warm kiss to the nape of his neck.

For the next half hour Sutton was suspended in sweet agony. Laurette's unbound hair teased and tickled him as she scattered kisses along his arms, across his shoulders and down his back. He moaned and folded his arms beneath his face as she kissed a line down his spine, her hands lightly gripping his ribs. And he tensed when he felt her face against the tight right cheek of his buttocks. He exhaled heavily when she licked his skin and groaned deeply when she teasingly bit him.

Laurette's teeth abruptly released Sutton's flesh. Her tongue deserted him. Her face lifted. Several seconds passed. Sutton ground his teeth, waiting, wanting more. Frowning, Laurette stared at the strange-looking scar on his left buttock. She laid a gentle hand on him and, with the tip of her forefinger, traced the scar's borders.

She felt his buttock flex beneath her hand. "What happened?" she asked. "How did you get this scar?"

"It's not a scar," he said, "it's a birthmark."

Laurette was immediately skeptical. "Really? It looks like the scar from an old wound and it—it looks like letters, the letters DC."

"You're imagining things," he said and lithely rolled over onto his back. He sat up and took her in his arms.

"I'm not," she said with a smile. "You, Sutton Vane, have the letters DC on your rear. Turn back over, I want to look at—"

"I've a better idea," he said and kissed her. When his lips left hers, he told her, "All day I've thought of nothing but how much I want you. Take off your clothes and let me make love to you."

Without a second thought she nodded, rose from the bed and, turning her back to him, began unbuttoning her wool dress.

"Why," he asked, "have you turned away from me?"

"I—I don't know, I just always…"

"Look at me."

Laurette slowly turned to face him. "Never be shy with me, Laurette. Never try to hide yourself from me. You have a beautiful body. Please allow me to admire it to my heart's content."

"All right," she said and began undressing while he gazed at her.

When she was as naked as he, he summoned her to the bed. She sat down on its edge, facing him. He took one of her hands and placed it on his hot, rigid flesh. Her slender fingers eagerly curled around him and she was awed by the heat and power she held.

"You're a slender, fragile woman and I don't want to hurt you," Sutton said, brushing her hair back off her shoulder. He lowered his hand to cover hers where it gripped him. He said, "I want to give pleasure with this, not pain."

She leaned up and kissed him and said softly, "I want you so much I'm certain there will be little or no discomfort."

Sutton felt his heart hammer in his naked chest. He shuddered when she released him, then agilely climbed onto the bed, threw a slender leg over and sat down astride his hips. At the first touch of her flesh against his, his erection surged upward, seeking her warmth. Laurette shivered at his involuntary response.

But, wanting to prolong the anticipation, she made him wait, did not immediately let him come inside her. Her hands lightly gripping his ribs, she leaned down, kissed him hotly and let her soft breasts brush back and forth against his broad chest. She felt his hands come up and cup the cheeks of her bottom.

"Ah, sweetheart," he murmured, "don't torture me so."

She raised her head, looked at him and said earnestly, "I would never do that. Never." She sat up straight and said what he'd said to her last night, "Watch me love me you, Sutton. Look at me. Don't close your eyes."

He didn't.

Aroused as he'd rarely been in his life, Sutton lay there on his back and watched as this beautiful blond temptress slowly raised up onto her knees, took him gently in both her hands and carefully guided the pulsing, blood-filled tip of his erection just inside her. To his amazement, she was so hot and wet that he realized she was as aroused as he. He liked that. He wanted her so excited she hardly knew what she was doing.

He loved it when she released him, tossed her wild hair back off her face, laid her hands on the tops of her thighs and slowly, sensuously rotating her hips and drawing in the taut muscles of her stomach, slid down the full, rigid length of him. Both moaned at the marvelous meeting and melding of hard male and soft female flesh. It was as if their bodies had been especially designed to accommodate and pleasure the other.

As it had last night, a wicked thought ran through Laurette's mind that she'd like to keep him forever just as he was now. Inside her. Filling her.

Much the same thoughts were going through Sutton's head.

He was totally dazzled by Laurette. Dazzled by her sweet, tight body so easily accepting him, taking him up inside, gripping him deliciously, making him her own. He waited indulgently while she carefully settled herself on him, getting totally relaxed, sighing as she found just the right position.

"Comfortable?" he finally inquired.

"Totally," she replied. "Heaven on earth."

"I know," he said, agilely rolling up into a sitting

position. He put his arms around her, drew his long legs up, crossed them, and sat Indian style.

"I like this," she said, wrapping her arms around his dark head and clasping his sides with her bent knees.

"So do I," he replied, moving his lips to the pale pink nipple rubbing against his bearded chin.

"Oh, yes," she sighed as he suckled her and began the rolling, thrusting motions of his pelvis.

The naked pair sat there in the middle of the bed on that cold, rainy afternoon and made passionate love. The first session didn't last all that long. They were so hot for each other that they had hardly begun the rolling, rhythmic movements of lovemaking before they felt their shared release overwhelming them.

Neither minded.

Both knew they had all afternoon.

After that first urgent climax had passed and they had calmed somewhat, they switched to a different position and began to make lazy, leisurely love, looking into each other's eyes as they came together.

For Laurette, the lovemaking was absolutely wonderful. Sutton enjoyed it too—so much so that he had to constantly remind himself, as she clung so sweetly to him, that making love with this particular woman was no different from making love to dozens of others. Pleasurable, of course, but that was all.

The fevered union involved only his body, not his heart. A heart once badly broken was forever immune to pain. His certainly was. This woman whose soft, yielding body accepted him so readily was no one special.

The lovemaking was nothing special.

While it might not have been special for Sutton, it was very special for Laurette. Utterly divine. She had never guessed that such physical pleasure was possible.

Now hours after they'd come upstairs, darkness was quickly falling. Laurette, lying warmly in Sutton's arms, was so stated and peaceful she fell asleep.

For a time Sutton continued to hold her and to gaze at her angelic face, her exquisite body. She looked so young, so innocent. He felt his heart squeeze painfully in his chest.

She had no idea what his true intentions were. She believed that he cared for her, wanted to be with her, was giving himself to her in the same sincere way she was giving herself to him.

Sutton closed his eyes. His jaw tensed. His belly contracted.

Perhaps what he was doing to her was too cruel, too inhumane. His eyes opened, then narrowed. He hardened his heart. He carefully untangled himself from Laurette and rose from the bed. He picked up the bedcovers and spread them over her. He placed one pillow beside her face.

Then he dressed to leave.

When Laurette awakened a short time later, she found a note on the pillow along with one white rose. The note read, ''Till tomorrow.'' Laurette sighed with happiness. Taking the note and the rose with her, she walked naked down the hall to her bedroom. There she placed the note on her bedside table and the rose in a crystal bud vase.

She drew on a robe and went downstairs. Starving, she hurried into the kitchen and ate a cold supper of cheese and bread and drank a glass of milk. When she had finished, she went back upstairs. She started toward the master suite at the front of the mansion but suddenly stopped.

Laurette decided that although it was surely shameful, she would skip her nightly bath. Sutton's kisses and his scent clung to her body and she was reluctant to wash him away. With a wicked grin she returned to the guest room where they had spent the lovely afternoon.

The rain had finally stopped. The moon had risen. Laurette opened the curtains to let the moonlight spill in. She took off the robe and crawled naked back into the love-tumbled bed.

Sutton filled her thoughts and she wondered at her deep and immediate fascination for this particular man. From the minute she'd seen him at the Ivys' party, she had been totally captivated. And, contradictory as it seemed, while he was a total stranger, he was, somehow, hauntingly familiar.

That mysterious feeling of familiarity drew her helplessly to him. Yet something about him frightened her, some elusive thing she couldn't put her finger on. He was not like any man she'd ever known. He could be incredibly charming and witty. He could also be quiet and somber. He could, she had noted with interest, sit perfectly still for an hour, not moving a muscle or blinking an eyelash. And, he was very powerful in his stillness. It gave one a sense that he was combustible.

Dangerous.

There was, Laurette felt, something secret, something hidden, something Sutton didn't want her to know. He asked her many questions, not just about herself, but about all her friends, to which she'd gladly supplied answers. But when she questioned him, she often got only vague replies. Why? What was he hiding? And why, she wondered, did he have such a poor appetite? His tanned body was beautiful to her, but it was lean to the point of thinness. And no wonder. No matter how tempting the meal, Sutton ate very little.

Laurette pulled the covers tighter.

She was suddenly trembling and it was with doubt and fear, not the recollection of shared passion. She was afraid of Sutton Vane and she didn't know why. She immediately chided herself for her foolishness. She certainly hadn't feared him enough to stay out of his arms, out of his bed.

And that worried her. She couldn't believe how she had behaved with this man. Was behaving. Would continue to behave for as long as he desired her. It made no sense. With the exception of the sweet, urgent loving she'd shared with Ladd all those years ago, Laurette had never enjoyed intimacy. She had loathed making love with her husband, had spent all the years with Jimmy dreading his touch, wishing he would leave her alone.

Then along came this dark, mysterious stranger and from the moment she saw him she couldn't wait to be in his arms. And when Sutton took her in his arms, it was as if she had always belonged there.

As if she belonged to him.

Twenty-Eight

"**I** passed a vacant lot on Canal Street last week. Find out if it's for sale. If it is, buy it. If not, locate another large, desirable lot downtown that is available," said Sutton to Bones.

Bones nodded and scribbled "Canal Street lot" on a page in the well-worn leather binder that was open on his knees. "We'll get right on it."

"Meet with the architect who designed the island house. Tell him to draw up plans for a floral shop with a large greenhouse in back."

Again Bones nodded, unquestioning. "Anything else?"

Sutton reached for the silver box that held his fine Cuban cigars. He took a cigar from the box and nipped off the end with the cigar clippers. Putting it into his mouth, he lit a match by striking it on his thumbnail.

Bones, seated across the mahogany desk, waited patiently for Sutton's next request.

The cigar now lit, Sutton blew out a narrow plume of smoke and said, "Have one of our men visit the Orphans Asylum on St. Francis. He is to speak with the director, Mrs. Abigail Young. Find out from Mrs.

Young if any or all of the children would be interested in taking piano lessons. Explain that the lessons will be free, but the benefactor has requested that his or her identity remain unknown.'' Sutton stopped speaking, drew on his cigar, exhaled, then tapped its ash in a crystal ashtray.

"That it?" Bones asked.

"For now," said Sutton. "How long will these little tasks take?"

"We should have some answers for you within forty-eight hours at the latest."

"Sounds good. Thanks, Bones."

"Don't mention it," said the burly man as he closed his leather journal and rose to his feet.

Declaring he could not stay away from her, Sutton made it a point to be with Laurette every moment she was free. And, he made love to her anytime he could manage to get her alone for a few minutes or a few hours.

Laurette was dazzled, overwhelmed, obsessed with him. Willing and ready to fall into his arms wherever and whenever, she savored every thrilling moment of their lovemaking. Every touch, every kiss was magical. She made no attempt to conceal the fact that she was wild about him.

Wanting desperately to believe that he felt the same way about her, Laurette pushed aside any lingering doubts about this man who had turned her humdrum world upside down. Sutton Vane had made such a wonderful difference in her life, she would be forever grateful to him. She told herself not to look ahead, not to worry about tomorrow, not to wonder where this passionate affair would lead. She cautioned herself not to assume that it would last. Something this wonderful rarely did.

At the same time she prayed that it would. Already the thought of losing him was unbearable. He was everything to her. Until she met Sutton, Laurette had felt as if her life was over, that she would never know true happiness again.

She had been wrong.

She had never been happier than she was now.

Sutton showed up at the Dauphin Street mansion a half hour early on a balmy evening in mid-February.

"Oh, no!" Laurette lamented as she grabbed a robe and raced down the stairs.

"I know I'm early," he said apologetically when she opened the door. Smiling, he reached out with both hands, gripped the satin lapels of her dressing robe, drew her slowly to him and whispered, "Forgive me?"

"I'll think about it," she teased, then nearly swooned when he drew her up on tiptoe and kissed her ardently.

"Know why I'm early?" he asked.

"I can't imagine."

"I was hoping I'd catch you like this, not yet dressed." His blue eyes gleamed and she read his meaning. "You have anything on under that robe? I don't think you do."

"No, Sutton," she scolded, smiling, as she pulled free of his arms. "There isn't time. If we're to meet the Ivys at eight, then I must hurry back upstairs and get dressed."

"Need any help?" His arched eyebrows lifted devilishly.

"Absolutely not," she said. "Wait in the drawing room and I'll be down in five minutes."

She turned away. He caught her arm and drew her back. He kissed her and said, "I can hardly wait to get back from the theater."

"Nor can I," she honestly admitted.

As she hurriedly climbed the stairs, Sutton moved toward the arched doorway of the drawing room, but didn't go inside. Instead, he turned and wandered aimlessly down the long corridor toward the back of the house. He paused when he reached the open door of the music room. Light from the hallway spilled into the shadowy room.

He smiled.

A sad, melancholy smile.

At the room's center sat the same large, square piano—ornately carved from black mahogany—upon which he and Laurette had learned to play while their teacher, the genteel Miss Foster, stood over them.

So many years ago.

A lifetime ago.

Sutton ventured inside. He let his hand sweep across the piano's top. The wood was dusty. The piano, he was sure, had not been played for a very long time. He sat down on the bench. His long fingers settled comfortably on the ivory keys. Without thinking, he automatically began playing the Chopin's polonaise that he and Laurette had learned when they were children.

He caught himself after playing only a few distinctive notes. He ground his teeth and his hands immediately stilled on the keys. His heart hammered.

Laurette, dressed and halfway down the stairs when the first familiar chord was struck, stopped abruptly, leaned against the bannister and put a hand to her fluttering heart. She shook her head as if to clear it.

She shivered and the fine hair lifted on the nape of her neck. Why, she wondered, should this upset her? Why should Sutton playing this particular piece upset her so? The polonaise was part of every talented player's repertoire. And Sutton was talented. At everything he did.

Feeling both chilled and flushed, Laurette forced herself to take deep, relaxing breaths. She told herself that she was behaving foolishly. Ghosts from the past were haunting her. Would always haunt her.

Finally she exhaled, began to smile and proceeded on down the stairs. A coincidence, that's all it was. Nothing more. She was being silly.

"Your piano is badly out of tune," said Sutton, now strolling back up the hall toward her, "I'll send someone around to work on it."

Laurette stopped on the bottom step of the stairs. She looked at him and said, "I didn't know you played."

"I don't," he said as he moved closer and put his hands to her waist. "Do you?"

"No, not really." She needlessly cleared her throat and started to ask why he had chosen the piece of music he had begun playing. But before she could speak he silenced her with a kiss. By the time his warm, smooth lips left hers, she had forgotten the question.

"We're late, love," he said, "Let's go."

After an evening at the theater where the renowned stage actress Ada Rehan gave a magnificent performance as Katherine in *The Taming of the Shrew*, Laurette and Sutton said good-night to the Ivys and went directly to Sutton's Government Street mansion. There they shared a late supper, complete with chilled champagne, upstairs in Sutton's private suite. After the sumptuous meal, they made love in the big, oversize bed while a fire in the marble fireplace cast a warm golden glow over their naked, entwined bodies.

By the time Sutton took the sleepy Laurette home in the wee small hours of the morning, he knew without a doubt that she—just as he had intended—was beginning to fall in love with him.

Laurette was surprised, but not alarmed, when Sutton wasn't waiting in his carriage near the hospital steps as had become his custom. She wrinkled her brow when she saw the empty street. She looked both ways, but saw nothing coming in either direction. She waited a few minutes, reasoning that he might have gotten away from his house late and would arrive any second.

When fifteen minutes had passed with no sign of him, Laurette began to feel uneasy. Then she laughed at herself for being anxious. He was probably on the way to her house this very minute. Laurette hurried down the steps and began walking fast, toward home. Once there, she built the fire, then freshened up, certain that Sutton would knock on the door any minute.

He did not.

Seven.

Eight.

Nine o'clock passed and still he had not come. Laurette tried to think back; had he told her that he was tied up this evening? That he wouldn't be able to make it?

No, he hadn't. He had said, as he had kissed her good-night, that he would see her the minute she was finished at the hospital.

Puzzled, Laurette restlessly paced the drawing room, wondering what could have happened. Where was he? Her stomach was beginning to churn and she felt as if she was going to scream if he didn't arrive soon. Surely there was a reasonable explanation.

Ten o'clock came and went, the chimes of the hall clock struck the late hour, startling her, mocking her. She finally realized that she might as well go up to bed. He wasn't coming. It was as simple as that.

Laurette shook her head in denial. He *would* come. He would. And soon. She would wait a while longer.

At eleven, a confused and disappointed Laurette

tiredly climbed the stairs. Once in bed, she lay awake, edgy and upset. She had the terrible feeling that something was very wrong, that Sutton had stayed away on purpose. That he hadn't wanted to see her that evening.

But she so wanted to believe that everything was all right, that Laurette convinced herself that one evening's absence meant nothing. After all, Sutton had been with her every night since their first evening out together. She didn't own him. He had other friends besides her. Perhaps some of those friends had shown up at his house unannounced. He couldn't very well turn them away; he was too kind and well-mannered to do that.

As she finally drifted toward slumber, Laurette assured herself that tomorrow Sutton would sweep through her front door, take her in his arms and explain everything.

It never happened.

Days passed and Laurette didn't see him, didn't hear from him. A full week went by and she was completely bewildered by his pointed absence. Hurt and heartsick, she wondered what she had done wrong. She couldn't go to him and ask, she could only wait and wonder.

In an elegant corner suite at the luxurious St. Louis Hotel in New Orleans's bustling French Quarter, Sutton lolled lazily in a tub filled to the brim with hot, sudsy water as the February sun set over the city.

In one hand he held a Cuban cigar, in the other a

snifter of brandy. His hooded eyes were almost closed, but his bearded jaw was ridged with tautness. He was, to his chagrin, bored and he was lonely. *She* kept intruding into his thoughts and that rankled him. He hadn't counted on thinking about her, missing her.

Hell, he *didn't* miss her; he was just suffering twinges of guilt from what he was doing to her. By now she was confused and upset at his sudden disappearance. Good! Let her worry and wonder and miss him. That was, after all, the purpose of this stay in New Orleans.

Sutton crushed out his cigar in a porcelain ashtray beside the tub. He drained his snifter of brandy, set the glass aside and rose to his feet. He began to smile as he toweled his lean body dry. Tonight he had a late engagement with one of the city's most beautiful raven-haired belles.

Gossip had it that the lovely, twenty-three-year-old Miss Caroline Summers, this year's Mardi Gras queen, was a bit of a tart who knew how to give a gentleman, married or single, an enjoyable time in bed. Sutton assumed it was true because, after being introduced to her last evening at a wine supper, the beautiful Caroline had leaned up and whispered in his ear, "Would you like to make love to me, Mr. Vane?"

Momentarily taken aback, Sutton had glanced warily at her father, who stood nearby and softly replied, "While I'm most flattered, Miss Summers, as you can see, I'm with someone." He nodded toward the wealthy widow he had accompanied to the party.

"Her? Why she's old enough to be your mother!" Caroline sniffed.

Sutton had chuckled softly. "Mrs. Sullivan is not exactly in her dotage, Caroline. She is a very young forty-one."

"I've been around as much as she has," said the brazen Caroline. "I'll show you a thing or two she's never heard of."

Sutton had nodded and said, "Tomorrow night?"

"Yes. Midnight. I have an earlier engagement."

"Midnight it is," Sutton agreed. "My suite at the St. Louis Hotel."

"I'll be there," she had said, dimpling prettily and fluttering her long, dark lashes.

Caroline Summers was exactly the kind of companion he needed tonight. A tempting young beauty with no inhibitions, no morals, no expectations.

Sutton glanced at the clock. Nearing nine. Caroline was to arrive at the stroke of midnight, so he had some time to kill. He dressed in a pair of pearl-gray trousers and matching frock coat, white starched shirt and maroon cravat with black pearl stickpin.

He poured himself another brandy, drank it down in one long swallow, then went downstairs and out into the street where he hailed a carriage.

"Toussaint's," he said to the driver, settled back and looked forward to a pleasant interlude at the plush gambling hall.

Once there, Sutton played high stakes poker with a quartet of well-heeled gentlemen. Lady Luck was with him. He won several thousand dollars. Remembering that he had an engagement at midnight, he subtly withdrew his gold-cased watch from his waistcoat pocket and checked the time.

He frowned. It was half-past midnight. But he couldn't get up and leave. Not when he was winning. He would be labeled a bad sport. He would have to wait until the others called an end to the game.

That didn't happen until almost 2:00 a.m. Sutton didn't rush to get back to the hotel. He felt sure Miss Summers had grown angry and left by now. To his astonishment, when he entered his suite, the lovely, milky-skinned Caroline was stretched out naked on his bed, striking a most provocative pose when he entered the room.

"My apologies. I didn't expect you to wait," he said, pointedly examining her plump, luscious body.

"Five more minutes and I would have been gone," she said, petulantly. Patting the mattress beside her, she said, "Now come here and make it up to me."

Sutton lay awake in the darkness.

Dawn was not far off. Caroline had left hours ago. She had lived up to her reputation—had been an eager and aggressive lover who couldn't seem to get enough. Brazen and experienced, she had, as soon as he'd gotten undressed, laughed at him and said, "You're not going to do me any good if you stay like that!"

"Maybe you can coax it to life," he had said, laughing with her, glancing down at his flaccid flesh.

"I guarantee it," she bragged.

And she had.

Why, he wondered now, had he tired of her long before she said good-night? It made no sense. She was everything a man could want in a woman. She was breathtakingly beautiful with a voluptuous body made for pleasure. When he'd first walked into the room and saw her lying there naked, he'd supposed that was it was going to be a most enjoyable night.

He'd had no trouble performing; Caroline had experienced several orgasms, but he had been oddly disinterested, detached. He had been able to hold his erection for a long time, a fact that had thrilled the greedy Caroline. It had been easy for him, because he was not fully engaged, not awed by her. He had learned, long ago, that he could hold his erection for an hour, sometimes longer, which made him a sought-after lover. It was a trick of control he was capable of with all women.

Sutton's brow suddenly knitted.

Not *all* women.

He was no longer able to hold an erection that long with Laurette. Even when he'd tried, he found it impossible. Sutton shuddered in the darkness. Why? Why was it different with her? Why did she make him so unbelievably hot that he could no longer control his body? Why could a simple look or touch from her bring him to the edge of climax?

No matter.

It was probably because she had—all those years ago—been his very first lover. When he was with her now, perhaps a part of him reverted back to being that bedazzled young boy who had been so much in love with her.

Well, he was no longer that gullible fool and would never be again.

Sutton was confident that this part of his plan—his unexplained absence—was likely working. He'd bet all the thousands he had won at the tables that he could go to Laurette this very night and she would willingly come into his arms because she was falling in love with him.

Sutton raised his long arms, folded his hands beneath his head. His heavily lashed eyes closed and he smiled to himself. He would sentence her to another week of loneliness and anxiety. Let her miss him so much she didn't sleep well, couldn't eat. Let her give up hope that he would ever return. Let her hear about his various escapades in New Orleans.

By the time he got back to her, she'd be on her knees, a willing slave to her beloved master.

Twenty-Nine

He felt as if they were closing in on him.

He jumped at the slightest unexpected sound or noise. He got the shakes often and for no apparent reason. Each time he went out on the street, he had the eerie feeling that he was being watched, that someone was following him, waiting to catch him alone.

The nervous, overweight, one-eyed Gilbert LaKid abruptly rose from the wooden eating table where he was seated. The hair on the back of his neck rising, he lumbered across the spartan, rented room where he lived alone. The old ramshackle building was located on a near deserted street in a seedy, run-down section of Washington, D.C. It was one of the many addresses he had had in the past several years.

He had kept on the move, drifting from city to city, taking odd jobs to get by, making few friends, hiding from the demons he was certain were after him.

LaKid stood unmoving for a long moment in front of the closed door, listening, waiting. He finally eased the door open and cautiously looked out, half expecting to see a figure waiting in the shadows.

A black cat, eyes flashing in the darkness, frightened by LaKid's sudden appearance, hissed and knocked over a full garbage can. The spoiled contents spilled across LaKid's front stoop and he cursed under his breath. He slammed the wooden door shut, bolted it and returned to the table.

Edgy, restless, he picked up an envelope resting on the table. The postmark was London, England. The date was March, 1881. LaKid took out the letter and read it through for the fourth time since receiving it that morning.

Dear Gilbert,

Thank you for sending some money. I truly appreciate the helping hand, as I am unemployed and in dire straits.

Let me warn you once more to be very careful. Dasheroon was responsible for my ruin, and he will come after you, mark my words.

The man is smart and he is ruthless. Combine this quality of ruthlessness with sterling administrative ability and you have Ladd Dasheroon, regardless of the name he now goes by. I have no idea what name he is using.

You must remember that one of the qualities which most of us carry around, usually a product of conscience, is mercy. Dasheroon is startlingly and completely devoid of any such civilized quality. He is hard and ruthless with a burning intensity usually reserved for the early Christian martyrs. Beware, old comrade, beware.

Sincerely,
James Tigart

LaKid carefully refolded the letter from Tigart and returned it to the envelope. The two had kept in touch through the years. Tigart was LaKid's only real friend, so he sent what little money he could afford to his former boss on occasion.

LaKid placed a cup of cold coffee atop the envelope, rose and paced the dimly lit room, feeling as if he were going to jump out of his skin. He had the strong premonition that something bad was going to happen. Tigart's letter had strengthened that unsettling feeling.

He mentally shook himself, then stormed over to the small cupboard, yanked open the doors and took down a bottle that had once held bourbon. It was empty. Only a few precious drops left. LaKid swore, uncorked the bottle, turned it up and drained the contents.

Angry that there was no more whiskey, he sailed the bottle across the room. It hit the slatted wooden wall, broke into a hundred pieces and scattered all across the floor. Barefooted, wearing only his dirty underwear, LaKid swore anew as his big toe touched a sliver of glass and bright-red blood appeared.

"Son of a bitch!" he bellowed, hopping around on one foot.

He sat down on the edge of his cot and wiped the

blood from his toe with the corner of his blanket. He lay down, folded his arms beneath his head and tried to sleep.

It was impossible.

He reached for a cigar on the night table at his elbow. Then remembered. There were none. He had smoked the last one after his unappetizing supper, hours earlier.

He had nothing to drink, nothing to smoke.

He raised up, looked at the clock. Almost midnight. Too late to go out. It wasn't safe. He lay back down and his thoughts turned—as they so often did—to Ladd Dasheroon.

LaKid ground his teeth in frustration. He should have killed the skinny Reb bastard when he'd had the chance! Why couldn't the bothersome son of a bitch have died in the dungeon the way they had planned? How could he have survived all those years in the dark cell?

Well, he had, like it or not. Dasheroon was alive, living under an assumed name and posing a constant threat to him. There was no doubt in LaKid's mind that Dasheroon was searching for him. He would have to spend the rest of his life looking over his shoulder.

LaKid rose from his cot. He went back to the table and searched for the butt of an unfinished cigar. There was nothing but cold ash in the saucer.

LaKid scratched his belly and thought how good a drink would taste. He smacked his lips. He worked up his courage, told himself he was being ridiculous.

Nothing was going to happen to him. He wasn't afraid. He was afraid of no man. He was not a coward. He would damn well go out and have himself a drink when he wanted to and the devil take the hindermost!

LaKid looked around for his clothes. They lay in a wrinkled heap on the wooden floor beside his cot. He picked up his trousers and shirt and starting getting dressed, humming tunelessly as he did so.

What was there to worry about? Not a thing. If Dasheroon hadn't been able to find him in all these years, he never would. He had probably stopped trying long ago. Hell, Dasheroon likely had forgotten he existed.

Feeling a little more like his old self, LaKid left his ground floor room and walked in the unusually warm March night the three blocks to Darcy's Tavern. A handful of men were in the saloon. All were familiar—he had nothing to worry about.

LaKid stepped up to the bar and was immediately joined by a flashily dressed woman whose full, heavy bosom was mostly exposed in a low-cut bodice. She was a fixture at Darcy's. For a five-dollar gold piece, she would take you upstairs for the night. She wasn't pretty. Her dyed hair was too red, her face too garishly painted, her figure too full.

She looked good to Gilbert LaKid.

Snapping his fingers to awaken the dozing barkeep, LaKid barked, "Whiskey. And leave the bottle." He turned his one eye on the smiling woman and said, "How much for thirty minutes?"

She giggled, hugged his huge arm and told him, "Give me a dollar."

An hour after arriving at Darcy's, a drunken Gilbert LaKid stepped back out into the darkness. He whistled merrily as he made his way home.

It happened so fast he never had time to react.

When he was only a few short steps from his front door, LaKid grunted in stunned shock as he was grabbed from behind and slammed back against his tall attacker. His pudgy hands clawing at the steely arm holding him immobile, LaKid felt the quick, deep slice of the blade as his throat was cut from ear to ear.

Blood spurting, gasping for breath, LaKid managed the words, "Damn you, Ladd Dasheroon!"

"Who the hell's Ladd Dasheroon?" said the assassin to his accomplice as LaKid fell to the sidewalk, dead.

Laurette was crushed and heartbroken.

She slept fitfully at night, a few short hours at a time. Many nights it was nearing dawn before she finally fell tiredly to sleep. Her healthy appetite was missing; she had to force herself to eat. Alone in the privacy of her empty house, she allowed the tears to fall. She sat before the fire, stared unseeing into the shooting flames and cried. Without Sutton in it, her life once again seemed dreary and unbearable.

Laurette had finally—after they had asked repeatedly—confessed her disappointment and despair to the Parlange twins. Both had genuinely sympathized and promised her they would say nothing, would tell no one. Worried about her, the sisters came to visit often, almost every evening. They brought foods to tempt Laurette, insisted that she eat and tried to cheer her up.

"Oh, dearest friend," said Johanna one evening, putting a comforting arm around Laurette's slender shoulders, "while Mr. Vane is a master charmer and sinfully handsome, he isn't worth your anguish. You must forget about him."

The wise, usually quiet Juliette looked sternly at her twin. "It isn't that simple or easy, is it Laurette?"

"No. No, it's not," Laurette replied, then said, "I am such a fool. You see, I have…I've fallen in love with Sutton Vane."

Johanna looked horrified.

Juliette nodded in understanding.

The twins said in unison, "In time, you will forget." Johanna added, "Just as you have finally forgotten Ladd."

"Yes, of course, I will forget," Laurette said, knowing that she would not.

At the Confederate Veteran's Convalescent Hospital, Laurette kept up a brave front. She made herself appear cheerful and relaxed, as if she had not a care in the world.

But she was further aggrieved when she heard from the sharp-tongued Nora Huffington, a gossiping nurse's aide, that the wealthy, devilish Sutton Vane was presently in New Orleans where he'd been seen out on the town with a different Creole beauty every evening.

The unkind busybody turned to Laurette with a sly look and said, "Oh, Mrs. Tigart, I'm sorry. I had forgotten, you've been seeing Mr...."

"I attended the theater with Mr. Vane and Colonel and Mrs. Ivy a time or two," Laurette stated calmly. "As a favor to the Colonel. I really don't know Mr. Vane very well."

Laurette smiled serenely and turned back to folding bandages. But she was shaking inside and counting the minutes until she could leave. She wanted nothing more than to flee to the blessed sanctuary of her home.

She was, she knew, behaving as a smitten, starry-eyed schoolgirl. Since she wasn't sixteen, but thirty-six, she should have known better. She should have had more sense. It was not surprising that a man like Sutton Vane would quickly lose interest. She could hardly blame him. She hadn't exactly played it smart where he was concerned.

She shuddered to think that the very first time Sutton had wanted to make love to her, she had quickly surrendered, eagerly giving herself to him. She had been an easy conquest, no challenge whatsoever.

No wonder he had become bored with her.

March had come to Mobile, but winter was making one last stubborn stand. On a raw, gray Saturday afternoon with a light sleet falling and the sky as dark as pitch, Laurette left the hospital after a long tiring day.

Shivering, she walked quickly home, the miserable weather matching her glum mood.

She let herself in the front door and immediately paused, puzzled.

The house was mysteriously warm.

Thirty

The door closed quietly behind her.

The only sound she heard was that of a crackling fire. Frowning now, Laurette anxiously stepped into the drawing room where a fire blazed in the grate and Sutton, totally naked, sat on the floor before the dancing flames. He sipped brandy from a crystal snifter.

Sutton looked up, smiled disarmingly, and raising his brandy said, "Welcome home, Laurette."

The sudden, unexpected sight of him caused her heart to miss a beat or two. Foolishly longing to throw herself into his arms and press kisses all over his handsome face, she glared at him.

"How did you get into this house? I always keep the doors locked and—"

"I have a key," he said with no apology.

Her eyes widened. "You have a...? You've no right to have a key to—"

"Ah, but I do," he corrected her. "I own this house."

She shot him a wilting look and shook her head. "For your information, a large company owns this house now. The Bay Minette Corporation." He nodded knowingly. Flabbergasted, she swallowed hard, then snapped, "Just what do you think you're doing without any clothes?"

"My clothes were wet," he replied, "as are yours."

Her chin elevated pugnaciously, she quickly shrugged out of her long, sleet-dampened cape and tossed it over his lap as she ordered, "Get dressed and get out."

To which he calmly replied, "Get undressed and get down here."

Insulted, she said, "You, Sutton Vane, are an arrogant bastard and if you do not vacate the premises at once, I shall summon the authorities!"

He tossed aside the cape she had thrown over him and agilely rose to his feet. He waited a couple of heartbeats before making another move and she realized that he was giving her the opportunity to turn and flee if she so desired. She strongly considered it. She knew that's what she should do.

But how could she leave when he stood gloriously naked before her, his tall, lean body, burnished by the firelight, a study in male perfection.

When she didn't move, Sutton reached out and took her in his arms, drawing her against his frame. At first she tried to free herself, but his will was stronger than hers. He kissed her then, and continued kissing her until she was short of breath and her heart was beating rapidly in her own ears.

In minutes they sank weakly to their knees before the fire and continued to kiss each other ardently, hungrily. When finally, after at least a dozen heated, probing kisses, Sutton took his lips from Laurette's, he gently cupped her flushed face in his tanned hands and said, "I cannot wait another minute to make love to you."

"No!" her inborn spirit rose and she declared hotly, "No. You can't just wander in and out of my life and expect me to—"

"There was a very good reason for my prolonged absence," he said.

"Fine! I'd like to hear it."

"And you will, as soon as we've made love," he replied as he bent and pressed his lips to her exposed throat. She felt the flick of his tongue against her flesh and it made her gasp.

Trying very hard to keep her wits about her, Laurette said, "Don't, Sutton. Stop it. Either you tell me why you—"

But his masterful lips silenced her and she soon surrendered to the searing passion he had aroused in her. Within seconds she was as naked as he and glad that she was.

While the sleet tapped against the windowpanes and the winter darkness engulfed the river city, Sutton stretched out on his back and drew her to lie atop him.

For the next half hour Sutton made love to Laurette the way he knew she best liked it. His weight supported on stiffened forearms, he watched her beautiful face change expressions as he teased and aroused her.

Finally, he flexed his firm buttocks and drove deeply into her. She sighed with building ecstasy. He changed the tempo of his lovemaking, thrust more seekingly until he totally possessed her. She responded with a wild sweetness that gave him the same kind of pleasure he was giving her.

The lovemaking was incredible. Their shared orgasm wrenching. But when at last both were satiated and drowsy, Laurette said, "I'm still very angry with you. You should leave now. Go home."

Never raising his dark head from where it rested comfortably on her breasts, he said, "You don't mean that."

"I do," she said as she made a halfhearted attempt to rise.

He tightened an arm across her waist and accused, "You're behaving like a child."

"What would you know about being a child?" was her retort.

"Even I was a child once," he said with a yawn. "And I remember my childhood well."

"And yet you've never spoken of it."

"Some other time," he said as he lifted his dark head and looked at her. "I thought you wanted to know why you haven't seen me lately."

Laurette, snared by his merciless blue eyes, held her breath. "I do and this had better be good."

He rolled over onto his back beside her, drew her close and put a supporting arm beneath her head. "Sweetheart, I'm not going to lie about it. I stayed away from you because I am afraid."

"Afraid?" she murmured, incredulous. "You? Afraid of what?"

"Of falling hopelessly in love with you," he whispered against her temple.

Laurette's heart immediately pounded with joy. She was elated by his honest and touching confession. She understood exactly how he felt because she felt the very same way.

She didn't see the smug look of satisfaction in the depths of his eyes when she hugged him and purred, "Don't be afraid to love me, Sutton. I want you to love me." She raised her head, pushed her wild golden hair out of her eyes and said, "Darling, I love you, oh, I do."

To which he said, teasingly, "I hope you mean it, but I'm still not certain. Could you try to convince me?"

Wildly happy, Laurette laughed, kissed him and lovingly reassured him. "Darling, don't be afraid. Let yourself fall in love with me. You will never love me more than I love you. You're all I want, now and forever and I'll try to make you happy. As happy as I am now. I will never hurt you, my love. I love you, I love you! I've never loved anyone the way I love you."

"No one?"

"No one."

"Not even your husband?"

"No one, ever," she sighed. "Please, say that you feel the same."

"I do," he said, "I love you, Laurette. I'll never stop loving you."

Thirty-One

The unusually chilly winter of 1881 finally turned to a warm, beautiful spring in Mobile. The sweet heavy scent of magnolia and wisteria drifted in through the open windows of Laurette's home and the maidenhair ferns just beyond the veranda were a bright, brilliant green.

Laurette was a content, happy woman.

Since his admission that he was falling in love with her, Sutton had insisted that Laurette spend her every free minute with him. She sometimes wondered how Sutton passed the time while she was working at the hospital or calling on old friends. He had remarked that on occasion he played cards with Colonel Ivy at the Camellia Club.

When he was not with her, Sutton *was* occupied. But he never mentioned anything about his business to Laurette. He spent a great deal of time working quietly behind the scenes, meting out his brand of justice to those who had betrayed him.

His philosophy was that if a man—or a woman— had made you suffer for an untold number of years, then you did not wish to avenge yourself instantaneously. He believed you should make your enemy endure prolonged suffering.

Sutton was intensely frustrated that he had not been able to locate Gilbert LaKid. However, he had no intention of giving up the chase. If it took the rest of his life, he would find the cruel Captain of the Guards. And when he did, he had a very special punishment in mind for the monster who had tortured, beaten and branded him.

While Sutton believed in punishing his enemies, he was just as intent on helping out old friends who had been wronged or were in need. At the top of that list were Melba and Lydia Adair who had been swindled out of the money they'd made from the sale of their home.

Sutton suddenly smiled with satisfaction.

His team had been successful in locating Jackson Tate, the unprincipled cad who had bilked the trusting Adair ladies out of their meager savings. The thief had been returned to Mobile, stood trial and was now cooling his heels in the state penitentiary at Montgomery. Mr. Tate would be a guest of the state for at least the next ten years.

Unfortunately, Tate's apprehension and punishment had been of no help financially to the Adairs, since he had spent all of the stolen money within a few short weeks of getting his hands on it. Sutton felt very sorry for the Adairs. He wanted to help them while carefully allowing them to maintain their pride and dignity.

He had given the situation a great deal of thought

and had finally come up with a suitable solution. He would build and open a floral shop with a greenhouse—and hire the Adairs to operate it. Beautiful gardens had always been the ladies' passion and Laurette had told him that the impoverished pair now lived in rented quarters with no place to plant flowers or bushes.

Construction had already begun on the greenhouse, and when it was nearing completion he would have an agent visit the Adairs. The agent would offer them the position of running the floral shop for salaries that would be quite generous.

Sutton knew what their answer would be.

He rubbed his bearded chin and his eyes crinkled at the corners. His scheme for offering his old music teacher, the dear, patient Miss Foster, a helping hand had been even more successful than he'd hoped. As it turned out, nearly all the children at the Orphans Asylum had been eager to take piano lessons. It had been reported to him that Miss Foster, when approached to teach the children, was so overjoyed by the offer that tears had welled up in her eyes. It had happened again when the aging music teacher arrived at the orphanage and was shown the brand-new cherrywood piano upon which she was to give the lessons.

Sutton always had several irons in the fire, but his most important campaign, the one that took up the majority of his time and thoughts, was the justice he had planned for the deceitful Laurette Howard Tigart.

He had to be absolutely certain that Laurette had fallen deeply in love with him before he made his move. When that time came—a time to which he was eagerly looking forward—he would coldly leave her and quickly marry another woman. Any other woman.

So long as she was young and beautiful.

But the time had not yet come. It was too soon. Laurette was falling more in love with him each time they were together, but she was still not completely in his thrall. He wanted to be certain that his leaving her would completely break her heart. Just as she had broken his.

It was springtime and he was seeing to it that the golden days and silver nights they spent together were filled with fun and laughter and intensely pleasurable lovemaking. He made love to Laurette often and everywhere. At his Government Street mansion. At her Dauphin Street home. On his private yacht in the middle of Mobile Bay.

She was, he had learned, a very sexual being. She had never refused him, no matter how often he took her. No matter how he took her.

Sutton leaned back in his chair and clasped his hands behind his head. His eyes clouded slightly.

By summer's end, it would be finished.

"Looks like you've been cheated, boss," Bones said as he stepped into the shadowy study carrying his leather journal under his arm.

The statement snapped Sutton out of his deep reveries. He had been, for the past several minutes, mulling over the end of his affair with Laurette.

"I don't follow," Sutton said, looking up at his trusted lieutenant. "What has happened?"

"Somebody beat you to the punch. Gilbert LaKid was found murdered on the streets of Washington, D.C. His throat had been cut from ear to ear." Bones paused, took a seat and waited for Sutton to speak. Sutton, staring into space, said nothing. Bones continued, "Evidently you were not the only enemy he had. Somebody else wanted a piece of him. Makes sense. LaKid was obviously a sadistic bastard, so I imagine he tortured other prisoners the way he tortured you."

Sutton continued to sit, unmoving, unblinking, as if he hadn't absorbed what Bones was telling him. Bones grew slightly nervous. Should he repeat what he'd said. Had Sutton heard him? Understood what he had said?

Finally, Sutton looked up, focused and said softly, "LaKid is...dead?"

"Dead and in the grave," confirmed Bones, explaining that the news had come from reliable sources and the facts had been double-checked for accuracy. "It's all over, Sutton."

For a few more minutes, Sutton continued to sit quietly in his chair, saying no more, not moving a muscle. Bones remained silent, but he was growing increasingly nervous.

Sutton's hand lay atop the desk. Without a change of expression he closed it into a fist. When the knuckles were white, Sutton slammed his tight fist down against the desk with such intensity, Bones jumped, startled. As he watched, wide-eyed, Sutton shot up out of his chair so abruptly, the chair turned over.

His blue eyes gleaming as an animal's, his lean body coiled as tightly as a watch spring, the consistently calm, reserved Sutton Vane went into a rage. He kicked the overturned chair out of his way and charged the tall mahogany cabinet behind the desk.

He yanked open a drawer, reached in, scooped up a number of files and threw them to the carpeted floor. He reached for more, cursing loudly with frustration.

"That lucky son of a bitch!" he snarled, his face a dark mask of anger. "That cruel, evil bastard didn't deserve to die so easily!"

"I know," said Bones, on his feet now, "but maybe it's best this way. At least he—"

Sutton turned on his friend and bellowed so he could be heard throughout the mansion, "No, dammit, no! Hell, no! He deserved to suffer! Don't you understand, I wanted that bullet-headed, one-eyed bastard to suffer and suffer and suffer!"

Sutton whirled around and drove his fist into the cabinet, breaking the wooden drawer and bloodying his knuckles. The remaining files spilled out onto the floor.

"Stop!" said Bones, who hurriedly circled the desk and grabbed Sutton's fist in midair as he pulled back to throw another punch at the ruined file cabinet. His strength superior to Sutton's, Bones gripped Sutton's wrist, held it firm and said, "Sit down."

"I don't want to sit down, damn you," said Sutton. "Get the hell out of here and leave me alone!"

"I'm not leaving," Bones said calmly. "I'll get you a drink."

"I don't want a drink!" shouted Sutton. "Let go of my wrist!"

Bones refused. "Hit me if you must hit something," said Bones. "Hit me, my friend."

The two men stood toe-to-toe, the shorter, stockier Bones firmly gripping Sutton's wrist. Finally, the wildness left Sutton's eyes. His tall body slumped with relaxation. Bones released his wrist.

"Jesus, Bones, I'm sorry," Sutton said, shaking his head.

"No apology needed, boss," said Bones. "Believe me, I can understand your frustration and disappointment."

Bones went directly to the small bar in the study's corner. He took down a decanter of bourbon and two shot glasses. He filled the glasses, came back and handed one to Sutton.

"Drink up," he coaxed. Sutton nodded and downed his whiskey in one long swallow.

"Another?" inquired Bones.

"No, I'm fine now, really I am," Sutton assured him. "Better go upstairs and clean my bloody hand."

"Sure. I'll help," said Bones.

"Thanks, but I'd like to be alone for a while."

Bones, plucking nervously at the white crossbones stitched on the front of his shirt, said, "You're not going to do anything foolish, are you?"

Sutton finally flashed that million-dollar smile. He laid a hand on his friend's shoulder and said, "No,

I'm not going to hurt myself, so stop your worrying."
He turned and walked away. In the door he paused,
turned back and said, "I behaved like a child. It won't
happen again."

Bones nodded and said, "Look at it this way, Sutton, it is finally over. All over. LaKid was the last of
those who—"

"Not quite," Sutton interrupted and the smile left
his face. "There's one more."

Bones frowned and shook his head sadly.

Thirty-Two

It was a perfect evening for an outdoor band concert.

The temperature at 8:00 p.m. was a pleasant seventy-five degrees and a golden sunset over the Gulf promised fair skies and clear sailing for tomorrow. With the advent of spring, the woods beyond the city were bright with blossoms of wisteria, redbud, dogwood, magnolia, honeysuckle and yellow jasmine. Along the coast, miles of beaches, dunes, swamp, palmetto and moss-hung oaks created a magical world of tropical beauty.

It was simply the best season of all in the port city; the cold chill and gray skies of winter were gone and the hot, humid heat of summer had not yet set in. After being shut up inside for months, the citizens of Mobile were eager to get out and enjoy the mild weather.

Laurette and Sutton were among the appreciative crowd gathered downtown on Bienville Square on that warm May evening to enjoy the band concert and to mingle with friends.

The Old Guard of Mobile had quickly taken to Sutton Vane, something that rarely happened. They liked him and were eager to embrace him as one of their own.

And, those who knew her best, the friends who cared the most, all agreed that they hadn't seen Laurette so happy in years. There was a glow about her that had been there when she was a young, carefree girl. Her dark eyes sparkled with sheer delight each time she looked at her handsome escort.

Laurette made no effort to hide the fact that she absolutely adored this handsome man who had come into her life when she'd thought that there would be no more joy. Sutton had changed everything for her: the sun shone brightly, the birds sang sweetly and music was hauntingly beautiful.

As Sutton and Laurette moved closer to the band shell, a clearly excited Melba and Lydia Adair anxiously made their way through the crowd toward the hand-holding pair.

"Laurette, Laurette, dear," Melba said, reaching out to clasp Laurette's arm.

"Oh, hello, Melba, Lydia." Laurette was glad to see them. "You know Sutton Vane."

"Good evening, ladies," Sutton said with a smile.

Both women nodded to him and said, "Nice to see you, Mr. Vane." They turned their attention back to Laurette. "The most wonderful thing has happened to us, Laurette," enthused Melba.

"Oh? Tell us. We can't wait to hear, can we Sutton?"

"Indeed, we can't," he said.

"You two just won't believe what has happened,"

said Melba. She turned to her daughter and coaxed, "Tell them, Lydia."

Lydia, still uncomfortably shy, shook her head and lowered her eyes. "No, Mother, you tell them."

Melba said, "Lydia and I have been employed to run that new floral shop and greenhouse on Canal Street! We're so thrilled, we're like a couple of kids. The shop opens next week and we can hardly wait to get started!"

"That is wonderful, Melba," said Laurette, genuinely pleased for the two women. "I am so happy for you, that's the best news I've heard in ages."

"It is, isn't it? A miracle. A dream come true. You know that nothing gives us more pleasure than tending flowers and…and…just think, with the greenhouse, why we can have all kinds of exotic blossoms. Orchids and gardenias and roses in the middle of the winter. And, we'll get paid for our efforts! Can you believe it!" Melba finally let go of Laurette's arm and clapped her hands together.

"Yes, I can," said Laurette.

"I don't really know how it happened, but I suppose our talent for raising beautiful flowers and plants is well-known and that is why we were chosen to run the operation."

Nodding, Laurette said, "Yes, of course, that's the reason." She glanced at Sutton and explained, "The Adairs were once famous for their incredibly lush gardens, the most beautiful gardens in Mobile."

Sutton said, "Then the owner of the floral shop has certainly chosen correctly."

"Who is the owner?" Laurette asked.

"No single owner," said Melba. "As I understand it, a big company owns it. The Bay Minette Corporation, I believe it is."

"Oh?" Laurette replied and quickly glanced at Sutton.

His expression never changed, but his blue eyes flickered slightly. Laurette realized, with a rush of affection, that he was responsible for this fortunate turn of events for the desperate Adairs. Bay Minette owned the new floral shop? He *was* Bay Minette. He hardly knew the Adairs, yet he had done this expressly to help them out. Laurette was deeply touched.

After the Adairs moved on, she squeezed Sutton's hand and whispered, "You're a fraud, Sutton Vane."

"Am I?" His tone was casual.

"Yes. You, sir, are not what you appear to be."

"And just what do I appear to be?"

"A handsome, wealthy, selfish gentleman who lives only for hedonistic pleasure."

"Guilty as charged," he said with a devilish grin.

"No, you are not guilty. What you really are is a kind, generous, good-hearted man and what you've done for the grateful Adairs is admirable indeed."

"I have no earthly idea what you're talking about, love."

"Mmmm. Yes, you do, but don't worry. I won't say a word. If you prefer to keep your good deeds quiet, I will respect your wishes." She hugged his arm and whispered, "You have no idea just how

much I love you. More than ever before because I've
found you out."

Sutton smiled at her but said nothing. *You haven't
found me out, my dear. You have no idea who I really
am or what I intend to do to you.*

The couple moved leisurely through the growing
crowd as the concert continued, the violins in particular creating stunningly beautiful music.

A lady who appreciated nothing more than beautiful music stood near the band shell, hands clasped
to her heart, a dreamy expression on her wrinkled
face.

"Miss Foster," Laurette said, pulling the little music teacher from her reverie.

Miss Foster turned, smiled broadly and said, "Oh,
Laurette, have you heard about my good fortune?"

"Why, no, I..."

Eagerly Miss Foster told of the new project that
had so changed her life. "...and nearly every child at
the orphanage has shown an interest in taking piano
lessons! Isn't that surprising?" said the gray-haired
lady. "I tell you, dear, I haven't been this busy in
years." She laughed then and added, "Not since
those long-ago days when I taught you and Ladd."
The tiny woman looked up at Sutton and explained,
"Ladd Dasheroon was the boy who lived across Dauphin from Laurette."

"Yes, she's mentioned him."

"Such a talented boy," mused Miss Foster, her
eyes twinkling, "Remember, Laurette, how you
couldn't quite master that favorite Chopin polonaise

and Ladd could play it beautifully after only a few times.''

''I remember,'' said Laurette and was momentarily jolted by the recollection of Sutton playing that familiar polonaise in her music room. She frowned slightly.

Her expression grown wistful, Miss Foster said, ''Dear, sweet Ladd. Killed in the war in the prime of manhood.'' She shook her head sadly.

Quickly changing the subject, Laurette said, ''It's wonderful that the children have the opportunity to take lessons from you.''

''Bless their hearts,'' said Miss Foster. ''They're so well-behaved and eager to learn. And, the orphanage has a brand-new cherrywood piano; perfectly tuned and an exquisite piece of furniture.'' She looked thoughtful then and added, ''I have no idea who is responsible. Mrs. Young, the director at the orphanage, said the benefactor wishes to remain anonymous.''

Laurette's well-arched eyebrows lifted. ''Really?''

''That's my understanding.''

When the music teacher had moved on to greet other friends, Laurette gave Sutton a questioning look.

''I know nothing about music lessons,'' he said, but she didn't believe him for a minute.

Her heart swelled with pride.

Then raced with anticipation when he leaned down and whispered in her ear, ''I want to be alone with you.''

Breathlessly, she replied, ''Then let's go.''

* * *

It was very early the next morning when Bones, summoned by Sutton, walked into the study. The room was mostly dark. Only the lamp atop the desk, the one with the smoked-gray globe, burned low.

Seated behind the desk, Sutton's face was, as usual, in deep shadow. Bones took a chair across from his boss and waited for Sutton to speak. Sutton said nothing. Bones needlessly cleared his throat, then opened his leather journal. He flipped through several pages, then stopped when he found the one he was looking for.

He laid a big hand atop the paper, squinted in an attempt to see Sutton and finally said, "Shall I begin?"

"That's why you're here," came Sutton's low, deep voice.

"Very well," replied Bones. "On that afternoon last week when she begged off of seeing you, saying that she was busy, I did as instructed. I followed her."

"Good," said Sutton. "Let's have it."

Bones nodded and began to read his neatly written notes. "Mrs. Tigart arrived home from the hospital shortly after two o'clock. After spending only a few minutes inside her house, she left again, and this time she was carrying some sort of…of…"

"What? What did she get inside?" Sutton leaned up into the light.

"A small bag with a drawstring top," said Bones. "Carrying the bag under her arm, she immediately set off for downtown."

Sutton frowned and said impatiently, "Go on."

"Mrs. Tigart went directly to Bill's Pawnshop on Monroe Street. She was inside for a few minutes, and the man behind the counter greeted her as if he knew her, as if she had been there before. She opened the small bag she carried and took something out. I couldn't see what it was. The pawnbroker wasted no time studying or evaluating the item she handed him. He took it from her, placed in underneath the counter, opened his cash register and handed her a few bills. I couldn't see what the denominations were. She took the money, stuffed it into her reticule, turned and left." Bones looked up from his text.

"Then what happened?" asked Sutton.

"I ducked around the corner of the building, waited until she had gone, then went inside the pawnshop. I asked the proprietor what the lady had pawned. He shrugged, gave no reply. I pulled out a couple of bills and placed them on the counter. He said, 'Four pieces of heavy sterling silverware.' I said, 'Has she ever pawned anything else?'"

"And his answer?"

"Another shrug. So I placed another couple of bills on the counter and he revealed that over the years she had pawned the entire set of sterling—a few pieces at a time. And, in addition, a gold-cased pocket watch, some oyster shell, jewel-encrusted combs and a heavy silver frame."

Ladd's jaw immediately tightened. Vividly he recalled giving Laurette the silver frame containing a tintype of himself shortly before leaving for West Point.

"Was the tintype still in the frame?" he asked sarcastically.

"Pardon?" replied Bones.

"Nothing. Never mind," said Sutton. "Go on. What happened next?"

"I hurried out of the pawnshop and caught up with Laurette."

"She didn't see you, did she?"

"No, by the time I stepped outside, she was a couple of blocks away. I followed her at a safe distance."

"She didn't immediately return home, did she?"

"No, no she didn't."

"Why am I not surprised," said the cynical Sutton.

Bones's florid face broke into a wide grin. "Perhaps you'll be surprised when I tell you where she went."

Sutton felt his heart kick against his ribs. He wanted to know the truth and yet he didn't.

"Give it to me straight, I can take it. You see, I've known for years she's a deceitful little piece of work."

"Deceitful? What's deceitful about her walking all the way down to lower Water Street?" said Bones. Sutton's dark eyebrows lifted quizzically. "She knocked on the front door of a row shack and immediately the door opened and a black woman came out onto the stoop. The two embraced warmly, then laughed and talked like…"

"Ruby Lee," Sutton interrupted.

"Who?"

"Ruby Lee. She was Laurette's personal maid when Laurette was a child. Ruby Lee grew up in the Howard household."

"Then it makes sense. Laurette gave Ruby Lee the money she got from pawning the silver."

Sutton nodded, ground his teeth. "That it? Or did she go somewhere else after leaving?"

"No, she did not. She visited with the black woman for a few minutes, then she walked straight home. She arrived at Dauphin Street at a few minutes after four." Bones looked up and said, "I believe you arrived at her house shortly before five, which would have given her only enough time to freshen up and—"

"Okay, okay," Sutton waved his hand. "You're sure she didn't go anywhere else?"

Bone slammed his leather folder together with impatience. He said, "Sutton, you have sent me out to follow Mrs. Tigart at least a dozen times and I have never come back with any evidence of improper behavior. I don't know what you're expecting to uncover, but you're wasting your time and mine."

Sutton made no reply. He exhaled heavily and said finally, "You can go."

"Should I continue this foolish surveillance?"

Sheepishly, Sutton grinned and said, "I suppose it's pointless. No, you needn't follow her anymore."

"Well, thank heaven," said Bones, rising to his

feet. "I dislike spying on someone as open and honest as Mrs. Tigart." He turned to leave.

"Wait," said Sutton. "Can you remember the house where you saw Laurette with Ruby Lee?"

"Sure, I can."

"Visit the occupants of that house. See if Ruby Lee and her family would like to come to work here at the mansion. We can always use some extra servants. Blakely needs help in the kitchen and the upstairs maids are spread a little thin."

"Consider it done," said Bones and left the room.

For a long moment, Sutton remained seated behind his desk. His dark-blue eyes clouded. Abruptly, he rose from his chair, walked to the tall windows where he drew back the heavy drapes and gazed out at the summer dawn now breaking over the city.

He was, as usual, torn between being disappointed and relieved on hearing Bones's report regarding Laurette's private activities. He wanted, he had told Bones, every minute of Laurette's time accounted for.

Bones had reluctantly agreed. But Bones had never had anything undue to report. Not once.

Sutton sighed with frustration. It would make it so much easier to continue hating the luscious Laurette if on occasion she behaved like the devious, heartless woman he knew her to be. If only he could catch her in some underhanded act, but then she was far too cunning.

Chances are she had become aware that Bones was shadowing her, so she made it a point to demonstrate that she was, at all times, a genteel, generous lady.

He would have been pleased had Bones been able to relate that the beautiful blond divorcée had been caught rendezvousing with one or more of the town's known philanderers for an afternoon of sexual sin. It would help if he found out that he was not the only one with whom she was intimate.

Sutton suddenly shuddered at such a repugnant idea. While he didn't love her, the thought of another man making love to her made his stomach turn. No, he didn't want that to happen. Not that, God no!

All right, so she'd been caught doing nothing more sinister than helping out an old friend. Still, he wasn't fooled. He knew who she was, what she was. This was the woman who married the man he'd thought to be his best friend. There was no changing that. The two of them hadn't cared if he was alive or dead, hadn't bothered to find out.

He had to remember that, no matter how sweet and passionate she was in his arms, she was the shallow, selfish bitch who had promised she'd wait forever and then married Tigart the minute he proposed. He must never, never let himself forget what had happened. While he was rotting away in the prison's dark cell, Laurette was eagerly spreading her legs for the double-crossing Tigart.

Damn them!

Damn them both to eternal hell.

Thirty-Three

The newly constructed beach house was a charming, five-thousand-square-feet manse, all on one sprawling level. Its grand arched entrance was framed by two white columns and enough floor-to-ceiling windows to bathe the interior in constant daylight.

A wide veranda, with a shade-giving thatched roof, wrapped entirely around the circumference of the house. On the front veranda were a pair of white rocking chairs at one end and a huge white canvas hammock at the other. The chairs rocked and the hammock swayed gently back and forth in the mild sea breezes.

The gleaming white house sat on a natural rise at the very center of the island. Directly in front of the mansion stood an all-white signal mast made of flagstaff pine.

Located six miles off the coast, the island was five miles long and one mile wide. Below the house, tall sea oats gave way to sugary white beaches where the surf pounded rhythmically, the sound lulling to the fortunate occupants or invited guests of the home.

There was, and would always be, only one occupant, only one invited guest.

Sutton had no intention of sharing his private island paradise with anyone other than Laurette. And, of course, her presence on the island was to be temporary. By summer's end, she would be vanquished. Never again to set foot on the property.

A handpicked staff was ferried over to clean and cook as necessary, but none were allowed to spend the night.

Laurette was as excited as a child when Sutton took her to the island for the first time. She had been dying to go there while the house was under construction, but Sutton had said no. He explained that he wanted the house to be entirely finished and the furniture he'd had specially built floated over on a barge from New Orleans and put in place before she saw it.

The day had come at last. A sunny, beautiful day in mid-May. Not only was he ready to take her to his island retreat, he had persuaded her to spend the night. At first she had strongly objected. It would, she argued, be scandalous for the two of them to spend the entire night together. What would his servants think? What would their friends think?

There would be no servants, he promised. It would be just the two of them. Total privacy. No staff of any kind on duty and the yacht that would take them there would return to Mobile. As to what their friends would think, didn't she realize that everyone knew they were having an affair, so what difference did it make?

Laurette finally agreed.

Once they reached the island and hurried up to the

beach house, the yacht immediately backed away from the levee for its return trip to Mobile. Laurette was instantly charmed by the serenity, the privacy of the place. And she fell in love with the unique house that had been designed solely for casual, comfortable living. All the furniture in the front parlor—the many long, soft sofas and high-backed easy chairs—were upholstered in warm, rich shades of beige and brown. Fat, fluffy cushions galore in bright, vivid colors graced the sofas. Cut wood was neatly stacked in a marble-trimmed fireplace that had never been lighted. It was a large, handsome room meant for relaxing.

Taking it all in, Laurette walked through the homey room. She went directly to the very back of the house and stepped into a gigantic bedroom. Following just behind, Sutton told her that it was the only bedroom in the house.

She turned and said, "You're teasing me."

"Not at all. You and I are the only ones who will ever come here. One bedroom is all we need, is it not?"

"Yes," she said, pleased, then turned back to look around.

What a bedroom it was! Located at the very back of the mansion, the room stretched the entire length of the house. Three of its walls consisted of sets of tall, slated double doors, one right after the other. All those doors were presently thrown open, making it seem as if the bedroom was outside.

Most remarkable of all, there was only one piece of furniture in the spacious room. A huge, square, four-poster bed that was totally plain, the wood devoid of carvings or design. The sturdy quartet of posts rising high above the bed, were of heavy pine. The square mattress sat much lower to the floor than one on a traditional four-poster.

White linen sheets, matching bed hangings and an abundance of white-cased pillows graced the bed which, to Laurette's surprise, sat at an angle in the very center of the room. Gazing at the bed, it occurred to her that its occupant or occupants could lie upon it and idly watch the waves crashing against the shore. And, they would be able to feel the gentle sea breezes caress their warm bodies.

Amazed by everything in the house, Laurette looked around and saw a wide arched doorway that obviously led into the dressing room and bath. She crossed to it and stuck her head inside. A tall chest of drawers and heavy armoires lined the walls of the dressing room. She walked through the dressing room and into the bath.

And she smiled.

A square tub of gold-veined white marble dominated the room. A tub large enough for two. Meant for two. Heavy sterling candlesticks with tall white tapers sat on a wide marble ledge at the foot of the tub. Dozens of white towels were stacked neatly on shelves. Most amazing of all, directly above the square tub was a large, glass window. Sunlight poured in and high, fluffy cumulus clouds glided leisurely by.

Already imagining how it would feel to bathe in

that tub while the moonlight spilled in, Laurette blushed and went back out into the bedroom.

"Is the bath to your liking, my dear?" Sutton inquired.

"Yes, it most certainly is. I've never seen anything like it," she said truthfully.

"It's all for you, darling."

"Well, be assured that I'm totally enchanted with everything," she said and smiled at him. He was pleased with her answer. Then, all at once, Laurette frowned, puzzled.

"What? What is it?" he asked, anxious.

She shook her head, said nothing. Directly before her, in a set of the open-slatted doors, a matching pair of heavy chains with large steel loops at their ends hung suspended from the high door frame. The chains were spaced approximately two feet apart. Laurette stared, but hated to ask.

Sutton saw where her attention was directed. He chuckled, walked up behind her, slipped his arms around her waist and said, "Don't worry, love. While the chains may look like something from a Chinese torture chamber, they're really quite harmless."

Skeptical, she leaned back against him and placed her hands on his forearms. "I believe you, but what on earth are—?"

"I'll show you," he interrupted, released her and crossed to the open doors. He reached up above his head, clasped his hands through the steel loops, raised himself up from the floor by bending his arms. He then lifted his legs straight out in front of him and held them there. "This is how I exercise, it keeps me fit."

Laurette had ventured forward. She stood nearby, rubbing her chin thoughtfully. She stared as he perfectly balanced himself, his arms bent, the muscles standing out in bold relief. He looked at her, winked and said, "I have to keep my arms good and strong so I can hold you tight." Shortly, he straightened his arms and lowered his feet to the floor. Still holding the iron loops, he asked, "Want to give it a try?"

"May I?"

"Come here."

Laurette got into position and listened carefully as he instructed, "Now stretch your arms up and grab the iron rings." She nodded and, bottom lip caught beneath her teeth in concentration, raised up on tiptoe, grabbed hold of the heavy rings and looked to him for further instruction. "Now, bend your arms, try and pull yourself up."

She complied. "Ohhh," she complained, "that hurts!"

"I know. I'll help a little," he said and stepping closer, put his hands to her narrow waist and hoisted her up. "Now, sweetheart, raise your legs and stretch them out directly in front of you."

"Oh, good lord," she exclaimed, as she strained and pulled and attempted to lift her legs, which seemed as heavy as lead, up the way he had done.

"You're almost there," he encouraged, as she struggled.

She managed to hold her legs up and out for less

than a second before lowering them and admitting defeat. "I'll find some other way to exercise," she told him.

"I've a suggestion," he said with a devilish grin.

"Oh, you!" she replied in mock disgust. "I haven't even finished looking around yet. Where is the kitchen? I want to show you that I really can cook."

"Not necessary, love," he told her. "Before they left, the staff prepared our dinner."

She tilted her head and put her arms around his trim waist. Looking up at him, she said, "You are spoiling me, Sutton Vane, and I'm afraid that I am getting used to it."

"That's the idea, sweetheart," he said and kissed her.

It was dark.

Pitch-dark.

He could hear the rats scurrying inside the stone walls. He shuddered. He hated the rats. He tried to sleep, but couldn't. He lay wide-awake on his thin cot, fighting the panic that was threatening to overcome him. He felt as if he was losing his tenuous grip on his sanity. He'd been here alone in this deep, dark dungeon for too many years. He wasn't certain that he could stand one more night of the thick cloying blackness that enveloped him. That, and the never-ending loneliness.

All at once the heavy cell door opened and hope filled his heart as he leaped to his feet. The Captain of the Guards filled the portal. LaKid had one arm behind his back and there was a nasty grin on his ugly face.

"Please," Ladd begged, "let me out. Let me out for just a few minutes, then you can lock me up again. Let me go outside and see the stars and feel the wind on my face, then I'll—"

"Let you out?" mocked LaKid and he threw back his big head and laughed. "You'll never get out of this dungeon, Dasheroon! Tigart and I have seen to that! For crimes against the Union you will die here, you sorry piece of Southern trash." Licking his fleshy lips with anticipation, LaKid took his arm from behind his back and Ladd's eyes widened in fear and dread. In his huge hand, LaKid held a long poker with a fiery red tip.

"No, please, no. Dear God, not again. Show a little mercy," said Ladd. Suddenly too weak to stand, he sank to his knees before his beefy tormentor.

LaKid showed no mercy. He kicked Ladd over onto all fours, tore this tattered trousers apart and laughed maniacally as he slowly lowered the red-hot branding iron toward Ladd's thin buttock.

"Stop, damn you, LaKid! No more, no more!" Sutton shouted loudly, then screamed with unbearable pain as his flesh was seared. "I'll kill you, LaKid!" he shouted through his agony. "When this is finally over, I'll get out of here! I will, I'll live and I'll find you and kill you! So help me God I'll kill you!"

"Sutton, Sutton," Laurette cried as she shook her

lover. She'd been awakened by his screams and shouts.

He bounded straight up in bed, trembling, his heart hammering, his body drenched in perspiration. His breath was coming in shallow gasps and his eyes were wild.

Alarmed, Laurette wrapped her arms protectively around him and said, ''Darling, darling, it's okay. It's okay. You're safe. We're here alone on your island, nobody can get to you. No one can hurt you. I won't let anyone hurt you, I promise.'' She tightened her arms around his trembling body. ''It was a dream. A bad dream.''

Starting to calm a little, Sutton attempted to take deep, slow breaths. Finally he pulled free of her arms, lay back down and, annoyed with himself, said curtly, ''Sorry I woke you.''

Sutton gritted his teeth and silently cursed himself. He knew he shouldn't have brought her here to spend the night, to let her sleep in the bed with him. He had hoped that the nightmares were behind him. He hadn't had one in months, so he had thought it was finally safe. He should have known better. The bad dreams would never end. Never.

Laurette, holding him again, murmured soothingly to him, ''My love, it was a terrible nightmare. Nothing more.''

''Yes, just a nightmare.''

''What was it, Sutton? What was happening in your nightmare?''

''I don't remember,'' he lied.

"Who is LaKid?"

Sutton stiffened. "LaKid?"

"Yes, you were shouting at LaKid, telling him you were going to kill him. Then you screamed and—"

"I know of no one named LaKid and I have no idea why I was screaming."

She leaned down and kissed him. "Bad dreams are like that, they go away the minute you wake up. Thank goodness. You've already forgotten yours, haven't you?"

"Yes," he assured her. "Can't remember a thing about it."

"Good. That's good," she said. "Now you can go back to sleep."

Sutton reached up, clasped a portion of her loose blond hair, wrapped it around his hand and said, "I don't want to go back to sleep. I want to make love to you, Laurette."

"Oh, darling, of course." She kissed him and let her hand slide down his dampened chest to his groin.

As they had done earlier in the evening, they made passionate love in the big square bed as the moonlight slowly crept into the room and across their entwined bodies. The tide, controlled by the moon, was coming in, loud and fierce, pounding the sandy beaches below.

Sutton pounded into Laurette with the same fierce rhythm as the moon-driven surf. It was a wild, almost savage coupling that left both lovers entirely spent.

Afterward, Sutton fell tiredly asleep in Laurette's loving arms. She was no longer sleepy. She held Sutton to her, stroked his deeply clefted back and stayed awake for a long, long time, slightly troubled.

She wondered what horror had caused him such fear in his nightmare. She also wondered at the potent sex they'd shared following his nightmare. It was almost as if he were…punishing her instead of making love to her. He had gazed directly into her eyes throughout and held her wrists tightly, pressing them against the mattress. He hadn't murmured a word as he thrust forcefully into her, and when she'd cried out in ecstasy she was sure she'd caught a fleeting look of triumph on his handsome face before he groaned with his own release.

Laurette shivered inwardly and her forehead creased with concern.

She knew so little about this man she loved with all her heart and soul. His past was a puzzle. *He* was a puzzle. His abrupt appearance in her life seemed almost as if it had been planned, was not simply happenstance. It was if he had moved to Mobile for the sole purpose of seeking her out and making her fall in love with him.

Laurette gazed worriedly at his handsome face as he slept peacefully in her arms. She immediately chided herself for her foolish doubts. How could a stranger possibly know that if he came to Mobile he would meet her and they would fall in love? He couldn't. He didn't. It was simply the hand of fate that had brought them together and she was being silly to think otherwise.

Laurette finally sighed and smoothed a wayward

lock of raven hair back off Sutton's high forehead. This was, she suddenly realized, the very first time that she and Sutton had slept together all through the night. His handsome face would be the first thing she saw when she awakened in the morning. What a wonderful way to start the new day. Wishing that she could sleep with him every night for the rest of her life, Laurette exhaled heavily and stretched and pressed her naked body to his. She was where she wanted to be.

She yawned, closed her eyes and fell asleep.

Thirty-Four

The beach house became Laurette's favorite place on earth. The barrier island's beauty and privacy made her feel young and free and totally uninhibited. Indeed, when they were on the island, both Sutton and Laurette went about in a state of near undress.

With the coming of June, the humid summer heat descended with a vengeance and the only armor against the sizzling hot weather was to wear fewer clothes. Sutton was partial to low-riding white duck trousers, rolled up to his knees, an open shirt, no shoes. Laurette favored one of Sutton's fine linen shirts, sleeves rolled up past her elbows, with little or nothing beneath.

While the Old Guard spent the hot summer weeks across the bay at Point Clear, Sutton and Laurette were more than content to be alone at the beach house. Whenever Laurette had a day or two off from her duties at the hospital, the couple headed for the beach house where they could unwind and relax.

There, in their own private getaway, they played like happy children. They roughhoused and wrestled, tumbling about on the carpeted floor, pinning each other down, tickling, laughing and finally kissing until the child's game turned to adult lovemaking.

Their passion was such that often they didn't wait to reach the bedroom—they made love wherever they happened to be at the time. On the drawing room floor. In the big white hammock swinging back and forth on the front veranda. In the white marble tub. On the sandy beach. In the choppy waters of the Gulf.

They surrendered to every desire without reflection or shame. There was never an occasion when one wanted to make love and the other did not. There was a fierce heat between them that had nothing to do with the blazing summer temperatures.

When they were on the island, they were both selfishly hedonistic, living only for the pleasure of the moment. They were satisfied to do nothing but enjoy delicious food and drink fine wines and sip brandy after dinner while watching a spectacular sunset across the water.

It was like living in a beautiful dream and that sometimes frightened Laurette. She often wondered how anything so marvelous could possibly last.

It was a sweltering July evening, the heat intense even at the beach house.

The huge ball of fire that was ole sol was slowly sinking, turning the choppy waves of the Gulf to a bright golden hue. Laurette, just out of a bath, walked into the bedroom. She was wearing a white silk robe, but even that slippery, lightweight fabric was hot against her flushed skin.

She didn't hesitate.

She untied the sash and shrugged out of the robe, tossing it across the foot of the bed. She then crossed the room to the set of double doors where the chained loops hung. She reached up, grabbed the rings and stood there naked in the open doorway, facing outward, hoping to catch a breeze off the calm water.

There was none.

It was totally still. And hot. Muggy, sticky hot. So uncomfortably hot, Laurette was perspiring, her body moist from head to toe. She stood there clinging to the iron rings watching the blistering sun make its slow descent toward the horizon.

Just then Sutton entered the bedroom. He was wearing a black silk robe and nothing else. In one hand he carried a silver bucket filled with ice in which a bottle of champagne was chilling. In the other were two stemmed glasses, snagged between his long fingers.

He immediately saw Laurette standing naked in the open doors, clinging to the steel loops, perfectly silhouetted against the dying sun. And he was instantly aroused. He hurriedly set the ice bucket and glasses down. Laurette heard him, turned and glanced over her shoulder.

"Stay as you are," he said, shedding his robe. "Let's play a while."

"What will we play?" she asked and gazed back out over the golden waters of the Gulf.

Sutton gave no answer. He reached into the silver bucket and picked up a chunk of the ice. Walking up behind Laurette, putting his lips near her ear, he said, "Darling, I'm going to cool you off."

"Ah, that would be sooo nice. I'm most uncomfortable."

Sutton moved closer, put an arm around her narrow waist and said, "Lean against me, sweetheart." She did, letting her head fall back against his shoulder.

Sutton took the piece of ice and rubbed it to her lips, first the lower, then the upper. Laurette sighed her approval and licked at the cooling ice. When her lips were gleaming wet, Sutton moved the ice to the hollow of her throat.

"Mmmm," she murmured, "that feels good."

Sutton slowly slid the ice down to her breasts. Laurette held her breath as he teasingly circled, then gently pressed the ice to a sleeping nipple. He rubbed the ice back and forth over the nipple and it quickly awakened and became stiff and full of feeling. Laurette squirmed against him, enjoying this strange exercise. When her left breast was wet, he leisurely dragged the ice across her chest to give the right nipple a cooling caress. While he toyed with her, playing this new game with the ice, Laurette lifted her head and then, looking down, saw that her upper body was wet from the ice bath while her lower body was shiny with perspiration.

Sutton began to slide the ice down her rib cage to her flat stomach. He stroked the ice against her bare belly until it glistened.

"Cooler, sweetheart?" he asked huskily.

"Mmmm, yes," she murmured, but it wasn't quite

true. The ice was cold but, strangely enough, it was making her hotter.

Laurette started to let go of the steel loops. He stopped her. "No, baby, keep holding on, let me cool you all over."

The summer sun finally sank below the bay as Laurette watched Sutton's lean brown hand slip the ice into the blond coils between her thighs. She automatically moved her bare feet farther apart. He dripped the ice on her and rubbed until the curls were damp and springy. Then he kissed the side of her neck and slid the ice into place between her parted legs.

She lunged at its first touch against her hot burning flesh. Sutton caressed that tiny button of passion with the ice while Laurette gasped and trembled. She closed her eyes and totally gave in to the new sensation: it was strange, it was thrilling, it was cold and hot at once. It was unlike anything she'd ever felt before. She was being stroked deliciously with cooling ice and yet she was burning up from the cold.

"Oh, Sutton, Sutton," she whispered as her head again fell back against his shoulder. "This is surely decadent, isn't it?"

"Is it?" he said, sliding the melting ice farther back between her legs. "It's enjoyable, isn't it?"

"Yes," she admitted, clinging tightly to the steel loops, her grip on logical thinking dissolving by a well-placed piece of ice.

When Laurette was in danger of climaxing, Sutton took the ice from her. She moaned in protest. He released her and went around to stand in front of her.

Expecting him to take her in his arms and carry her to the bed, Laurette started to let go of her hold on the rings. Again he stopped her.

"Don't let go, Laurette. Whatever I do, just keep holding on. Tight."

"Yes, master," she teased, so hot and aroused she would have done anything he asked.

"Time for me to cool off," Sutton said, taking the rapidly melting chunk of ice and quickly wetting his chest and belly. Laurette watched, fascinated. As he had done with her, he dripped water into the raven-black hair of his groin. The dense curls were soon damp and beaded with diamond drops of water. He then began rubbing the ice up and down the length of his fully formed erection. When that potent male power was gleaming wet, Sutton tossed the ice away.

He stepped in closer, put his hands to Laurette's waist and kissed her ice-wet mouth. She clung to the rings and kissed him back. He bent his head and sucked her wet nipple. Holding her with both hands at her waist, he moved to the other breast. Raking his teeth over her nipple, he acted as if he was going to bite it.

Sinking to his knees, Sutton moved his hands down to rest on Laurette's hips. When he leaned forward and kissed her wet belly Laurette knew what was coming next and she tensed in eager anticipation. She would never in a million years have told anyone—not even Sutton—but the truth was, she was absolutely wild for the forbidden touch of his talented tongue on her sensitive female flesh. There was no greater ecstasy than that which she derived from this particular brand of lovemaking.

Her hands tightened on the steel rings when at last his nose and mouth nuzzled in the damp golden curls between her legs. She held her breath when he eased her right leg up and draped it over his shoulder. He turned his head and kissed the inside of her thigh, then lifted her other leg up over his shoulder. For a fleeting second Laurette considered with shame how indecent she surely looked, clinging to the steel bars with her legs draped over her kneeling lover's shoulders while he made love to her. And then, that exquisite moment when his hot mouth was upon her and his sleek tongue was stroking her into a wild sexual nirvana.

Her arms stretched above her head, her legs open to him, Laurette hung there in the pink and pastel gloaming of the dying light, gazing down on the man between her legs. The sight of him there, the feel of his mouth and tongue on her sensitive flesh, the knowledge that he would do this to her at her request, caused her release to involuntarily begin.

"Ohhh," she breathed, momentarily releasing her tight hold of the rings. "Sutton, Sutton," she called his name as her coming climax vibrated through her.

"Mmmm," he said, never taking his loving mouth from her.

Laurette's pale thighs squeezed his handsome head and she clung to the rings as the heat between her legs spread throughout her slender body and blinding ecstasy took her to new erotic heights. She cried out in her bliss and her body jerked spasmodically until the incredible joy began to subside. Then she went totally limp.

Sutton carefully removed her legs from his shoulders and lowered her feet back to the floor. He rose and looked at her. She was incredibly beautiful standing there—naked with her arms stretched up to the rings and her slender body wet. An expression of total bliss crossed her flawless face. He gently put his arms around her and drew her close, letting her feel his pulsating erection against her belly as he tenderly held her.

"Baby, sweet baby," he murmured as he caressed her back.

"Sutton," she gasped, "I'm so—"

"I know, sweet, I know."

Again he kissed her and he kept on kissing her until at last she was eagerly kissing him back. He spent several patient minutes arousing her again. She was shocked that, so soon after coming as she had, she wanted him—that she could hardly wait to feel him inside her once again.

He could tell she was ready. He kissed her one last time and cautioned, "Don't let go."

"No, no, I won't."

Sutton curled his hands beneath her thighs and easily lifted her up. When she was positioned directly above his hard male flesh, he carefully, skillfully lowered her down to the gleaming tip. Laurette was skeptical. He couldn't put it in without one or the other of them guiding it. Could he?

He could.

He did.

While they both watched, Sutton managed to lower Laurette onto his wet throbbing shaft. Both moaned as she eagerly slid down onto him and he clenched the twin cheeks of his buttocks before gently thrusting upward. When he was fully inside her, Sutton stood flat-footed and made love to Laurette. With his hands beneath her thighs, he controlled her, pressing her closer, then moving her back, as the pleasure increased.

"My lord," she said, on fire again, "tell me you'll make love to me all night. And all day tomorrow. I've seen you and now I feel you inside me and I want more and ever more."

Pleased, Sutton promised, "That's up to you, sweetheart. Any time you can get me hard, you can have me."

"I'll get you hard and keep you that way," she vowed, her dark eyes glazed with lust.

Sutton was not nearly as cool and controlled as he seemed to be. The truth was that her simple touch burned his flesh and made him thobbingly erect inside her. He was seized with an excitement that had him aching with his need to climax immediately. But he held himself in check. Caught up in the sensations trembling through his shaft, he purposely slowed his advance to prolong the building ecstasy.

For several thrilling minutes, the pair made love there in the open doorway with Laurette clinging to the rings and Sutton standing flat-footed before her, setting the pace.

As the lights of Mobile flickered on across the water and full darkness descended, it was Laurette who cried out first. Clinging desperately to the iron loops, she lunged and writhed and Sutton felt himself hotly enveloped in a sheath of blazing flame that quickly raged out of control, racing through his entire body. With a loud groan he held the now sobbing Laurette to him and let the flood pour out of him with a fury that left him weak and dazed.

For a long moment the two of them stayed as they were, trembling, breathing hard, stunned by the depth of their shared climax.

Finally Sutton spoke. "You can let go now, darling."

"Oh, oh yes. All right," Laurette sobbed and lowering her tired arms around his neck, laid her head on his shoulder and whispered, "But don't you ever let go of me."

Sutton smiled, kissed her temple but gave no reply.

Thirty-Five

It began as just another wonderful interlude for the lovers. In the final days of a sweltering, seemingly endless July, Laurette and Sutton spent a glorious weekend on the island. Late Friday evening when they arrived, they spread a blanket on the beach. Sutton gathered driftwood and built a fire. They had a picnic hamper filled with food. After they dined on cheese, smoked ham, boiled shrimp and French bread, they lay on their backs and searched the heavens for falling stars.

On Saturday morning they slept late and Sutton served Laurette hot coffee and chilled juice in bed. After which, she insisted on making him breakfast. They lolled lazily about all day, not doing much of anything. Late that afternoon, they went for a long walk on the beach, holding hands, saying little, silently enjoying the beauty and serenity surrounding them. When they returned from the stroll, they sat down on the front steps.

As they talked quietly, a huge butterfly landed on the braids of Laurette's upswept hair. Sutton raised his hand, placing his palm near her head. The delicate-

winged creature fluttered into his cupped palm and he
held it out for Laurette to see.

"What a lovely butterfly," she said.

"It's known to lepidopterists as the great purple
hairstreak."

"Really?" She tilted her head and gazed at him.
"Lepidopter…ah…"

"Lepidopterists. Specialists in the study of butterflies and lepidopteran insects."

"How do you know so much about butterflies?"

"I had years to study them," he said and, continuing to hold the powdery purple butterfly in his palm,
vividly recalled the day in the dungeon when just
such a butterfly came into his cell and sat on his hand.
It was the same day he had vowed to serve justice to
all those who had betrayed him.

"Oh, no," Laurette said, as the butterfly abruptly
took wing, sailing off into the gathering twilight.
"Come back," she called.

"It won't come back," he said.

"Mmmm." A few seconds passed, then she asked,
"And where exactly did you study butterflies?"

"It was a long time ago," he replied. "Let's go
inside. I'm hungry."

"Me, too!"

Arms around each other, they went inside. An hour
later, they dined by candlelight, drank wine and went
back outdoors to lie in the hammock as the moon rose
over the water.

Late Sunday afternoon, as the long, lovely weekend
was coming to a close, Sutton lay stretched out in the

hammock on the front gallery, hands folded beneath his head. Laurette had insisted he get out of the house and leave her alone while she prepared an early dinner.

Sutton was half dozing when all at once Laurette came dashing out the house, skipped down the steps and headed for the beach. She wore a plain pink cotton dress. Her blond hair was pinned haphazardly atop her head and she was barefooted. She was laughing as she raced across the sugary sand toward the water.

Sutton sat up, swung his long legs over the side of the hammock. He rose to his feet and went down the gallery steps to watch her. He stood with his feet apart, hands on his hips. He threw back his head and laughed gaily, his white teeth flashing when, a few yards from the water's edge, Laurette stopped abruptly, stripped off her dress and dropped it to the sand. She wore nothing beneath. She raced forward and dove naked into the surf.

Sutton continued to laugh merrily. What a playful nymph she was, what a joy to be with. When his laughter subsided, he shaded his eyes with one hand and continued to watch her splash about like a happy child. He stood stock-still and watched, mesmerized, when moments later Laurette emerged from the sea, dripping wet and breathtakingly beautiful.

And in this moment, at the sight of her running toward him, her beautiful body glistening in the sunshine, the base of power shifted. It was now all hers, not his.

He was, he realized with a jolt of shock and sadness, still very much in love with this woman he'd known since the day she was born. He watched Laurette approach, laughing and pushing her damp hair back off her lovely face, and he felt his chest tighten.

God, he couldn't leave her.

Not again.

At such a prospect there came a terrible sinking sensation, an unexpected feeling of loss. The heart he had thought immune to pain would break once more if he left her again. If he lost her again. The remembrance of his past love for the young Laurette conquered any lingering desire for vengeance. All his money, power and influence paled and became nothing in the face of love. He loved Laurette even more now than he had when they were young. His heart hammering in his bare chest, Sutton slipped off his white duck trousers and ran to meet Laurette.

She squealed with delight when he swept her up into his arms and dashed into the sea. While the waves lapped gently and the blazing July sun beat down on them, the pair made love in the water and when Sutton said, "I love you, Laurette," he meant it.

"And I love you," she said. "Carry me back to the house?"

"It will be my pleasure."

Sutton was very sure of his love for Laurette, but he was now faced with a serious dilemma. He had to tell her who he really was. He couldn't allow her to spend the rest of her life believing he was Sutton Vane. Or could he? Would that be so unfair?

He seriously considered doing just that because he was greatly troubled at the thought of telling her the truth. Would she forgive him, knowing what his cruel intention had been? He wouldn't blame her if she never spoke to him again.

"Sutton, what's wrong?" Laurette asked later that evening as they dined on the veranda.

"Wrong?" he replied, swallowing with difficulty.

"Yes, wrong," she said. "Ever since we came in from our swim, you've been withdrawn. You haven't said two words all evening. Something is bothering you. Tell me what it is."

He took a bolstering drink of wine, nodded and said, "Laurette, stay right where you are, I'll be back in a minute."

Now she was really curious and half-worried, but she smiled at him and promised, "I'll be right here waiting, my love."

Sutton rose and hurried inside. Shortly he returned to the veranda and, for the first time since she had met him, he was clean shaven. The black beard was gone. His handsome face, devoid of hair, was a smooth olive hue. Her lips parting, Laurette stared at him, her brows knitting, a chill skipping up her spine.

He came around the table, crouched down beside her chair, took her hand in his and said, "Dearest one, there's something that I—I have to tell you. Promise you won't be too angry with me."

Unsettled, continuing to stare at him as if seeing him for the first time, yet realizing that there was something hauntingly familiar about him, she said quietly, "Darling, I could never be angry with you. Tell me."

He looked at her for a long moment, dreading having to admit the terrible truth. He could wait no longer. He prayed she would understand and forgive him.

"I'm not Sutton Vane," he said simply. "I'm Ladd Dasheroon."

Her forehead wrinkled. She made a face. She shook her head as if to clear it. She examined him closely as his startling confession rang in her ears.

"No. No, you're not Ladd," she said, refusing to believe him. "Ladd died in a Yankee prison during the war."

"I was in prison, but I didn't die. I escaped."

"No, it can't be. You're not Ladd, you're not. I know you're not."

"I am, sweetheart. I really am. I'm the same Ladd that made love to you down by the river in the darkness the night before I left for West Point. You and I took music lessons from Miss Foster when we were kids. We were born on the same day, a year apart, and we always had our birthday parties together. It was at one of those parties when we first kissed, first confessed our love for each other." He stopped talking, waiting for it all to sink in.

He saw bright tears spring to her dark eyes, but she did not cry, nor did she speak. For a long, tense moment Laurette said nothing. She sat perfectly still, rigid and silent, shaking inside, torn between the strong desire to throw herself into his arms and kiss his handsome face and the equally strong impulse to hurt him badly, to hit him and scream at him and banish him from sight.

Ladd, on his knees beside her, held his breath. He realized that it could go either way.

Her teeth firmly clamped together, Laurette thought back over all the sad, empty years that she had grieved for this man who was kneeling beside her. Dear God, he had been alive all along and had never let her know. Damn him! Damn him! Damn him to eternal hell!

Thirty-Six

Her anger swiftly rising, Laurette wrenched her hand from his. "You cruel, heartless bastard!" she said through clenched teeth. "Just what is this evil game, Ladd Dasheroon? Why the pretense? Tell me, I'm a bit confused."

He rose to face her. "Oh, Lollie, I can explain if—"

"Don't call me that!" she interrupted. "Never again. I want an explanation and I want it now! What was your reason for doing this? Why did you pretend to be someone else?"

Ladd exhaled heavily. He couldn't avoid the truth. He had to tell her. "Let's sit down and—"

"No! I don't want to sit down," she fumed, hugging her arms to her chest and moving a step back from him. "I want you to tell me what's going on and why you have lied to me all this time."

Ladd knew he had to confess. But he began by saying, "I will tell you. I'll tell you everything. But first let me say that there has never been a day, an hour, a minute in my life that I didn't love you, Laurette."

"Liar!" she accused. "If you loved me—"

"I do love you, so help me God." He drew a deep breath and said, "Laurette, I was wounded in the war and captured by the Union forces. They threw me in a terrible place called Devil's Castle prison. I spent many long years in prison, most of them down in a dark dungeon alone. Perhaps I wasn't strong enough, I don't know. All I know is that such an experience made it hard to think straight, to keep a grip on one's sanity."

He looked at her, hoping to read her emotions. She stared at him and revealed nothing.

He continued, "After I had been at Devil's Castle for a year, Jimmy was installed as commandant of the prison. With his arrival, I was sure everything would be better for me. Easier. I was wrong. So wrong." Again he paused. Then he declared simply, "It was Jimmy who had me thrown into the dungeon."

"No, that can't be...Jimmy wouldn't...he was your best friend."

"Jimmy had me locked up in the dungeon. He did it so that he could have you. I hadn't known, but apparently he had always wanted you." Her lips fell open and she stared at him in horror. He hurried on, "When the war ended he came home to Mobile and you immediately married him. You married him not knowing if I was alive or dead."

"That's a lie!" she defended herself. "Jimmy said you had died in prison. I had no reason to believe otherwise. I hadn't heard a word from you in ages and—"

"Devil's Castle allowed no incoming or outgoing mail."

"I believed that you were dead," she repeated.

"Even so...you married him within weeks of learning I was dead." Ladd said.

"What was I supposed to do? Bury my heart with you? I did that, damn you, but my body, unfortunately, had to survive. I had no parents, no money, I was destitute. I hadn't heard from you in over two years. Jimmy was there at time when I needed him, offering help and understanding. Federal occupation and their ruinous reconstruction taxes had left me a pauper." She drew a quick breath and continued, "Maybe I'm shallow and selfish, but I didn't want to starve like some people I knew. So, yes, yes I married Jimmy. How was I to know he had lied? I had no reason to doubt him. I didn't know you were alive!" She was shouting now, her face growing red with emotion. Her hands went to her hips and her dark eyes flashed fire. "I believed that you were dead, that I would never see you again. Had I known the truth, I would never have married Jimmy or anyone else."

"I wasn't dead and I vowed that I would live and get out of prison and—and—"

Cutting in, Laurette said, "All that aside, the war has been over for sixteen years. Why did you wait all this time to come home?"

"I was in prison long after the war ended," he said. "I finally escaped in '75."

She frowned, but said, "Why didn't you come home then? And why have you used an alias? Why

have you allowed me to believe that you were someone else?'' He opened his mouth to speak, but she
silenced him with a hand up, palm out and screamed
at him, ''Why? Why? Why?''

Ladd started to explain, but his justification
sounded unsatisfactory even to himself. Only weeks
ago his judgment had seemed quite sound; now, he
questioned his sanity. He wished he had never
hatched the cruel plot. He repeatedly apologized and
begged for Laurette's forgiveness.

She staunchly withheld it and when he attempted
to take her in his arms, she coldly ordered, ''Don't
touch me. Never touch me again.'' Her eyes narrowing, she said, ''You were in prison? Well, so was I.
You'll be happy to know that I was miserable with
Jimmy. I never loved him, didn't even like him very
much.''

His heart aching with regret, Ladd said, ''Oh, God,
darling, I'm so sorry for everything. Please try to understand how I felt when I heard that you had married
Jimmy. I couldn't believe that the precious girl who
was mine, who had promised to wait forever, had forgotten so easily.''

''I didn't forget. Never, ever. I had no other
choice!''

''I believe you and—''

''I don't give a damn what you believe, you callous, calculating son of a bitch. This evil charade is
coming clear to me now. You destroyed Jimmy for
betraying you. It is you who owns the bank where he
was president. You who had him caught for embez-

zling. You had him divorce me and leave the country. It was you! Admit it!''

''I do admit it. And I admit that I would do it all over again. As far as I'm concerned, Jimmy got off lightly. He could have spent the rest of his life in a prison dungeon.''

Her head beginning to throb from the shock and the hurt, Laurette stated sadly, ''You took care of Jimmy and then it was time to take care of me. The wealthy, urbane, mysterious stranger who I just happened to meet at Colonel Ivy's party. It was all thoroughly planned, wasn't it? You came back to punish me.''

''Laurette, I was—''

''And what better way to punish me than to make me fall madly in love with you. And then to cruelly abandon me. That was your intention, wasn't it?'' He gave no reply. She shouted, ''Wasn't it!''

He sadly shook his head, admitting his plan. Then he asked again for her forgiveness, swearing that he loved her and wanted to marry her. Desperate, he reached out and clasped her wrist.

''Let me go,'' she said.

''Laurette, please listen. I'll spend the rest of my life making it up to you and—''

''Let me go,'' she said again.

He released her.

She looked at him with naked hatred flashing in the depths of her dark eyes and said, ''You let me believe that you were dead. Well, now you *are* dead to me, Dasheroon. I never want to see you again! I hate you more than I ever loved you and I will hate you to the grave and beyond!''

With that, Laurette turned, hurried down the front steps and raced across the sand to the levee. It was almost nine and the yacht was to return to the island at nine o'clock to pick them up. Ladd remained on the veranda, knowing she was far too angry and upset to listen to him right now. Hopefully, she would change her mind in time.

When the sleek white craft came alongside the dock, Ladd stepped off the porch, crossed the beach and made his way to the levee.

"No!" Laurette warned Ladd as Bones took her hand to guide her up onto the yacht's teak deck. "You are not coming, do you understand me? I want you out of my sight now and forever!"

Stunned, Bones gave Ladd a questioning look. "It's okay," Ladd said. "I'll spend another night on the island. You can come for me tomorrow."

Bones nodded as Laurette anxiously disappeared below deck. The yacht pulled away from the levee. Hands in his trouser pockets, wide shoulders slumped in despair, Ladd stood on the sandy beach and watched until the yacht was swallowed up in the darkness. He turned and walked slowly back up to the beach house, the darkness seeming to envelop his aching heart.

Aboard the yacht, Bones stood at the railing, his face somber. There was a deep feeling of sadness in his heart for Laurette. And a strong feeling of animosity toward the man responsible for her unhappiness.

Bones supposed that Ladd had chosen this hot summer evening to tell Laurette he was done with her. Tired of her. Didn't care to see her again. Bones's firm jaw tightened with outrage. He knew the next part of the plan. Ladd would, within days, marry a beautiful young belle whom he could parade about Mobile so that the cruelly jilted Laurette would suffer even more than she was suffering now.

The big man felt his eyes burn with tears. He loved Ladd like a brother, but what Ladd had done to Laurette was inhuman. This sweet woman whose heart Ladd had purposely broken didn't deserve such dreadful treatment. Bones raised a hand, rubbed his face and blinked away his tears.

When the yacht reached the port of Mobile, Bones called out to Laurette. "We're home, Mrs. Tigart."

Laurette came topside and Bones immediately saw that she had been weeping. Her eyes were puffy and red. It broke his heart to see her so unhappy. He wished there was something that he could say or do to comfort her, but he knew that there wasn't.

When Laurette started down the gangway, Bones followed close behind. "Mrs. Tigart, this old Mobile wharf is full of splinters," he said. "I'm afraid you might—" She looked down at her bare feet in half-surprise, forgetting that she had left in such a hurry that she hadn't bothered with her shoes. He said gently, "If you'll allow me, I'll carry you to the waiting carriage."

She nodded and the gentle giant lifted her up into his arms as easily as if she were a little girl. He crossed the wide wharf, climbed the steps up the riverbank, handed her into the waiting carriage and closed the door.

When the brougham rolled to a stop before her residence, Bones hurried to her aid, saying he'd be honored to carry her up to the house. Weary as she'd never been in her life, Laurette agreed.

When Bones opened her front door and lowered her bare feet to the foyer floor, it was dark inside. "You stay right here," he instructed, "I'll light a lamp."

"Thank you," she said and leaned weakly against the wall.

A lamp soon flickered on in the drawing room and Bones returned to the foyer to say good-night. But before he left, the tenderhearted man couldn't help but ask, "Is there anything I can do?"

"No, but thank you, Bones. You're a kind, good man." She smiled sadly and added, "There are very few of you left in this world."

Thirty-Seven

Laurette paced the confines of her bedroom through the long and sleepless night. Again and again she went over everything that had happened, recalled everything that Ladd had said and done. And she realized with growing fury that his foremost intention had been to break her heart and make a fool of her.

It was impossible to believe that the sweet, loving boy she had known and loved as a child had become this cold, devious seducer who had made of her his willing wanton. She cringed at the recollection of how she had behaved with him, freely and eagerly giving herself to him, body and soul. She'd been his to do with as he pleased. It was inconceivable to her that the incredible ecstasy they had shared involved only his body, never his heart.

Laurette stopped pacing.

She climbed up into the windowsill the way she'd done as a girl. She sat hugging her gowned knees, gazing out at the twinkling lights of the city and the bay beyond. Out there in the Gulf was a private island where she had spent the happiest moments of her life.

A sense of terrible emptiness struck her, a deep despair that was like a physical pain.

God, how she loved him.

God, how she hated him!

On that private island out in the Gulf, Ladd restlessly paced the veranda through a long and sleepless night. Again and again he went over everything that had happened, everything she had said and done. And he realized with a growing sense of despair that she would never forgive him. Should never forgive him.

There was no excuse for what he had done, no justification for hurting her so badly. He wished he had never come back to Mobile, wished he had left her alone.

Ladd shuddered at the recollection of her eager lovemaking and of the times she had lain totally open to him, offering him not only her lovely body, but her very soul as well. What incredible ecstasy they had shared, a kind of rare, sweet bliss that had totally possessed his heart as well as his body.

Ladd stopped pacing.

He climbed into the canvas hammock and folded an arm beneath his head. He gazed out over the waters toward the lights of Mobile. On Dauphin Street in the heart of the city was a big white house. Inside that mansion was the woman who had given him the happiest moments of his life.

Ladd's bare stomach contracted sharply. He felt as if he were going to suffocate. A sense of terrible emptiness struck him, a deep despair that was like a physical pain.

God, how he loved her.

God, how she must hate him.

At midmorning the next day, Bones returned to the island with the yacht's crew to pick up Ladd. Bones went up to the house to get him. Ladd was on the veranda, lying in the hammock. He was wide-awake, but he looked like he hadn't slept all night. Bones had no sympathy for him. In fact, it was all he could do to keep from yanking Ladd up out of the hammock and throwing a well-aimed right cross at his jaw.

Ladd rose wearily and followed Bones down the front steps. The two men headed across the beach toward the dock. Neither had said a word.

Finally, a few yards from the dock, Bones stopped, and, biting out the words, said, "So you told her last night you were through with her." It was not a question, but a statement.

"You have it wrong," the careworn Ladd corrected. "She told me."

Bones made a face. "What do you mean, she told you?"

Ladd shrugged, gave the big man a sad, self-deprecating smile and said, "Looks like the last laugh is on me and I'm the one who gets a dose of well-deserved justice." He hung his head, kicked at the sand with a bare toe. "I fell in love with her all over again, so I decided to come clean, to tell her the truth, the whole truth."

His eyes widening, Bones said, "You mean, you admitted you're Ladd Dasheroon."

"I did," said Ladd, raising his head and looking

Bones squarely in the eyes, "and because I did, I have lost her for good."

"No," said Bones, "don't say that. You don't know that. You have to go to her immediately, make her understand."

"Understand what?" was Ladd's reply. "That I am a heartless bastard who came back here for the sole purpose of making her pay? She knows that. Laurette's a very clever woman. She figured out the reason for the pretense, realized that I planned to seduce and abandon her."

"But—but you admitted the truth, that should stand for something," Bones said hopefully.

"My friend, I intend to do everything in my power to get her back," said Ladd. "But I know her well. She's stubborn and prideful and I'm sure she would like nothing better than to get even with me. And who can blame her?"

"Not me," Bones said truthfully.

"Nor me," said Ladd, tiredly. "She will hate me forever for what I've done. I deserve it, but God, how I wish I could change everything."

"Well, you can't, but maybe you can repair the damage. She's a fine lady and she loves you."

"No, she loved me, past tense."

"She loved you twice—the young Ladd Dasheroon and the mature Sutton Vane." Ladd nodded sadly. "You can't convince me that she loved you yesterday and that she no longer loves you today," continued

Bones. "She's hurt and confused and angry, but surely she still loves you."

"I hope you're right."

Ladd swallowed any pretense of pride.

He loved Laurette, he wanted her back and he was bent on doing everything in his power to persuade her to forgive him.

After an interminable day of waiting and wondering, a tired, anxious Ladd, who had finally shaved, bathed and put on fresh clothes, climbed into the brougham for the short ride to the Veteran's Convalescent Hospital.

As nervous as a young, insecure boy, Ladd waited for Laurette to walk out the front doors and come down the hospital steps. He kept watching, looking for her, but didn't see her. He was early, he told himself. It was still several minutes to two o'clock. She got off duty at two.

Feeling the perspiration bead in his hairline and above his lip, he kept reaching into his waistcoat pocket, fishing out the gold-cased watch, flipping it open and checking the time. He repeated the exercise at least a dozen times, until finally the watch read two-fifteen. Where was she? She usually skipped down the front steps at a minute after two. What was keeping her?

No longer able to sit still, Ladd opened the coach's door and climbed out. He stood in the broiling July sun, leaning against the brougham, arms folded over his chest, one well-shod foot nervously tapping the cobblestone street. Doctors and nurses, one at a time, or two or three together, had been exiting the big hospital since straight up two.

Laurette was not among them.

At two-thirty Ladd could stand it no longer. He pushed away from the carriage, hurried toward the hospital's steep steps and quickly ascended them. Inside, he stopped the first person he saw, a tall, stout nurse with a stiff white cap on her head.

"Excuse me," he said with a smile, "Would you happen to know Laurette Tigart?"

"Sure, I know Laurette," said woman. "She didn't come in today. Sent word that she was ill and—"

Before she finished the sentence, Ladd turned and hurried back toward the entrance. He rushed down the hospital steps, shrugging out of his hot coat as he went. Instructing his driver to take him to the Dauphin Street mansion, he swung up inside and closed the door.

At the mansion, he ran up the front walk, climbed the veranda steps and, standing before the closed door, took a deep breath and ordered his heart to stop racing. It didn't listen. He knocked firmly on the door. He waited patiently. At last the door opened and Laurette, looking pale and wan, stood in the portal.

"Laurette, I—" he began, but she cut him off.

"I thought I made it clear. I never want to see you again." She closed the door in his face.

He banged on it and pleaded, "Just give me five minutes. Please don't let it end like this, Lollie. For God's sake, give me a chance. Remember all we've been to each other."

Desperate, he banged on the door again. It remained closed to him, just as Laurette's heart remained closed to him. She had already gone back upstairs.

In the following days and weeks, Ladd didn't give up. Each day he came to the hospital to wait for her, to beg for her forgiveness. He never got the chance. She pointedly ignored him, refused to listen or to talk to him. Each day Ladd had three dozen white roses delivered to her home with a note that read, "I'll never stop loving you. Forgive me."

But Laurette, who had been hurt enough in her life, had successfully hardened her heart. She no longer cared if he loved her or not. It was of no importance to her. She never read the notes that came with the roses. She threw the roses in the trash the minute they arrived.

She had told Ladd that he was now dead to her and she intended to make it so. She didn't care about him. She didn't care about anything. She was aware that the entire city had learned of their breakup, but she was not bothered by the whispering and the looks she drew when she was forced to go out in public. So she was the topic of gossip? Well, it wasn't the first time and it made no difference to her. Nothing made any difference to her. She confided in no one, not even her best friends, the Parlange twins. They, like the rest of the gentry, were left to wonder and speculate.

Laurette had convinced herself that she was now incapable of feeling anything. She performed her duties at the hospital just as always, but she was no longer deeply concerned when she came upon a seriously sick patient who needed a cool hand on his brow. She refused to get involved, to allow her patient's misery to touch her anesthetized heart.

Alone for so many years, Ladd, like Laurette, confided in no one.

But unlike Laurette's, his own heart was very much alive and capable of feeling. Indeed it ached persistently. His hope of winning Laurette back was growing dim and with the passing of each long, lonely night, he grew more morose. He rarely bothered going up to his bedroom at night. He knew he wouldn't sleep, so why bother? He sat in his office in the quiet early-morning hours, drinking whiskey straight and cursing himself for what he had done.

He, too, knew that the city was gossiping about Laurette and him, although no one else knew his true identity, only that the affair had ended. He didn't care about his own reputation. But he did worry that Laurette was being hurt by the meddling and slander. By the scandal he had brought down on her head.

Bones was worried about Ladd. Although he had soundly disapproved of Ladd's treatment of Laurette, he was now concerned for Ladd's welfare. Ladd had never had much of an appetite due to the long years in prison when he'd been starved. But lately he often refused to eat at all. An entire day would pass without

Ladd ever lifting a fork or taking a bite of food. The only thing he lifted was a shot glass of bourbon.

One warm September night as Ladd sat drinking alone, Bones came into the study. He tried to talk to Ladd. But his attempt was shut off with a dark look and a wave of Ladd's hand.

"Get the hell out of here and go to bed!" Ladd said, slurring his words.

"I was going to suggest the same thing to you," said Bones.

"You've suggested it, now go. Leave me."

"Look, Ladd, I know it's none of my business, but—"

"You're absolutely right," said Ladd. He took a long swing of whiskey, wiped his mouth on the back of his hand and added, "It is none of your business."

Bones pressed on. "Drinking is not going to get her back, boss."

"I know that," said Ladd sadly. "Nothing is going to get her back. I've lost her for good, Bones."

Thirty-Eight

The summer of '81 finally ended and a cool, crisp autumn arrived in Mobile. With the change of seasons, the leaves began to fade and then fall to the ground. The sun seemed to come from a different direction and it no longer burned quite as brightly. The nights had grown decidedly chilly.

But not as chilly as Laurette Howard Tigart.

She remained inflexible.

She staunchly refused to have anything to do with Ladd Dasheroon. After weeks of doing everything he could think of to gain her forgiveness, Ladd finally gave up. He would no longer try to win her back. It was not going to happen. He knew Laurette too well. And, if he couldn't have her, he didn't want to live in Alabama. He'd go to New York, or perhaps London or Paris. It made no difference to him.

When he mentioned leaving to Bones one cold, clear November night, Bones said calmly, "Not a bad idea. Give me a few weeks to wind things up here."

"Sure," said Ladd. "No hurry."

Upon learning that Ladd planned to leave Mobile, Bones allowed no more moss to grow under his feet. After that evening when Ladd casually mentioned moving, Bones was out of the house a great deal. Which was not like him. Ladd was mildly curious, but not curious enough to ask Bones where he spent his time.

Bones was very careful not to arouse her suspicions, but he took great pains to run into Laurette with increasing regularity. The first time he bumped into her was at the downtown market. She was friendly enough and put up no protest when he offered to see her home.

Wisely, he spoke only of the weather, of her work at the hospital, of the rising price of the vegetables she had just purchased.

He never mentioned Ladd's name.

A couple of days later, Bones happened to be walking past the hospital when Laurette came down the steps. Again, he saw her home. Again he didn't mention Ladd.

Laurette liked Bones, had liked him from the first time she met him. He was a good, kind man and as the winter winds blew and she worked longer hours at the hospital and darkness fell early, she was glad to see him when she came out of the hospital. To have him escort her safely home.

On a cold, gray afternoon in early December, Bones was waiting outside the hospital. Laurette smiled when she saw him. Bones protectively took her arm and walked her home as the winter darkness descended.

But this time, he didn't say good evening and leave her at the door. When they stepped onto the veranda,

Bones said, "Let me come inside for a few minutes. I want to talk to you."

Laurette looked up at him skeptically. She knew what he wanted to talk about and she didn't want to hear it. She began to shake her head.

"I'm sorry, Bones. But, no. I know your intention, but nothing you can say or do will change my mind about Ladd."

"That's entirely up to you," he said, "but there's so much that you don't know. So much you should know. So much that the modest Ladd would never tell you. Would never tell anyone."

Laurette frowned, but he ignored her. And not taking no for an answer, he followed her inside. He hung his topcoat on the coat tree and went directly into the drawing room where he lit a lamp and built a fire in the grate.

Laurette sighed in defeat, took off her wrap, hung it on the coat tree, and followed him into the drawing room. She stretched her hands out to the warmth of the fire and said, "You're a good, loyal friend, Bones, but you're wasting your time."

"It's mine to waste," he said. "Why don't you sit down?" When she made no move to do so, he took her arm and guided her to the sofa that faced the fireplace. Laurette sat down and crossed her arms over her chest, not wanting to listen to what he had to say. Nothing he could tell her would change her mind about the unscrupulous Ladd Dasheroon.

Bones did not sit down. He stood by the fireplace,

facing Laurette. And he began to talk. To tell her about the years that Ladd had spent in prison.

"Ladd had it awfully rough in Devil's Castle," he stated firmly. "The Captain of the Guards was a sadistic man who had known Ladd at West Point and had made Ladd's life hard at the academy. You can well imagine how he treated Ladd in prison. He singled Ladd out for punishment. Ladd was starved, tortured, beaten and even branded by the guard."

Laurette's lips parted and her eyes widened slightly. She recalled the scar on Ladd's bare buttock. When she'd mentioned it to him, he'd said it was a birthmark.

"He was lucky to live through the kind of cruel abuse the evil LaKid meted out."

"LaKid?" she repeated, thinking out loud. "The guard's name was LaKid."

"Yes, Gilbert LaKid. Why?"

"No reason. Just an unusual name," she said, shrugging slender shoulders, vividly remembering the first time she'd spent the night at the beach house. Ladd had awakened from a terrible nightmare shouting, "I'll kill you, LaKid."

Bones continued, "After a hellish year, Ladd was overjoyed when Major James Tigart was awarded the top position at Devil's Castle. Naturally, Ladd assumed that his old boyhood friend would call off the cruel guard and that his days in prison would be easier." Bones looked at Laurette to see if she was paying attention. She was, but she showed absolutely no emotion. She knew what was coming next. "Ladd's life didn't get better, it got much worse. Tigart's first order as prison commandant was to throw Ladd in the deepest dungeon, where Ladd stayed for the next eleven long, lonely years.''

"But how could that be?" Laurette asked. "The war ended in '65 and—"

"Tigart had Ladd charged with a serious crime against the government. Labeled him a dangerous political prisoner. So Ladd was not released when the war ended—was never to be released.''

"What was Ladd's crime?"

"Ladd committed no crime. Tigart lied. He meant for Ladd to die in prison.''

"Jimmy told me that Ladd had died in Devil's Castle. He said Ladd died shortly before he came to the prison to take command. Said that if only he'd been there before Ladd died, he would have put his name at the top of the prisoner exchange list.''

"Tigart lied so that you would marry him.''

Laurette released a weary sigh. "Dear lord, I didn't know Ladd was alive, I swear it.''

As if she hadn't spoken, Bones asked, "Did Ladd tell you how he learned about your marriage?"

"No. No, he didn't,'' she said.

"He didn't find out that you had married the man who so coldly betrayed him until years after the wedding took place. One day the guards tossed the page of a yellowing newspaper on the floor of Ladd's cell, then forked a piece of rancid meat atop it for Ladd's meal. It was the society page of an old copy of the

Mobile Press from June 9, 1865. Your wedding announcement was in it.''

Bones waited for her response. She said nothing. But he could see the brief flicker of pity in her dark eyes. Pity for the poor, lonely Ladd learning that she had married Jimmy.

''You can well imagine how he felt, how hurt and heartsick he was,'' said Bones. ''And why he vowed to get even with Tigart. And, yes, with you as well.'' Laurette did not comment; she was determined to remain completely composed, to act as if she didn't care what had happened to Ladd.

Bones continued trying to reach her. ''Ladd finally escaped by sewing himself in a dead man's shroud. He and a fellow prisoner had found each other by tunneling from one cell to the other. Both were so lonely they were about to lose their minds, so they quickly became good friends. The older man, Finis Schafer, counseled Ladd, educated him in history, philosophy, art, music and the theater. And, he told Ladd of a shipment of Yankee gold that he had stolen and buried. The two decided to tunnel their way to freedom. They worked hard, but it took too long. The older man got sick and died. Before he died, he told Ladd where he had buried the gold. When he passed away, Ladd moved his friend's body into his own cell, went into the dead man's cell, sewed himself into the shroud and let the guards bury him.''

Bones paused and stared at her. Surely that would get a response. It did not. She sat there on the sofa with her arms folded and her face set.

"When the guards had buried him and returned to Devil's Castle, Ladd fought his way out of the shallow grave, shed the shroud and jumped into Chesapeake Bay so that prison bloodhounds wouldn't catch his scent. Trouble was, the poor, emaciated bastard was so weak and sick, he couldn't continue to swim. He kept going under. So he headed for the banks, but was too tired and weak to pull himself up. He knew he was going to die, to drown."

"Obviously, he didn't," was all she said.

"No, he didn't. And that's were I came in. I was having troubles of my own and had decided to end it all. My intent was to jump into the icy waters of the bay and die. But I saw this pour soul struggling, so I reached down and saved him." Bones smiled then and said, "We saved each other that day. So you can see why I'm fond of him."

Laurette merely nodded.

Bones continued to talk for the next half hour, to tell Laurette how he'd pulled the freezing Ladd from the water and nursed him back to health. How the two of them had searched for and found the Yankee gold.

He talked and talked and when finally he stopped, Laurette rose and said, "It's getting late."

"Yes, yes, I've overstayed my welcome. I'm sorry," the big man apologized and headed for the foyer. He was disappointed. He had hoped—truly believed—that if Laurette learned all that had happened to Ladd, knew how badly he had suffered, she might soften. He was wrong. He could tell by her manner that she was not moved. Ladd was right. She was never going to forgive him.

Hurriedly shoving his muscular arms into the sleeves of his topcoat, Bones was taken aback when Laurette softly asked, "Bones, why did you want to die that day you saved Ladd?"

"Oh, it doesn't matter. I was a long time ago. I'm fine now."

"Please," she said and touched his forearm, "tell me."

Bones closed his eyes and then opened them. In a clear, deep voice he said, "I had lost my wife and child. I was a seaman back then and I was out at sea when my sweet Amanda, pregnant with our first child, went into early labor. She delivered my son, but he lived only a few hours. Amanda died minutes later. I wanted to die with them."

"Oh, Bones," Laurette said, genuinely touched, "I'm so sorry."

"Don't be," he said with a smile. "Amanda brought me great happiness, bless her sweet heart. I am blessed, for I have known a love that few are fortunate enough to find." He pointedly looked at her and said, "When you find a love like that, you should—"

"I'm really quite tired," she said, cutting him off.

He understood. "I'm going," he replied. "But after I'm gone, when you're alone, you think about what I've told you today. I don't expect anything I've said to change your mind, but maybe it will at least help you understand why Ladd did what he did."

"No, no it won't," she stated emphatically. "While I sympathize with what he endured, I will never forgive him for what he's done to me." Her dark eyes grew wintry and she told the big man, "As you know all too well, Ladd Dasheroon is not the only person on earth who has ever had to suffer."

Bones nodded and headed for the front door. He opened it, started to step outside, paused in the portal and turned back to look at her. His florid face a study in frustration, he said, "Just let me say one last thing and then I'll go."

"Yes?"

"Ladd loves you very much."

"That," Laurette said coldly, "is his misfortune."

Thirty-Nine

Laurette Howard Tigart had always possessed a defiant pride and rebellious strength. That innate pride and strength had seen her through numerous troubles and tragedies through the years. She had survived her share of loss and loneliness and would continue to survive and press on despite this latest heartbreak.

Laurette had convinced herself that when she'd told Ladd he was dead to her, she meant it. Still, she hadn't been entirely unmoved by all that Bones had told her about Ladd's terrible years in prison. And she could fully understand that it had broken Ladd's heart when he had learned—in the cruelest possible way—that she had married Jimmy.

Fate had definitely been unkind to Ladd.

But then it had been unkind to her, as well, and she couldn't bring herself to forget or forgive the fact that Ladd had returned to Mobile with the sole purpose of further hurting and humiliating her.

Laurette had told no one that the man claiming to be Sutton Vane was actually Ladd Dasheroon. All she had said—when pressed—was that she and Sutton Vane had mutually agreed to no longer see each other. The Parlange twins begged her to tell them what had happened to cause the breakup, but she had not been forthcoming. Furthermore she let them know, in no uncertain terms, that she didn't want to hear Sutton Vane's name spoken in her presence ever again.

Apparently Ladd had told no one else of his true identity, because she heard whispered gossip about the now mysteriously reclusive Sutton Vane. It was said that the only time he left his Government Street mansion was to slip away to his private island getaway. The gentry was puzzled by his uncharacteristic, antisocial behavior. There were those who were bold enough to question Laurette about it. She assured them that she had no idea why Mr. Vane chose to remain sequestered.

Nor did she care.

As the Christmas season rapidly approached, Laurette put on a good front to the world. She bought little gifts for those closest to her and sat on the floor before the fire to wrap the treasures in tissue paper and tie them with red ribbons.

She didn't, however, get a tree for the house. It was, she realized with a twinge of sadness, the first year of her life that a tall, fragrant spruce hadn't stood in the corner of the drawing room for the holidays. The Christmas ornaments would remain packed away in the upstairs linen closet. Decorating a tree when she was to spend Christmas alone hardly seemed worth the effort.

Christmas itself hardly seemed worth the effort.

"Why, Laurette," exclaimed Johanna Parlange Ford. "You don't have a Christmas tree!"

"How quick you are," was Laurette's retort as the twins came in from the cold and into the warm drawing room as darkness fell over the city.

"What are all those boxes stacked in the foyer that Johanna almost tripped over?" asked Juliette.

"My things," stated Laurette with no further explanation. The sisters exchanged looks.

It was six days before Christmas, but the twins, as was their custom, were going to New Orleans to spend the holidays. Both had begged Laurette to come with them. They assured her that their cousins had a big roomy home in the Garden District and would be more than glad to have her. But she had declined, stating that she was scheduled to work at the hospital. They, and she, knew that if she'd really wanted to go to New Orleans, she could have gotten some time off.

Since she refused to accompany them, they had come to spend this evening at her home, to celebrate an early Christmas with her. They went out of their way to be agreeable and cheerful.

It was Juliette who reminded her sister, as they'd come up the front walk, "Now, remember, Johanna, you are not to mention Sutton Vane's name!"

"I know that," said Johanna. "You think I want to spoil Christmas?"

So they came to the Dauphin Street mansion to exchange gifts, drink hot cocoa by the fire and enjoy the evening together. The twins gave Laurette a warm wool shawl that they had knitted themselves. She oohed and aahed over it and immediately wrapped it around her shoulders. Laurette gave Johanna a box of

perfumed soap knowing how Johanna loved to loll in
the tub. She had chosen Henry James's masterpiece,
Portrait of a Lady for Juliette. The twins were delighted with their gifts.

The three old friends talked and laughed and when
Laurette brought down a bottle of cognac she had
saved for the occasion, Johanna applauded and Juliette smiled and nodded her approval. They sipped
freely and soon their conversation grew more ani-
mated, their laughter louder. They ended up lying on
their stomachs before the blazing fire, singing and
giggling like children.

They had finished the bottle and were starting to
yawn when the clock in the corridor struck the hour
of midnight.

"Good heavens," said Juliette, rising to her knees
and sitting back on her heels. "I had no idea it was
getting so late."

"Nor me," agreed Johanna. "We must go, the
steamer leaves at dawn for New Orleans."

Minutes later, the twins had donned their wraps
and, carrying their gifts, stepped out into the cold
winter moonlight that spilled across the veranda.

"We so enjoyed the evening," said the gracious
Juliette.

"I did, too," said Laurette. "Thanks so much for
coming."

"We'll see you in ten days," said Johanna, slurring
her words slightly, then laughing about it.

Laurette laughed, too, as she stood shivering in the
open doorway, seeing the twins off. On the steps, Jo-

hanna stopped, turned abruptly and said, "Oh, guess what, Laurette? *He* is leaving town."

Laurette's heart kicked against her ribs. Forcing a laugh, she asked, "And who is he?"

"Johanna Parlange Ford!" scolded her sister. "I told you not to—"

"Sutton Vane," said Johanna, ignoring Juliette's frantic tugging on her arm. "He's leaving Mobile for good. Moving. New York or Paris, I've forgotten which. We heard that this is his last night in Mobile."

"Will you come on, Johanna," said Juliette, urging her sister down the steps. She turned, said over her shoulder, "Good night, Laurette."

"Good night. Have a wonderful time in New Orleans," Laurette said calmly.

She closed the door, locked it, turned and leaned back against it. So Ladd Dasheroon was leaving Mobile? Good! Great! Wonderful! She was glad he was leaving. With him gone for good, she could stop losing her breath every time she glimpsed a tall, raven-haired man that might be him. Her life could return to normal. Soon she would forget that he had ever come back.

Yes, she was glad he was going away.

Laurette went back into the drawing room, picked up the brandy snifters from the floor and carried them into the kitchen. She returned, lifted the empty bottle, turned it up to her lips and let the last few precious drops slide down her throat.

She shrugged out of the shawl the twins had given her, sat down on the sofa and gazed into the low-burning fire. She sighed, stretched out on the sofa and stayed there until the fire had burned completely down and was no more than dying embers.

She rose and told herself she was going to bed. But she didn't climb the stairs. Instead, she nervously paced back and forth in her silent, lonely drawing room, thinking, remembering, regretting.

All at once she abruptly stopped pacing and began to tremble. For an instant time turned back and she was sixteen again and it was the night before her seventeen-year-old sweetheart was to leave for West Point.

Laurette moaned as she recalled the sweetness of their urgent lovemaking that night. And she remembered the nagging fear she'd had that once Ladd left her, she would never see him again.

"Dear God, I can't lose him again," she said aloud. "Not again."

Laurette rushed out of the room and out of the house without bothering to grab a wrap. She ran through the freezing December night straight to the big white mansion on Government Street. Chilled to the bone, her teeth chattering, breath coming in labored gasps, she frantically banged on the heavy front door.

Minutes passed.

Bones opened the door.

"Laurette," he said, eyes wide with surprise. "Come in out of the cold. What are you doing out so late?"

Laurette hurried inside. "Where is he?" she asked,

a hand to her painfully throbbing heart. "Has he already gone? Am I too late?"

Bones began to smile. "Ladd's spending his last night out on the island. Alone."

Laurette reached out, grabbed Bones's muscular arm. "I have to see him, Bones. I have to go to him. Will you take me?"

Grinning broadly now, glad she had come to her senses before it was too late, Bones told her, "You'll have to wait until tomorrow, Laurette. Ladd took the yacht. It's at the island." Seeing the disappointment in her eyes, he asked, "Are you afraid to take a small craft across the water at night?"

"I'm afraid of nothing but losing Ladd forever."

Nodding his understanding, Bones said, "I'll get you one of Ladd's warm cloaks." He went out into the foyer, took down a heavy woolen cloak and swirled it around her trembling shoulders. "I'll wake up the coachman, have him drive us to the levee."

"Hurry," she said, "please hurry."

"Ten minutes at the most," he said and hurried toward the servants' quarters.

Nine minutes later Bones was handing Laurette up into the brougham for the ride to the harbor. When they reached the docks, Bones attempted to engage a steamer or a private yacht or a sailboat, without success. Laurette waited impatiently.

"I'm sorry," Bones said, returning to Laurette, "looks like we can't get to the island tonight. Tomorrow, we can..."

"I have to get there tonight," she stated emphatically and, pointing, said, "What about one of those row boats?"

Bones rubbed his chin thoughtfully. "Well," he said, "the bay looks pretty calm tonight, but still…"

"Please, Bones, I'll help row. I have to see Ladd."

"Come on," he said, taking her arm and guiding her toward one of the small row boats.

The strong, powerfully built Bones rowed Laurette across the six miles of water to Ladd's private island. When they reached the island's dock, Bones rowed the tiny craft up alongside the wharf, tied the rope line to a post and stepped onto the wooden wharf. He extended his hand and helped Laurette out of the boat. He gave her an affectionate pat on the back and started to climb back into the boat.

"Wait. Aren't you coming with me?" she asked.

"No," he said. "This is between the two of you. I'm going to row myself right back to Mobile."

Momentarily overcome with doubt, she said, "You're going to leave me alone? What if Ladd doesn't—?"

But Bones was gone.

Laurette stood alone on the levee. She offered up a prayer, then turned and looked toward the beach house. Ladd was inside. Would he welcome her? Or banish her from sight? She drew a deep breath of the cold night air.

With Ladd's long black cloak billowing out behind her, Laurette began to run eagerly across the sandy shore toward the house where one lone lamp burned. A full moon shone down from the cold night sky.

Ladd, gazing wistfully out the window, blinked with disbelief when he saw Laurette coming. He leaped up, rushed out of the house, down the steps and across the sand.

By the time they met, both were laughing and crying with joy. Ladd lifted Laurette up into his arms and swung her around while she clung to his neck and declared, "Ladd, my darling, I lost you once. I can't let it happen again."

Elated, Ladd replied, "Lollie, my love, my own, you'll never lose me again this side of paradise."

BARBARA

NEW YORK TIMES BESTSELLING AUTHOR

DELINSKY

Diandra Casey and Gregory York, childhood rivals and long-term adversaries, are vying for the same powerful position at the posh Casey and York department store. Intensely competitive, they are shocked to find themselves confined—together!—for one week in an elegant Boston town house. Away from the pressures of corporate life and alone with each other, they discover their feelings are suddenly taking unexpected twists and turns. Does the old house hold a surprising fate that they cannot resist? Dare they surrender to the pull of its mystery and the lure of a legend that binds their two families together, a legend too powerful and magnificent to understand...or deny?

Fulfillment

"Barbara Delinsky knows the human heart and its immense capacity to love and to believe."
—*Washington (PA) Observer-Reporter*

GWEN HUNTER

A Dr. Rhea Lynch Novel

PRESCRIBED DANGER

Working in the E.R. in a small South Carolina hospital, Dr. Rhea Lynch
has seen it all. But when an interracial couple is rushed in, beaten and
bloodied by a mysterious hate group, the patients show symptoms of a
fast-acting pulmonary infection Rhea has never seen before. Within
hours, it proves fatal.

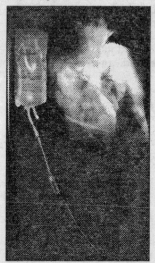

Soon more victims are rushed in,
and an epidemic has Dawkins County
in an icy grip of terror. As the
puzzling illness claims more lives
by the hour, every second counts as
Rhea desperately tries to fit the
pieces together—and soon realizes
that she is dealing with something
bigger and more terrifying than she
could ever imagine.

*Available the first week
of April 2002 wherever
paperbacks are sold!*

NAN RYAN

66814 THE SEDUCTION OF ELLEN ___ $6.50 U.S. ___ $7.99 CAN.
66591 THE COUNTESS MISBEHAVES ___ $6.50 U.S. ___ $7.99 CAN.
66521 WANTING YOU ___ $5.99 U.S. ___ $6.99 CAN.

(limited quantities available)

TOTAL AMOUNT	$_____
POSTAGE & HANDLING	$_____
($1.00 for one book; 50¢ for each additional)	
APPLICABLE TAXES*	$_____
TOTAL PAYABLE	$_____

(check or money order—please do not send cash)

To order, complete this form and send it, along with a check or money order for the total above, payable to MIRA Books®, to: **In the U.S.:** 3010 Walden Avenue, P.O. Box 9077, Buffalo, NY 14269-9077; **In Canada:** P.O. Box 636, Fort Erie, Ontario, L2A 5X3.

Name:_____
Address:_____ City:_____
State/Prov.:_____ Zip/Postal Code:_____
Account Number (if applicable):_____
075 CSAS

*New York residents remit applicable sales taxes.
  Canadian residents remit applicable GST and provincial taxes.

MIRA®